TURNING POINT

PAULA CHASE

TURNING POINT

GREENWILLOW BOOKS

AN *IMPRINT OF* HARPERCOLLINS *PUBLISHERS*

Turning Point
Copyright © 2020 by Paula Chase

All rights reserved. No part of this book may be used or reproduced in any manner whatsoever without written permission except in the case of brief quotations embodied in critical articles and reviews. Printed in the United States of America. For information address HarperCollins Children's Books, a division of HarperCollins Publishers, 195 Broadway, New York, NY 10007.
www.harpercollinschildrens.com

The text of this book is set in Sabon MT. Book design by Sylvie Le Floc'h

Library of Congress Cataloging-in-Publication Data

Names: Chase, Paula, author.
Title: Turning point / Paula Chase.
Description: First edition. | New York, NY : Greenwillow Books, an Imprint of HarperCollins Publishers, [2020] | Audience: Ages 8–12. | Audience: Grades 4–6. |
Summary: "Best friends Rasheeda and Monique navigate the ups and downs of a teenager's summer, Mo at home in the Cove; Sheeda at a sleepaway ballet intensive"— Provided by publisher.
Identifiers: LCCN 2020024445 | ISBN 9780062965660 (hardcover)
Subjects: CYAC: Best friends—Fiction. | Friendship—Fiction. | Ballet dancing—Fiction. | African Americans—Fiction.
Classification: LCC PZ7.C38747 Tu 2020 | DDC [Fic]—dc23 LC record available at https://lccn.loc.gov/2020024445
20 21 22 23 24 PC/LSCH 10 9 8 7 6 5 4 3 2 1

First Edition
 Greenwillow Books

To all of my Black and Brown Ballerinas
changing the world one jeté at a time,
keep leaping

TURNING POINT

RASHEEDA

The Summer of Lonely.

The Lonely Summer.

She wasn't sure which one to call it.

The second that her best friend, Mo, had come to her, excited about getting into something they called an "intensive" (why not just call it "dance camp," for real?), Sheeda's summer was turned on its head. But then Mila got in, too. And Chrissy was going away to spend time with family in Virginia. The entire squad was ghost for the summer. That just left her.

Well, and Tai. Tai wasn't going anywhere. Low-key, a summer with Tai, who had exactly one speed—bossy—

wasn't any better than a summer totally alone.

Rasheeda Tate hadn't had a Lonely Summer (That sounded better. Summer of Lonely was too fancy.) since her very first in the Cove. It was home now. She almost, *almost* couldn't remember a time when it wasn't.

When she first left North Carolina to move in with her aunt, she mumbled to hide her slow drawl to fit in with the Cove kids whose words streamed strung together. Mo was the one who hadn't teased her. Who had taught her the dead-eye stare when grown men hollered, "Hey, little momma, what's your name?" Mo was the one who stood up to older girls who ordered them to do stupid stuff, like fetch snacks from the Wa.

The last six summers were hanging together out at the basketball court, even when it was scorching hot.

Going to the carnival together and eating funnel cake until the powdered sugar gave them a headache.

Hanging out at the rec's open gym nights with their squad.

Now what was she going to do?

Stupid question. Because she was going to end up in church every day. Just like she was at this moment, sitting lonely in the second pew waiting until Sister Butler made everyone stop all the foolishness and get up in the choir loft. Sheeda knew she looked antisocial. Good, 'cause she felt that way.

For real, it always took her a few minutes to be all right with being stuck at church. Today she was feeling more standoffish than usual. Yola and Kita, her two closest church friends, were used to it and let her be until she felt like dragging herself up the three tiny stairs that led to where the choir sat staring out into the big sanctuary. Sitting alone on the long pew that could hold fifteen people, while everybody else bulled around, Sheeda might as well have been invisible.

Again.

Just like when she hadn't made it into TAG.

Jealousy burned her chest. She didn't want it to. But it did.

She danced, too. Not that anybody would know it, since she was the only one in their clique whose dancing wasn't good enough outside of church. That's how it felt. She'd been praise dancing for years and was good. Still, it hadn't gotten her into the school's talented and gifted dance program. Now Mila and Mo were going away for three weeks to dance. And Sheeda was bursting with why's. Why hadn't she been good enough to get into TAG dance? Why hadn't their dance teacher from the rec center at least recommended her for the summer intensive thingie? And why in the world had she been stupid enough to admit how she'd felt to her aunt?

Auntie D wasn't having any of her whining. She'd put her hands on her slim, barely there hips and said, "Rasheeda Tate, listen to yourself. The Bible says, 'But each person is tempted when they are dragged away by their own evil desire and enticed.'"

Sheeda had wiped her face of any expression. Her aunt paused, just enough to let the Bible verse sink in. "That's from James, first chapter, fourteenth verse. If He wanted you in that school program for dance, you would have gotten in. Nothing good is going to come from you wanting something that wasn't meant to be."

Usually after a lecture, Sheeda thought about doing better. Not that time. Evil desire. Really? She'd been dancing at church forever and everybody swore she was good, but now, suddenly, wanting to dance was evil?

She'd almost said as much to her aunt. Instead, she'd quietly muttered, "Yes, ma'am." There was no point. When Deandra Tate's mind was made up, it was a wrap.

With no alternatives for summer, Auntie D would 100 percent fill any free second Sheeda had with church. And Sheeda hated that she didn't have any choice in it.

Hated it like a chair scraping across the floor. Hated it like when the teacher volunteers you to read something out loud because she can sense you don't want to. Hated everything about the never-ending schedule of choir and praise dance rehearsals, youth activities, Bible study— repeat, repeat, repeat.

A stony pebble of annoyance lodged in her heart at the thought of being stuck the whole summer inside the walls of First Bap, where the bright red carpet made the pews and pulpit look like they floated on a river of blood and there was an elder around every corner wanting to ask how your grades were, like they were gonna tutor you on the spot if you said you were failing.

Sister Butler plunked away at the piano, warming up her fingers. Squeals of laughter came from the back of the church, where the fifth graders were playing some game that consisted of them racing up and down the pews. Never mind that running in the sanctuary was forbidden, ten-year-olds had a way of making the best of being in church.

First Baptist was her second home since she'd moved in with her aunt. Six years ago her, Yola, Kita, and Jalen were the only kids in the whole church. The First Bap Pack, Sister Butler had named them. They all knew what it was like to be the entire choir and youth ministry.

She should have felt closer to them. Honestly, the four of them should hard-core be a clique by now. If five years at Bible study, youth nights, and Vacation Bible School didn't make you close to somebody, what did?

Rasheeda was still trying to find out. She liked the First Bap Pack, but calling them friends felt like an exaggeration. Even a lie.

All total, there were twenty kids in the choir now. Most were fifth graders. Sheeda had loved choir and running the then brand-new church's halls when she was that age, too. Now, at thirteen, it wasn't the same. Maybe because they couldn't be all wild like the fifth graders anymore.

Or . . .

She stopped herself from even thinking it. Because she was ready to think "hate" again and if she didn't know anything else, she knew sitting in church thinking about hating was wrong. She mentally blinked the word away and focused on Yola and Kita pretending to be going over the lyrics for today's songs. Sheeda knew they were really looking at the text Jalen had sent to Yola.

Jalen stood on the altos side by himself. Eventually she, Carlos, and Anthony would join him. First it bothered her to be the only girl alto, but whenever she tried singing in a higher voice Sister Butler smiled and said, "All right now, altos gotta alto."

Jalen had his lyric sheet in his hand, lips moving as he read the words—no doubt trying to impress Sister Butler. Sheeda had no idea what Yola saw in him. He had a thick head of wavy hair and skin the shade of coffee that had too much cream in it. It wasn't that he wasn't cute, but he thought he was all that because he got all the leads in the songs and the Christmas play. Pastor's favorite. All the women in the church acted like he was a prize. To them he was a "nice young man." Outside of the view of grown-ups, he was mad cocky. It erased his cuteness.

Sheeda stared past him to the back of the pulpit at the big gold cross. There was a glint to it, like the cross knew she was dreading a summer inside First Baptist and was shining itself on her spirit. She wanted to duck from its presence.

Her Auntie D's voice played like a sermon on demand—*God knows your heart, Luvvie. Can't hide from that.*

The nickname usually had a way of taking the bite off her aunt's constant Scripture quotes and sermons. But lately, there were two Auntie D's—the one who saw that Sheeda meant well and the one giving side-eye as if every little wrong was the world's worst sin. Sheeda never knew which Deandra Tate was going to show up. For sure, the Auntie D who called her "Luvvie," with affection, wasn't around as much.

If she was keeping it a buck, the only time Auntie D was truly happy was when they were at church.

Shocker.

She leaned her head back and sighed toward the ceiling. Her thick rope Marley twists slid on the pew's glossy wood. She adjusted until her neck laid flat. Her phone suddenly glowed beside her. Sheeda glanced at the message: whatchu doin? just as Sister Butler clapped her hands. "Okay, let's get started."

Ugh, of course. She couldn't torture the keyboard for three more minutes?

Sheeda made her way into the choir loft. She debated if she had time to answer Dat Boy Ell back. His profile picture, eyes piercing the camera and throwing not one but two middle fingers, made her face even hotter. Middle-finger pic shots in church was most definitely wrong. She didn't need her aunt to tell her that.

His pic wasn't the only thing wrong, though. And since God didn't like a liar, she admitted to herself that her church friendships, a little jealousy, and how she felt about church weren't the only things complicated these days.

Dat Boy Ell was Lennie Jenkins, Mo's older brother. She'd known Lennie since she was eight years old and he was ten. Then, he spent so much time being punished for one thing or another that Rasheeda had been afraid of him. Afraid that merely being in his presence might get her in trouble. Especially since Mo's other three brothers were locked up. It took her a while to realize that Lennie only had a big mouth and mainly got in trouble for talking back at school.

That felt forever ago.

He was fifteen now and had never gotten in trouble like his brothers. Him and Mo were the "good" ones according to her aunt.

Actually she'd said, "Their mother finally caught a break. I *guess* they're the good ones."

Auntie D stayed waiting on people to go wrong.

Anytime her aunt threw shade at Mo and her family, Rasheeda felt two-faced. The only thing that comforted her was her aunt threw shade to pretty much anybody who didn't go to First Bap. She definitely would have never approved of the message Lennie sent commenting on a picture on Rasheeda's FriendMe page: all growed up like . . . and a GIF of a nearly naked model slo-mo walking down the runway with wind in her weave.

It made Sheeda take a closer look at the picture he was talking about. In it, she wore a white sundress with pink and green flowers. The dress had ruffled straps (three fingers wide, no more, no less), fitted her waist tight then flowed over her wideish hips. She guessed Lennie was referring to the length of the dress. It stopped a few inches above her knee, which was new. Until she'd turned thirteen, every dress she owned came to the middle of her calves.

Sheeda thought it made her look fat. She didn't need help looking thick. But Lennie had liked it. Well, not liked it on her page but at least privately. And the only person in the world she would have shared it with, she couldn't tell.

That had been a few weeks ago. He'd been texting her ever since.

A few times she almost admitted it to Mo. Felt like she should and let Mo say whatever she was going to say because Mo was forever honest. Then that would be that. Only, she still hadn't.

She wasn't worried about Mo getting angry and dramatic. Well, at least not dramatic. Mo was one of the realest people Rasheeda knew. And that was it. Mo could be too honest. Like, pointing-out-your-flaws-to-the-world honest.

Sheeda wasn't sure what truth Mo would tell her once she found out about Lennie, but she knew with all her heart it was one she didn't want to hear.

She glanced at the message, tempted to answer, then shut the screen down and placed the phone in her back pocket.

Sister Butler hit the first note for the song, and Sheeda sang out with all her energy, "Yessss, I'm a believer," hiding behind the lyrics.

MONIQUE

When Ms. Noelle opened La May at the rec center—La Maison de Danse for the bougie at heart—a lot of the older girls in the Cove had joked on it. "What kind of fancy name was Lah May-zon Duh Dance?" They wanted to learn hip-hop or something that would get them on tour or in a music video. And most of them dropped out, with the quickness, when they realized the classes were strictly ballet and jazz.

Until then, Mo had never been in a dance class. That first year Ms. Noelle (Mademoiselle, to her face) forced Mo's body into the craziest most annoying positions. Mo had wanted to quit. Then, one day, they watched a video of Alvin Ailey American Dance Theater and the screen swallowed Mo whole. She was there, in the dark auditorium, watching all those Black bodies move like they didn't have bones.

Ms. Noelle asked, "Who can see themselves doing this?"

And every hand went up. There was a satisfied look on Ms. Noelle's face as she went on to say, "Good. I know that ballet is hard. But its technique is the foundation of modern dance. Want to do that?" She pointed at the screen. "Then you've got to learn ballet."

Monique had been hooked ever since. And good thing, because right about now she felt like her body was ready to break.

"Cambré side."

Monique repeated the word in her head: *calm-BRAY*.

She leaned toward the barre, feeling the stretch in her side.

Knowing the term made her feel like she could go to France and just start talking.

She couldn't, for real, unless everybody around her was going to talk in ballet terms. But when she was in class, it made her feel smarter. Like she'd spent an entire hour in another country.

Every new position change was a command from Ms. Noelle. Yet somehow the words were silky, floating into Mo's ear and slipping through her body so her arms, legs, and torso did the right thing. The tinkling piano music boomed so loud from the speakers, it demanded you follow it. And even though her ballet teacher wasn't yelling, Monique heard her over the music, like it was magic trick.

"Now, back. Cambré." Ms. Noelle held the word out to make sure her tiny class of two understood to stay in the pose.

No cheating. Make the body work, Mo told herself.

She knew she'd never be considered the best dancer. Not as long as her and Mila were competing for the title. Mila was long and lean and looked like the dancers Mo had seen in the ballet videos they watched. Mo was good and she worked hard. Ms. Noelle always praised her for her dedication and how focused she was in class. Mo took the W however she got it.

She couldn't see Mila, but she knew her friend's back was arched as far back as it could go. Mila probably wasn't straining, either. She slid so easily into positions that Mo found herself clenching her teeth to back down the jealousy. In a few days, Mila would be the only person she'd know at the Summer Experience, a ballet intensive they had gotten scholarships to. They needed each other.

Her back straining in the deep arch, Mo gripped the barre, loosened her jaw.

How in the world did Mila look like she could stay leaned back like this all day?

She exhaled slowly through her mouth, feeling the tension in her spine. Seriously, it felt like it was going to crack.

Just as she was about to lift out of the position, Ms. Noelle's hands guided her arm.

"Your arm should be just a little behind your face, Monique. No?"

Which of course meant yes. Ms. Noelle was Canadian. Her French accent took the edge off the gentle command.

Mo's body went along with the adjustment.

Barre work was hard. The movements were so slow.

Ah-dah-gee-oh, she repeated in her head. The ballet terms were still tricky for her sometimes. But she couldn't go all the way to Philly and look crazy, not understanding the right words.

Adagio required patience. Something Mo didn't have a lot of. She charged that to the game.

A) She lived in the Cove, which the local paper had once called "a jungle of narrow, brick row houses that give local drug dealers an all-too-easy escape route." Really? A jungle, though?

B) If the Cove was a jungle (not that she was claiming all that), then her court, K Court, was the deepest, wildest part of it. It was the very last cul-de-sac of homes, surrounded by a half mile of trees, and it hid any dirt people wanted to keep on the low too well.

Being from the last court (what she called it instead) meant having dudes assume she was just another "thirsty bae from the K" who was willing to be on some stupid stuff for a little cash, jewelry, or attention. Mo wasn't. Never had been. Linda Jenkins wouldn't have it. She worked too many shifts at Bay Memorial to keep her kids clothed and fed to have them fall prey to the siren call of street dealing. Well, two of her kids, at least.

The real reason Mo had a shortage of patience was simple.

With four older brothers who swarmed the house like locusts when meals were ready, being patient in the Jenkins household meant not getting anything to eat or going to school with your breath humming because you never got into the bathroom to brush your teeth.

Everything Mo ever did had been about getting it done before her brothers beat her to it.

The Jenkins boys. Every one of them two years apart, like her mother had either kept trying until she got one boy who could stay out of trouble or was trying until she got a girl. She'd finally gotten both.

It was just her and Lennie home now. Rennard and Dante were in jail, a two-hour drive away. Low-key, she always tried to make sure she had dance class when her mother announced the weekend's plan to visit them. Mo loved her brothers but didn't get why her mother spent what little bit of time she got off from the hospital visiting them.

And Josiah was in Boys Town, the juvenile lockup. Even if he got out, he'd probably waste the free time he had long enough to turn eighteen, get into nonsense, and end up with their older brothers.

Mo didn't think about them a lot. That was probably wrong. But they'd been in and out of juvvie or jail since she was five years old. Whenever Rennie and Dante had been home, which wasn't much, to her they were extra bodies in the house and random big-brother advice that she sometimes remembered but mostly didn't.

Lennie wasn't no angel. But, so far, he had enough sense not to get into big trouble. At fifteen, he was (of course) only two years older than her. And they were as close as any other brother and sister, always competing to get the things they wanted from their mother. People swore they were twins. Mo had stopped reminding people they weren't. People remembered what they wanted. They were as close as twins, though.

He was the one who taught her how to fight. The one who somehow slid their mother eighty dollars for her first pair of pointe shoes. "Don't be asking me my business, Monique. You needed 'em. It's whatever," he'd said when she'd questioned him, worried he was dealing.

And he was the only one left to give out big-brother advice. Which, for real, was tiresome. Lately, it was his full-time job to remind Mo not to "mess with these hard heads out here."

First of all, Mo didn't have any interest in any of the dudes from their neighborhood. Half of them were Lennie's friends—so hard pass. And the others, her age, Mo had known since they were little. Knowing too much about a person made them 100 percent un-dateable in her opinion. Though based on some of the crushing going on among her clique—Tai liking Rollie, Simp liking Tai, Mila liking Chris—she was the only one who felt that way.

Not that she was going into all that with her brother. That's why her and Lennie had got into it when she pointed out that getting with a dude didn't make her a bird. That's what Lennie and his friends called girls who they gamed into whatever they wanted to game them into. She could guess what they wanted but didn't want to think about her brother doing It with anybody. Ugh.

He had turned his mouth up in disgust, arguing back, "It do though."

Mo had cocked her head to the side, mouth upturned in as much disgust. "So, basically you spend all this time schemin' on somebody and when it work, she the one wrong?"

"It's wack when you put it that way . . ." Lennie had said, then laughed. Still, he held his ground. "But Ioun care. Good girls don't let themselves get played."

She'd walked out of his face. Lennie was barely passing school each year. And when he passed, it was probably because the teachers were pushing him through. But if there was a way around and into something he wanted, he had plans for days. Mo didn't get how he could be smart when he wanted to and dumb when someone else needed him to be smart.

Her mother had always said, because he's slick like y'all father.

A father Mo had never met. She had no idea if she was

slick like him or if that was why she was so competitive. Maybe. If so, then wherever he was, he was one of the reasons she worked so hard at dance and had gotten that scholarship to Ballet America's Summer Experience.

Shout out to that.

She arched back a tiny bit more, proud of the screaming she felt in her muscles as she pushed them to do the impossible. That screaming meant she was focused and ready (almost) for the intensive.

She'd be gone for three weeks.

Three weeks in a new city. Around girls who had probably been dancing since they were two. Her stomach fluttered.

She lifted out of the arch and let her body follow Ms. Noelle's instructions while her mind drifted to the summer ahead.

She was nervous about going away for the first time. But the closer it got, the more she thought about what life would be like if Ballet America offered her a scholarship to stay the whole year. She had never heard of a ballet conservatory until a few months ago. But if going to one made her dance like the Ailey dancers, she needed that— screaming muscles, calloused feet, all of it.

Ballet was crazy hard. You had to hold your head at

a certain angle and make your feet do the wildest things. Even your hands had to be held a certain way—index and pinky fingers long, thumb under the first finger.

There was a time, not that long ago, when she didn't get it. For some reason she kept wanting to extend the middle finger. Ms. Noelle would tease her. "Monique, let's not insult the audience."

Like, who in the world can see what your hands are doing from the audience?

But now, three years later and after a year in the talented and gifted dance program, when she watched herself compared to some girls who had danced longer, she had it. She wasn't as good as Mila, but for real, she was getting close.

Mila was good at adagio and the graceful stuff. She was five-foot-eight and had skinny stick legs like most of the White ballet dancers had. Mo was five-foot-five with muscular thighs and wasn't mad at 'em. She could turn and jump her butt off thanks to her thickety thighs.

Mo was the best at allegro, the fast movements.

The music stopped. Chest heaving, she listened as Ms. Noelle commented on the things needing work.

She hoped the Ballet America teachers would be as patient as Ms. Noelle. Sometimes, in class, if they forgot a term, she'd call it out by the descriptions she'd made up to help them understand when they'd first started. No matter how patient her summer teachers were, they probably weren't going to tell her to put her arms like she was making a basketball hoop. So, Mo had made a cheat sheet of terms. She'd been studying them every night for weeks.

Her chest swelled with pride thinking about the work she'd been putting in. She was about to beast this Summer Experience.

RASHEEDA

Sheeda wasn't used to how the Kay—K Court—where Mo lived felt like a land time ignored. The Cove had eleven courts, named by alphabet. All the other courts overflowed with loud activity, sometimes late into the night. The Kay was always eerily quiet, even when plenty of people were out, like no one wanted you to know they were back there.

Sheeda lived in E Court, but everyone called it fifth court.

The Kay (eleventh court?) was far away from the rest of the nabe's activity and backed up by a thick band of woods. Rumor was the woods led to a deep trench cut by a stream. Sheeda had no idea if it existed since her aunt barely let her come visit Mo, much less go tramping through the woods.

According to the Book of Auntie D, you don't go looking for trouble. To her the Kay was trouble. She preferred that Sheeda stay near the basketball courts and the rec center—both right across from their row house. And, for the most part, her and the squad did. Her house was just closer to everything. But her best friend was about to leave, so instead of her usual "Why can't Monique come here?," Auntie D had sighed like the words were heavy when she said, "Text me when you get there . . . and tell Monique I said good luck."

Mo's house was a whole fifteen-minute walk. But Sheeda obeyed and texted her arrival.

Anything to prevent a sermon.

She rapped on the door hard. The tattered screen rattled in the frame like it was about to fall out. One hole was big enough for her to stick her hand through and open the locked door. She resisted, then dared to put her face closer to peer inside.

A chorus of "Ohhhh" went up from a few feet away inside.

Four guys were in the darkened living room, their faces trained to the television. Lennie was closest to the door, standing, his back to her. A pair of denim shorts barely held on to his thin waist, showing blue and red boxer shorts. His baby locs spiked all over his head, too short to lie down and behave. He was shirtless. He always was in his pics on social media, too. The thought of his bare chest made Sheeda's cheeks burn.

She tapped the doorframe lightly with her fist and the raggedy screen clattered at the same time that the room quieted down for a second.

Lennie spun around, scowling at the door. "Who is it?"

"It's Rasheeda." Her voice trembled at his growl. She spoke louder. "Hey, Lennie. It's Sheeda."

Recognition flickered on his face.

"Ay." He yelled back into the living room, "Ain't none of y'all ready for me, though." He turned the lock on the door and it swung open. "What's up?"

"Nothing. Mo upstairs?" Sheeda stepped inside, eyes searching the stairwell.

Lennie's smile was sly. "Would you be here if she wasn't?"

Sheeda's heart raced. "I mean, probably . . . n-n-not."

She waited for him to say something, anything to confirm the messages they exchanged had been real. Standing in front of him made her stomach float.

His finger grazed her bare arm. "I'm playing with you. Yeah, she upstairs." He hollered in the general direction of the upper level, "Mo, your friend here," then was back at the edge of the video game action.

The word *friend* smacked Sheeda in the face.

His flirty messages replayed in her head. If she was honest with herself, it wasn't anything he'd said specifically that hooked her. It was that he'd hit her up at all. Guys never kicked it with her like that. She had a mass of brown, ropey twists that always felt out of control and a face that was losing its battle with pimples—she was never the one guys paid attention to. Between Tai's confidence and phat booty, Mila's smooth chocolate face and skinniness, and Mo's always-laid hair and dancer's body, Sheeda didn't stand a chance being noticed. When they were out, dudes regularly hollered at Mo asking her to slide her number into their phones.

When Lennie hit her up, of course she'd thought . . .

Never mind what she'd thought.

Before disappearing up the stairs, Sheeda glanced back, hoping Lennie was watching her walk away. She'd read that dark colors on the bottom could make her hips look smaller. She'd put a lot of time into picking out her outfit—a white tank top with the words *Girls Rule* across it and a pair of red denim shorts that looked good against her brown skin. They normally stopped right above her knee. She'd rolled them up until they gripped her thighs— the fastest way around Auntie D's no-booty-short rule. Still, it hadn't made any difference. Lennie hadn't looked back.

Her entire body felt the disappointment like a weight in her belly.

She lurked at the top of the stairs and considered going back home. Mo's door was closed. She hadn't heard Lennie and didn't know Sheeda was there.

She didn't want to watch Mo pack, anyway. It would make her leaving too real.

It was hard to believe that it had only been a year ago that her, Mo, Mila, and Tai had all been part of La May, dancing several nights a week. Sheeda had never been as good as Mo and Mila at ballet, but their teacher, Mademoiselle Noelle, always complimented her for being graceful. Graceful just hadn't been good enough for anything except La May and church. That hurt. Watching Mo pack would only be a reminder that she didn't have whatever it took to do real dance.

She hesitated on the landing, trapped between the silence of the upstairs and the rowdy bass of the boys' laughter behind her. Thank God Ms. Linda was at work. Sheeda didn't have to worry about her popping out of her room, wondering why she was standing there in the dim hallway. Which was another reason Auntie D didn't like her hanging at Mo's. Ms. Linda was usually either asleep during the day or at work during the evening, leaving Mo and Lennie on their own a lot.

Lennie's voice made her jump. "You good?"

Sheeda looked back down the stairs. "Oh. Yeah."

Yes. He'd peeped up the stairs. He'd looked for her.

"Just go head in." He called out louder, "Monique, your friend here, girl."

He slid back off as Mo's door swung open. Her face was twisted in a frown. "What you sa—" she screamed back. The frown U-turned into a grin when she saw Sheeda. "Hey. I didn't know you was here. Why you ain't just knock?"

Sheeda laughed to cover up her giddiness. "Lennie didn't give me time to."

After standing in the darkened hallway, the brightness of Mo's room was blinding. Music played from a tiny lip-shaped speaker. Leotards, tights, and shorts were strewn everywhere. Sheeda scooted worn ballet slippers and shiny, barely worn pointe shoes to the side and plopped onto Mo's bed.

"Hey, sorry," Mo said.

"You fine," Sheeda said.

Mo waved toward her dresser. "No, I'm talking to Mila."

Sheeda noticed the phone propped up. Mila's chocolate face smiled back at her.

"Hey, Sheeda," Mila said.

"Oh, hey." Mila was going to have Mo half the summer. Couldn't this time with Mo be hers? The selfish thought shamed Sheeda into a fake, high-pitched, "So do your room look like Mo's? There's stuff everywhere. I barely have any place to sit."

Mila chuckled. "Believe it or not, mine looks worse. Plus, my aunt brought me a good year's worth of pads and tampons. It's like a drugstore over here."

"I'm not mad. Now I can borrow from you and not bring as much," Mo said. She scooped up an armful of T-shirts and dropped them beside Sheeda. "Can you fold these, please?"

"No fair, you have help," Mila said.

Mo's fingers raked through her hair. It hung straight to her shoulders with enough bend at the end to say it was curled. Until she got really into dance, Mo was the type that went to the hair salon every two weeks. Now her hair was in a bun most of the time. Still, it always looked neat and sleek, not like Sheeda's full head of fuzz. Sheeda followed her gaze, wondering what Mo was looking for.

"I should have got braids." She took a step toward the dresser, talking at her phone. "Now Imma have to wash my hair at intensive. That's dunk."

Mila's mountain of tiny braids shivered as she laughed. "So then, it's official. You're really keeping 'dunk' in rotation?"

"I'm definitely keeping it in rotation. 'Cause it's messed up and for real, nothing says messed up like *dunk*," Mo said, her half smile disappearing as she fretted again. "I know my scalp gonna get nasty after dancing all day, every day. What should I do? I don't even have a blow-dryer anymore."

Sheeda had never seen Mo worry about anything. More importantly, Mo hated braids. She said they took too long to get done and hurt her scalp. She'd been on a mission all middle school to get Sheeda to change up her twists. "Your hair gonna start breaking off. You should give them a rest."

Wasn't like it was Sheeda's choice. Her aunt didn't have money to send her to the salon every other weekend or time to do the hair herself. The Senegalese and Marley twists were all Sheeda knew. And for the record, her real hair was long and healthy—something she'd never bothered to remind Mo. When Mo thought she was right, there was no real point in arguing. That's why seeing her look worried made Sheeda want to hug her friend.

She picked up a T-shirt that had the silhouette of a dancer on her toes, arms above her head in what Mademoiselle called "high beach ball." She creased it down the middle and began folding, then tried to get into the conversation, "You don't like braids, though."

Mo looked Sheeda's way, then Mila's voice drew her away.

"It's only three weeks. I keep my braids in longer than that without washing. I think you'll be fine."

"You probably right," Mo said. She swooshed her hair into a messy bun, then patted it. "This stuff gonna be wooly as I don't know what when we get back, though."

Sheeda sped up folding the shirts. "I think you'd look cute in braids. The box kind would be perfect for you?"

Mo's nose wrinkled. "But I don't want them snobby ballet girls to think I'm ghetto."

"Why—" Sheeda started.

"So, wait. I'm ghetto?" Mila asked, shaking her skinny

braids at the camera. She laughed at the look of busted embarrassment on Mo's face.

"My bad. I didn't mean it like that," Mo said. She sighed toward the ceiling. "I don't want to be worried about impressing nobody. But, ugh. I am."

"You're a good dancer, Mo. Mademoiselle says intensives aren't about competing. You're there to strengthen your technique," Mila said.

"Girl, please. Everything's a competition," Mo said with a snort. "I mean, Ms. Noelle know better than I do. But, like, no, it's still a competition." She pulled shorts out of her dresser and laid them in a sliver of empty space to Sheeda's left, the request to fold clear.

Sheeda obeyed, robotically. The Mo she knew never cared what anyone thought. The tremor in Mo's voice, her deep breath like the air in her chest was heavy, was all new.

A tiny pile of T-shirts rose up against her leg, a wall between her and the clutter of ballet slippers. Her eyes lingered on the pointe shoes. Once Mo and Mila started what they called pointe work, they had a language only the two of them understood. Sheeda had no idea what jet glue was, or why they'd ever spray shellac in them. She'd had to look up what that even was.

She had a million questions about them. Did it hurt?

How did they stay up on their toes like that? She'd never asked them, though.

She was thinking how to get herself into their conversation when her phone dinged once. She grabbed it, greedy for the distraction.

Before Mo could see Lennie's profile pic shining from the screen, Sheeda cuffed the phone closer to her face. She shook her head, smiling at his message:

> what u gon do when u don't have
> my sister as a excuse to come
> see 'bout me?

She pretended to listen to Mo and Mila while they talked about lamb's wool—whatever that was—while she tried to think of a cute or flirty response. It took her a few seconds to realize Mo was talking to her.

"What did you say?" Sheeda clicked her screen off.

Mo frowned. "What you grinning so hard for? Who dat?"

"Nobody grinning." Even though the smile pulled her cheeks hard. "It's just one of my friends from church. They tripping."

Mo plucked the pile of T-shirts off the bed and laid them in a suitcase. "Is it that basket boy? Jalen?" She fussed playfully. "Tell him I wasn't trying get with him last year and you not trying this year."

Jalen most definitely had tried to holler at Mo during the teen retreat. He found a way to sit next to her every night at revival and called himself helping Mo weave a basket at arts and crafts. He really had thought he was getting somewhere until, after one direction too many, Mo had said—loud enough for everybody to hear—"Boy, look, I don't care nothing about this basket. Please take your basket-weaving, naw-it-go-like-this-not-that self somewhere else."

He'd kept his distance after that.

Sheeda giggled. "Naw, it's not him."

Mo folded her arms. She was used to being answered. "Who is it then? I mean, let us in on the juice. I need something to take my mind off this intensive. I'm starting to trip a little bit."

Sheeda had bad-mouthed all the First Bap dudes to the squad. They were all cocky (Jalen), geeky (Carlos), or not committed enough to the youth ministries—Auntie D's words (Gerard). It was her own fault the squad clowned on First Bap. Sheeda rarely stopped them. And sometimes she started it. She fumbled to get herself together. Mila's voice floated through the air, saving her from making up something.

"She never said it was a guy."

"Oh, true." Mo sat down on the floor and rearranged clothes. "Your clique from Saint Baptist happy they have you to their self this summer?"

First, Sheeda corrected in her head, deflating at the reminder that she was stuck alone. "They hardly my clique."

"They are your church clique, though," Mo said.

Sheeda rolled her eyes. "You sound like my aunt."

"Hey, let me hit you back later. My father is calling me," Mila said.

"All right," Mo called out from the floor. "See you."

With Mo to herself, Sheeda was anxious to talk about something other than dance. "Can you still go to the youth retreat with me when you get back from dance camp?"

"Summer intensive," Mo corrected. For an instant her head cocked to the left, like she was going to say one thing before she said, "Yeah, my mother said I could."

Sheeda's brows crinkled. "You still want to go, don't you?"

"For real, I was surprised I had a good time last year. Shoot, clowning on basket boy was the best part." Mo laughed. "Your church friends act like they don't know how to talk to nobody who don't go church with 'em."

She rubbed the neat stacks of clothes in her suitcase, then patted them. "But, yeah, I'm still going."

Sheeda couldn't dispute a word Mo had said. Sometimes she felt like the only person at Baptist that had friends outside of the church walls. She couldn't lie; it made her feel above them that she'd brought a friend along to the retreat. Having Mo there was the only thing she had to look forward to this summer.

"This year, they're letting us go to the go-kart place and skating," Sheeda said, hopeful that it didn't sound weak.

"Oh, speaking of that." Mo jumped up and grabbed a glossy brochure. She thrust it at Sheeda. "Look at the field trips we're going on during intensive. I can't wait to go to Smash Time Park. They have this roller coaster that goes backward."

"I thought all you did was dance?" Sheeda asked, looking at the photos of kids splashing at a water park, squealing on a roller coaster, and playing volleyball on a beach.

"Basically, yeah. We only off on Sundays. That's when we do field trips."

Sheeda let Mo chatter on. The retreat wouldn't be as much fun as the intensive. They would be staying in a building that looked like a log cabin, eating in a big dining hall with other churches at the site, and having revival every night, which was basically a church service that they pumped with extra songs from the choir to hide that there would be a sermon. The best part was usually being at the pool, when the adults sat back and let the lifeguards babysit them.

When Sheeda's phone dinged twice in a row, she slid it under the pointe shoes so the screen wouldn't show, but the noise caught Mo's attention.

"Somebody blowing you up."

Sheeda blurted, "It's Lennie."

When Mo's forehead creased in confusion, Sheeda pumped the words out fast, her hands nervously folding shorts into too-small squares. "I commented on one of his pictures a few weeks ago, and we started following each other. So he be hitting me up sometimes."

Mo put her hands up, took on a tone Sheeda knew well, the all-knowing teacher to Sheeda's constantly confused student that couldn't be taught. "Girl, Lennie be racking up likes and friends like it's a game of round ball. You was probably part of some stupid contest him and his boys had to get their eight-hundredth girl to follow them."

Hallelujah. Mo wasn't mad.

Sheeda laughed along as Mo teased her brother's weak game. She was genuinely relieved that Mo hadn't gone off. Except, did it have to be that she was just another thumbs-up Lennie had schemed on? Sheeda wanted to show Mo some of his messages. They didn't feel like part of a bet to her.

And if it was just that, wouldn't a bet be over by now? He'd gotten her to follow him back. End of bet.

"Tell him don't be hitting your phone, like some lame, while you just up the stairs," Mo said.

"I don't want no parts of that," Sheeda said.

Mo clipped her phone out of her hand. "I do it."

Mo typed the message so fast all Sheeda could do was force a laugh at Lennie's response.

Oh Imma lame? 😠

Sheeda groaned. "Now he gonna think I'm tripping."

Mo's eyes rolled. "Girl, so what." She tossed the phone back, then sat within the clothes scattered on the floor, hugging her knees. "You and Tai making any plans while we gone?"

"Not really," Sheeda said.

"You sure?" Mo frowned. "You didn't see the last message in the chat?"

"Oh goodness. No." Sheeda scrolled and found it.

I can't believe y'all bit'cis leaving us
for the whole summer. First Mila was
ghost last year 🙄 Now both of y'all
going? My bad and Chrissy too. The ish
is played out. But me and @RahRah be
alright. Zoo. Carnival. Cove Days. So we
good out here.
Bye wenches.🖤

"The heart was a nice touch." Mo howled at her own sarcasm.

Sheeda pleaded, "Y'all can't leave me."

"I mean, it sounds fun . . . ish."

"You got so many jokes." Sheeda read over the roster of activities. Tai had every week covered. "The thing is, I probably can't do any of them."

"Why?" Mo had gone back to packing and only half paying attention.

Sheeda talked it out anyway.

"Vacation Bible School is the same week as Cove Days."

"True. You never do go with us, do you?"

Sheeda nodded. "And unless Ms. Nona plan on going to the carnival with us, Auntie D probably not down for that, either."

"Tai gonna be hot," Mo said, chuckling.

"No probably in it," Sheeda said, not seeing the humor.

"Facts," Mo said.

"Any advice?" Sheeda asked, but Mo was packing and muttering to herself. All Sheeda caught were the words "trash bag pants." She had no idea what those were and didn't care to ask. Mo was already half a world away.

Sheeda was now, apparently, officially Tai's babysitter.

Fact was, they all had a role. Even if nobody admitted it. Mila was the one who kept the peace. Sheeda was wishy-washy (Tai's words for it). She wasn't; she just hated picking sides in an argument.

Mo and Tai were in a forever battle to be the leader. Chrissy had only been there a year. She always let things play out. But Sheeda secretly believed Chrissy was Team Mila and would swing whatever way Mila went.

Sheeda could take Tai in small doses, and that was with Mila and Mo along. Three weeks with her alone was too much. She didn't need to experience it to know that. Now Tai had their lives planned out and Sheeda had nowhere to hide from her bossiness except church.

Tai or church.

Now it was gonna be the lonely and depressing summer.

MONIQUE

Mo loved spaghetti night. The smell of the fat from the ground beef mixed with the sweetness of the tomato sauce made her stomach happy. In honor of her last meal at home, she was going to have two pieces of toast with a big pat of butter. Who knew what the food tasted like at Ballet America. Something told her it probably wouldn't be anything like how her and Lennie cooked—lots of sugar, plenty of salt, enough butter for her mother to fuss that butter didn't grow on trees and no, she wasn't going to stop on her way home to pick some up because they'd run out.

For real, that was Lennie's fault. He ate grilled cheese

like other people ate snacks and put so much butter in the pan, his bread came out soggy. The first time he had to make grilled cheese without butter he learned, though. They always did. Their mother didn't play when it came to them sharing chef duties.

Mo didn't see how her brothers ever got away with the things they did. To her, their mother was not to be messed with. She wasn't a big woman and though her hands were super soft from constantly washing, sanitizing, and moisturizing during her late shift at the hospital—those hands could backhand you quick and hard if you called yourself smart mouthing. At least that's the mother her and Lennie knew. So, if their mother said do something, they always did.

"I buy the food; y'all cook it. Unless you don't want to eat," was Linda Jenkins's favorite phrase, the second anybody complained. If Mo and Lennie hadn't learned to cook, they would have been some starving somebodies.

Mo expertly drained the beef's slippery juices into the empty spaghetti sauce jar, making sure not to drip any into the sink. When she first learned to cook, and by learn she meant teaching herself, she dumped everything down the sink. Didn't it just wash away?

Apparently not. The sink clogged and no matter how

much Lennie plunged it, the water wouldn't drain. The maintenance people ended up pulling a nasty glob that looked like dragon snot out of the pipe. The dude had complained that people didn't know how to take care of anything. Mo had stood by quietly, unwilling to admit she had regularly poured burger and bacon grease down the drain. What did she know? She was only ten. Now she knew better.

As she mixed the sauce into the beef, she pulled herself up into relevé onto her toes and then slowly rolled down. Ms. Noelle said it was important to build up the strength in her feet. She did it anytime she was standing still and barely knew she was doing it until Lennie burst into the kitchen.

Based on the number of girls always sliding into his DMs, her brother wasn't a bad-looking dude. To Mo, he was a little too skinny with a bird chest. Why he never wore a shirt, Mo didn't know. And his pants never sat on his waist, but that's what happened when you never bothered to pull the pants up. Little twists dotted his head like coily worms reaching for the sun trying to grow into full locs. Like Mo's, his skin was the color of almonds, brown with a tiny hint of red, and his eyes were slender ovals, a little too far apart.

His voice boomed unnecessarily loud, "What you doing?"

She pretended he hadn't startled her. "Toe lifts."

He stood behind her, trying to slip a spoon into the sauce. "Ioun even wanna know what that means."

Her elbow connected, softly, with his gut. "Get away. It's almost done." When he took a second too long to step back she lifted her arm ready to crack him good, but he stepped back in time. She called out, "Ma, dinner ready."

"'Bout time," Lennie said, but without his usual frustration. Let him tell it, Mo always took too long to get food on the table when it was her turn to cook. He groused as he brought plates out and put them on the table. "So now I gotta cook dinner every night myself while you gone?"

"I mean, unless you think I'm gonna come back from Philly every night," Mo said, hand on her hip. She dumped the boiling water and noodles into a colander. "You only cooking for yourself. Mommy only home to eat two nights anyway."

Their mother floated into the room, refreshed after her shower. About five-foot-five, she and her two children were height triplets. Her almond-colored skin was a richer brown than theirs, but there was no mistaking them as family. It was almost as if, by the sheer power of keeping her two youngest at home out of trouble, she, Mo, and Lennie looked more alike.

In place of her work scrubs, she wore a pair of cotton cheer shorts and a T-shirt with *Sam-Well Trojans* across it, a relic from the days of one of Mo's older brothers who played basketball once upon a time. She pecked Mo, then Lennie, on the cheek and took her seat at the table. It was a given that they'd serve her. She worked twelve-hour shifts, and on the few nights she was home, dinner as a family was mandatory. Mo didn't mind. Her and Lennie were home alone a lot. She loved the few days her mother was around.

"What's this about I'm only home two nights," she asked, sitting with one foot folded beneath her.

Mo twirled spaghetti onto the plates, trying to be fancy like on the food channels, then drowned the mini-mounds in beef sauce. She put a plate in front of her mother, then filled her and Lennie's plates as she explained. "Lennie was complaining about having to cook while I'm gone."

"I wasn't complaining." He wiped the scowl off his face at his mother's raised eyebrow and softened his tone. "Just saying, why I still gotta cook while Mo gone?"

"Grace on your own," their mother said. She bowed

her head, lips moving silently. Mo and Lennie did the same. She waited until everyone's head lifted before continuing. "So, wait, just because your sister not here you not trying cook for me?"

Mo cosigned, "Ain't that something, Mommy?"

Their laughter went on too long, irritating Lennie. "I ain't say that," he mumbled.

"I think you just mad because you'll miss your baby sister," their mother said, spinning her fork until it bulged with spaghetti. Her smile was sly.

Lennie's eyebrows went up then down like he wasn't sure whether to be mad or sad. They stayed raised. "Ain't nobody gonna miss her. She only be gone for three weeks anyway."

Spaghetti wiggled as their mother stabbed her full fork his way. "Exactly. You get to cook for me all of, like, six times. I carried you nine months. Let's see." She pretended to think before nodding. "We almost be even."

Lennie chomped on his food. A noodle hung out of his mouth as he talked. "All right, Ma, dang." He shoveled his fork under his spaghetti, determined to get as much on it as possible. "That mean Mo gotta cook extra when she get back, right?"

Mo's mouth tightened. "How does that make sense, though?"

"'Cause I'm pulling your slack, yo," Lennie said, before inhaling another forkful. Full mouth and all, he pleaded with his mother. It came out as, "Mah, she gah mae up for beingone, righ?"

Their mother shook her head in disapproval. "Stop talking with your mouth full. But, no, she doesn't need to make up for being gone. When she gets back, y'all split the work like you always do."

Lennie's fork clattered softly against his plate, enough to show dismay, not enough to make their mother go off on him. "You haven't even left for this fancy camp and already things changing." He argued, "That's not right, Ma. Why can't I get a vacation, too?"

"I make a bet with you. Soon as you learn ballet, I'll send you too, hear?" Their mother's small frame shook as she laughed. She grew serious. Her fork hung, foodless, suspended in the air as she spoke in what Mo considered her work voice—firm but caring, like they were patients she was giving medical orders to. "Be happy for your sister. It's exciting that Ms. N think she's good enough to go away to dance."

Mo's heart leaped at the words. She suddenly felt bad for her brother. Lennie wasn't really good at anything, except hustling people out of whatever he wanted and playing video games. With her gone. who would help keep him out of trouble?

He ruined it by keeping up the fuss.

"I'm happy for her. Just saying don't be coming back home thinking you all special or you gon' get back to the hood and get your feelings hurt."

"It takes a lot to hurt my feelings," Mo said, meaning it. Yet it hurt hearing Lennie doubt her. Like she'd ever change just because of dance. She'd been in the talented and gifted dance program the whole school year and hadn't changed. Had danced at La May for three years and hadn't changed. She wanted to point that out, but it would only make him think he was right. And he wasn't.

"Is it even gonna be any other Black people up there besides you and Bean?" he asked, giving her the side-eye as he dug into the rest of his food.

Mila hated being called Bean. But the last time Mo had corrected her brother, he'd gone off about people being bougie. Tonight definitely wasn't the night for corrections.

She took the bait. "I don't know, Lennie. And so what if it's not? I'm there to dance. That's it."

A smirk spread across his face. "So you gonna come back speaking all proper and stuff?" His fork swayed in the air, a conductor's baton emphasizing his words. His lips pursing and stretching in exaggeration. "Hell-er, my name is Monique. How are you, today?"

"Stop, Len," their mother said, but she chuckled. "Leave your sister alone. Going away for the first time is a big deal. Don't fill her head with nonsense." She reached over and rubbed Mo's arm. "Everyone is going to this intensive for the same reason you going—to work on their technique. You and Bean are going to have a great time."

Mo sipped a noodle into her mouth so she wouldn't need to speak. She'd been afraid to admit she was worried about the same thing. All the brochures of Ballet America were stick-legged White girls, suspended on their toes so high she wondered if there wasn't an invisible string holding them in place. Maybe they had Photoshopped it out. Even the one or two Black girls in the pictures looked more like Mila than her, taller and thinner.

Her middle school was nearly all Black and Latino. The few White people at school were in the TAG program. When the school year started, she'd seen them walk down the halls quiet, beating feet to class like the hall was a dark alley where they could be jacked. She couldn't lie, she'd laughed whenever somebody joked about it or yelled out, "What, you scurred, White girl?" But, the teasing got old pretty fast, and by Christmas break things seemed better. She guessed everybody had made enough friends and realized nobody messed with them if they didn't mess with anybody. And she had made friends (sort of) with a few of the girls.

If Ballet America was like that, she could handle herself. Though she couldn't imagine a bunch of ballet dancers coming for her that way. If they had any sense they wouldn't. One good thing about having older brothers, Mo knew how to take care of herself. Words, fists, whatever.

Still, the thought of feeling out of place made the food in her stomach churn. She hoped her mother was right.

Her mother was saying, "I think this is a good time for you to experience something new, Monique." She sat back in her chair, fork down, food forgotten. Mo didn't know how long she'd been daydreaming, but it must have been a minute. Lennie's eyes were glazed. His plate was empty.

Mo uttered, "Mm-hm," unusually loud. It worked. Her mother turned her head just enough to focus her words Mo's way. Lennie sent her a silent thank-you.

"When your little friend, Roland, got shot a few months ago, it just hit too close for me." Her mother's eyes closed. "I'd send you away all summer if I could. Both of you. But I can't." Mo thought she was about to cry. The moment passed. Gone were the three crinkles in her forehead that meant she was trying to solve a puzzle. She beamed at Mo, then Lennie. "So, look, if it means you come back with a little bit of the culture erased, we'll just have to take that."

Lennie jumped on the chance to lighten up the moment. "All right. Go 'head and see. I'm gon' straight clown you if you come back different. I'm telling you now."

"What if she comes back and doesn't want mayo in the potato salad, Len?" their mother said, howling.

"Man-n-n-n." Lennie's head reared back, in horror, as if Mo had already committed the crime.

Mo took their teasing. Usually she and her mother teamed up against Lennie. It didn't take much to make him mad, which made teasing him easy. The least she could do was let him win this one. She let them have their jokes, because reality was, nobody was going to change her. Not in three little weeks. Not ever.

RASHEEDA

Gospel music floated from Auntie D's bedroom, filling the row.

The lead singer's growly scream was accented by the choir's melodic but powerful voices. Sheeda brushed her teeth, stroking back and forth to the song's beat, as if the toothbrush were a violin. She loved this song. The mass choir (the oldsters and youngsters combined) had sang it at the regional cluster and absolutely killed it. Auntie D had gotten so happy that she'd swooned, and Sheeda watched from the loft as the ushers stood over her fanning, nodding along themselves to the music, used to the spirit reducing people to puddles.

The first time Sheeda had seen that happen, she'd been scared. Thought her aunt was hurt. Yola had teased her later. "Girl, she was all right. She just got the spirit." She had started imitating Auntie D, pumping her hands and bending her knees like she was trying to lift an invisible boulder off her head before fake fainting into Makita's arms.

The elders stayed getting the spirit and the First Bap Pack stayed imitating them when nobody was looking. Auntie D was the swayer. Sister Butler did the head shake and run in place. Brother Patterson was the shouter and holy dancer. For real, Sheeda had seen an usher chase him to make sure he didn't hurt himself because he'd start tearing down the aisle so fast.

Probably Auntie D was in her room now palms up to the heavens, swaying along, her lips mouthing the word *hallelujah* over and over like she was in a trance. She never said it aloud, just formed the word. One time, Sheeda had counted thirty *hallelujah*'s in a row—each one coming out faster than the one before until it became one long string: *hallelujahhallelujahhallelujah*.

Much as she went along with the First Bap Pack's teasing, there were plenty of times she'd been in church and felt her emotions bouncing off each other like they were working up to something. She'd never actually gotten "happy" shouting, crying, or jumping. But sometimes, if it was a song she loved or when the congregation shouted and waved them on as they danced, her heart felt so full she thought it would burst. At those times, her throat would clog with tears that never fell.

By the time she'd finished brushing her teeth, she was feeling that way. She wanted to go hug her aunt. Hold on to her. Do something to release or pass on some of the feeling inside. It didn't feel bad. Sometimes it just felt like it had nowhere to go. She guessed that's why people let it out.

A new song came on, one she didn't know, and like water swirling down the tub the emotions slowly drained away as she stood in front of her small closet packed with neatly hung dresses. She put her hand on one she'd been dying to wear. Every time she tried, something else was happening at church that required a specific outfit. Praise dance uniform or the red polo and khaki pants for the choir, which she hated because the elastic in the pants made her look like an oversized ten-year-old.

It was a burgundy fit and flare dress with three-quarter length sleeves. It came slightly above her knees—mid thigh, really, but she didn't like to describe it that way. Auntie D had thought it was too short, but the dark color made up for its length enough that she'd given in. Sheeda went to pull it down from the hanger. Finally.

Her aunt's voice came from the hallway. "Rasheeda, don't forget today is women's and children's day. The color is navy."

Ugh. Of course.

She patted the dress, as if consoling it instead of herself and hurriedly grabbed a navy blue, short-sleeved dress with a white Peter Pan collar. It was so boring compared to the burgundy one. It was bad enough having a whole closet full of dresses that Auntie D had basically hand selected as GFC—good for church. But it was women's and children's day so the church would be awash in navy, making her disappear in their sameness.

It ended up worse than that. She walked into church and Yola and Kita had on dresses nearly the same as hers. Only Yola's was much shorter—Sheeda couldn't believe Sister Carla let her wear it—and Kita's had a white stripe going around the bottom of hers that, unfortunately, made her hips look bigger than Sheeda's.

"I'll meet you in the kitchen after," her aunt said. Before turning she stopped, gave Sheeda a raised eyebrow. Sheeda recited in her head as her aunt added, "Don't be acting up in service."

"Yes, ma'am," Sheeda said.

Yola giggled. "Like clockwork she make sure she say that, huh?"

Sheeda wanted to roll her eyes but was too afraid one of the elders would see and report back. Instead, she snorted her frustration.

It was the same lecture each Sunday. For no reason. Sheeda had never acted up in church. But her aunt felt the need to say it anyway.

And it wasn't like her aunt wasn't going to be there, too. She was the kitchen manager and always spent the first twenty minutes of service in the back making sure things were good for any after-service refreshments. But once she was done, she'd take her seat on the left side of the church, fourth row. Which was only two rows in front of where Sheeda, Yola, and Kita sat every Sunday when they weren't part of the service.

They made their way to their seats. Yola always made it a point to sit between Sheeda and Kita—needing to be the one in the middle of any conversation at all times. There wasn't a children's section, but most of the young people sat in the sixth and seventh pews stuck with the ushers behind them—to ensure they didn't get too rowdy—and their parents spread out in front of them.

Sister Butler banged on the organ's keys and everybody

stood as the men's and women's choir strolled in. The women were sharp in their navy blue dresses, the men in white shirts and navy blue slacks. They took their time, making sure they were seen doing a new two-step down the aisle—right foot, left foot, right step back. Right foot, left foot, right step back.

It was going to take them a while to reach the loft.

Sister Butler went HAM on the organ. She always seemed to play harder when the men's and women's choir sang, like everybody was hard of hearing or something. Sheeda guessed most of them weren't much older than Auntie D—in their late thirties. Still, the organ was turned up to a thousand.

While the congregation sang, Yola started talking like they weren't standing in the middle of pounding music and offkey voices. "Y'all down for going to the Park Heights carnival with me?"

Sheeda leaned in, head ducked into her hymnal, pretending she was trying to sing along. Yola's voice was a loud murmur among the singing.

"My mother said she'll take us. Y'all can sleep over, and then she'll drop us at rehearsal the next evening."

"Funnel caaaaaake," Kita said. She pumped her hand. No one would ever know she was praising sugary confections instead of the Lord. "Is Jalen going?"

Yola frowned. "I don't know."

Kita laughed. "Lies. I already saw his post on FriendMe—'bout to go down at the PHC this year."

Yola cheesed. "Umph. Busted, one hundred percent."

"It sound like he bringing some friends." Kita leaned in and locked eyes with Sheeda. "They better be cute, right, Sheeda?"

Sheeda could only nod. She wasn't trying to yell like they did. No one had ever told them to be quiet, but she didn't need somebody snitching: "Your niece was talking the whole time in service."

Yola raised her hymnal in front of her face as she fussed. "He can't help how his friends look, so don't trip."

Makita rolled her eyes and repeated, "They better be cute."

Yola turned her head to Sheeda. "Are you gonna come with us?"

The choir finally made it to the loft. Their voices raised for the grand finale, then it was quiet. The church burst into applause. Pastor Weems beamed, then signaled for the congregation to sit. As he spoke, the sanctuary was too quiet for Sheeda to answer.

They each brought their phone out, laying them

discreetly on their laps so they could keep the conversation going in the Bap Girls Do chat.

Sheeda hated the chat's name. It had been Yola's idea of a joke. "Just because we go to church all the time don't mean we wack," she'd said, looking up at Sheeda, then Makita, for confirmation. Confirmation of what Sheeda didn't know. Maybe to the other kids at Baptist the three of them were cool, but real talk—not to anyone else in the world. She'd gone along, of course, and spent most days trying to keep the chat near the bottom of her screen. Because, if Auntie D ever caught wind of that name, she'd flip.

Sheeda could already hear it: Baptist girls do what? What do they do, Rasheeda? You better not be messing around with these little boys out here. I'm not about to be taking care of you and a baby—from the Book of Auntie D, first chapter, second verse.

The lectures were so annoying. She wasn't even out here checking for no dudes like that. Lennie didn't count. That was just a crush.

The chat rolled on without her input. She wasn't sure she wanted to go to the carnival. She just didn't know how to say it, but didn't want to boldface lie in church, on Sunday.

Yo-La:

You in @RahRah?

CutieKita:

It's fun. Last year

Gerard and Los went.

Yo-La:

And almost got us kicked out

Sheeda finally dropped in with her go-to jewel:

I need to ask my aunt.

Yo-La:

😒 It's us. I know she'll say yes. She

loves us 😍

Rah-Rah:

No lies told. Still gotta ask tho

She didn't want to go. For a lot of reasons.

Hanging in church or at church functions with Yola and Kita was fine. That's really where she wanted to keep it. Also, everybody from the Cove went to the Lake Hill carnival. Park Heights was closer to her church, which was twenty minutes away. Something about going to another community's carnival felt wrong. Like she wouldn't be able to come back to her own, if she did. She knew that was stupid. Still, it didn't feel right.

The sit down, stand up portion of the service had started. They stood, at the pastor's command. Sheeda's phone lit up. Lennie.

The grin on her face was as bright as her phone's backlight. She had been afraid to hit Lennie up to tell him that Mo had been playing on her phone. Had hoped he'd text her, so she could explain. She was relieved to see his message.

DatBoyEll:

So imma lame?

Rah-Rah:

Mo wrote that. Sorry. She was
playing around.

DatBoyEll:

I shoulda known. She on one

DatBoyEll:

U had a brotha low-key pressed in
those red shorts

She put a Bible on top of the phone and followed along with the Scripture as the pastor read. As soon as they were allowed to sit again, she balanced her phone on her lap, sitting erect, eyes (never the whole head) cast down as she tapped away.

Rah-Rah:

DatBoyEll:

probly not gonna see u once my sister
gone, huh?

Rah-Rah:

My aunt definitely would not be

down for me hanging out if Mo

isn't there

DatBoyEll:

kinda figured. I can still hit u up tho,

right?

Rah-Rah:

Yes

DatBoyEll:

Thas whas up

Yola's head was all in Sheeda's phone as she stared down. "Who's that?" she whispered loudly.

"Who?" Kita asked, her eyes but nothing else stretching Sheeda's way.

"Nobody. My best friend's brother was asking me something," Sheeda said, happy when the phone dimmed.

Going to the carnival with them was one thing. And she wasn't sure she was saying yes to that. She definitely wasn't ready to have Yola and Kita up in her business. What in the world kind of wacky summer was this going to end up being?

MONIQUE

So, this was college?

The entire campus was stuck in the middle of a forest. At least it felt that way to Mo.

In a way it was like the Cove. Trees enclosed the buildings, making it feel like there was no world beyond it. Except instead of hip-hop and go-go music blaring from cars or houses, the sounds of chirping birds and crickets—definitely, honest to God crickets—filled the air. Everyone she passed seemed to be whispering. As Mr. Jamal was moving their stuff into the room, anytime someone spoke to him it was in a hushed voice like even the outside was under some sort of library inside-voices rule.

Mo wanted to yell out *hello* to see if it would echo back but had serious worries that the campus police she'd seen in a golf cart would roll up and give her a ticket. Though how fast were they rolling up on anybody in a golf cart? Right then and there she knew there probably wasn't any crime to speak of. Even if his golf cart got to the crime, all he'd have was a ticket pad and a pen to punish anybody.

Even though their dorm building was one of the newer ones (according to their resident advisor, or RA as she called herself) and made of brick instead of the large gray stones like others she'd seen, it looked like a housing project to Mo. It had fifteen floors and the slowest elevator on earth. Their room was on the sixth floor. Poor Mr. Jamal took the stairs, and by the fourth trip proclaimed that Mo and Mila were plotting to kill him—mostly because they had carried tiny things like a lamp and duffel bags while he beasted suitcases in both hands and comforters under his arms.

Every time Mo went to the truck to get more stuff, she counted. She was stuck at three. She scanned the parking lot, the lobby, the stairs, and people getting in and out of the elevator and was still only on three by the time Mr. Jamal, soaked with sweat, hugged them both and told them to be good and have a good time.

Three Black people. Her, Mila, and Mr Jamal. That was it.

Watching Mila's father's taillights as he drove off, she had muttered, defeated, "Well, two, now."

Lennie was right. Which was bad enough.

It wasn't that she hadn't expected it to mostly be White people. But her mind had a hard time with the math. Fifteen floors of rooms, two people per room, sometimes four, and her and Mila were it? She felt surrounded. Even more when she realized that they had to share a bathroom with the two girls in the next room. Their suitemates.

Sometimes the White girls in TAG had asked the stupidest questions—like, why do you need lotion? Lotion. The thing that's advertised all over TV by a White model. One girl had legit asked her that. Mo wasn't for it. If somebody asked to touch her hair, she was going off.

While they were still unpacking, a White woman had peeked her head into their room, scaring the daylights out of Mo.

"Oh, hi. I didn't know anyone was here yet," she'd said, trying to play off her nosiness. "I'm Brenna's mom. She's over there making up her bed. I'll have to send her over to meet her new suite buddies."

Mila said hello. Mo didn't. Like, who just busts into a room they know isn't theirs?

The woman asked fifty eleven questions, none of which Mo answered.

"Where are you girls from?"

"Are you girls sisters?"

"How far is Del Rio Bay from here?"

"How long have you been dancing?"

If it wasn't for Mila, it would have been dead silence after every question. Mo went right on unpacking, not even bothering to look up anymore. She was still listening, though. The woman went on nonstop—Brenna was an only child, Brenna had been dancing since she was two, five other girls from Brenna's ballet school were now with professional companies.

She didn't seem no ways tired of sharing and probing and probably would have kept on if a man's voice from the other side of the bathroom hadn't called out, "Hon, let's let the girls get to know each other. We have a long drive back."

Her lips had crimped, like she was mad that he'd blocked her investigation, then spread into a smile as she chirped, "Well, let me get back over and help make up this bed. I'll send Brenna over to meet you ladies."

Mo had locked the door behind her. If Brenna was

coming over she was going to have to knock.

Mila giggled. "You're wrong."

Mo scowled. "This our room. How you just gonna come in uninvited?"

"True." Mila took her time placing clothes into the dresser across from her bed. "She scared me."

"Me, too." Mo had cleared her throat, unsure whether to go on. But decided if she couldn't be real with Mila, then it was going to be the longest three weeks of her life. "Did you hear her gasp when she stuck her head in?"

Mila frowned in thought. "No. But I guess she was surprised to see us in here."

Mo sucked her teeth. "Surprised we was Black, maybe."

"You think so?" Mila asked.

"How she surprised that people in here when everybody checking in?" Mo challenged. "Aren't all the rooms gonna have people in them eventually?"

Mila didn't take the bait. She knew Mo and hadn't earned the unofficial title of peacekeeper for nothing. She kept unpacking as she answered. "Well then, she can give her daughter the heads-up."

"I know that's right," Mo said.

They laughed about it, wondering aloud how many

other people would be thrown off to meet them. Mila guessed no one else. Mo figured just about everybody would be. They balanced each other out that way.

At La May they were the two best dancers and were always in the front line during center work. At first all Mo had wanted was to be better than Mila. But Mila had never once returned that same energy. She had always been one of Mo's biggest cheerleaders, helping her fix her form and whispering encouragement before they performed. Mo couldn't imagine doing something like this with anybody else.

The entire ride up, Mo had gone between excitement and fear. By the time they'd arrived, it had settled into a bubbling uncertainty. Having Mila there kept the bubbles from rising into her throat and belching nervousness everywhere.

With their clothes put away, Mila ventured into the bathroom to claim a spot for toiletries. Mo sat on her bed against the two new fat pillows she'd brought. They pushed against her back as she texted Sheeda.

Mo'Betta:
OMG . . . help!!! 😩

Rah-Rah:
Heyyyy. Missing you already.
What's up?

Mo'Betta:

we just chillin before dinner. I think me
and Mila are for real the only 2 black
people here. 😔

Rah-Rah:

wait how many people in the
program?

Mo'Betta:
girl IDK.

Rah-Rah:

that's wild.
Tell Mila I said hey!!!!

Mo'Betta:

she's 🤚 and frfr all these girls skinny
the same and white the same. 😆 I can't
tell nobody apart.

Rah-Rah:
😂

Mo'Betta:
Whut u doing? 👀

Rah-Rah:
What else, for real? Still at church
waiting on A.D. to close the
kitchen. 🙄

Mo'Betta:

😄 Oh I thought maybe it was Praising
Him on High bible study time

Rah-Rah:

Wow. You wrong for that. 😂

Mo'Betta:

A.D. would flip if she saw that. Delete
that text!! 😂

Rah-Rah:

You already know. LOL But how is
it though? What your room look
like?

Mo'Betta:

The room hella big. Mila took the best
bed by the window. 😠 We have mad
space though. Its bigger than the rooms
in our row for sure.

Rah-Rah:

Pics please!

Mo'Betta:

so we share a bathroom w/two other
girls. White . . . of course. So why the
advisor call them sweet mates and I'm
all—white people always be making up

cute names for crap. But she was saying
suite cause the 4 of us share the same
bathroom. LMAO

Rah-Rah:

Sweet mates. 💀 How are they?

Mo'Betta:

IDK only met the one girls mother. I
swear her eyes popped when she saw
me & Mila was Black.

Rah-Rah:

you think they prejudice?

Mo'Betta:

they can be on some nonsense if they want
and catch these hands. But IDK. Mila think
she was just surprised cause she was being
nosy sticking her head in our room and didn't
know we was in here already. So 💀

Rah-Rah:

I mean even if the mother is racist
don't mean the daughter is

Mo'Betta:

Don't make me no difference. If she
don't like black people then she don't
need come in my room. It's w/e

> **Rah-Rah:**
>
> I'm kind of tripping that you living
> with white people.

Mo'Betta:

You?! Girl I'm on another planet right
now fr fr

> **Rah-Rah:**
>
> just promise you won't replace me
> with Becky

Mo'Betta:

I won't . . . cause my sweet mates
names are Brenna and Katie

> **Rah-Rah:**
>
> Of course Katie. It had to be Katie.

Mo'Betta:

Right? And Brenna's mother did a real
life "Jamila? Oh that's an interesting
name."

> **Rah-Rah:**
>
> Jamila is an interesting name?
> Umph imagine if I was there.
> She'd be like, Rah-She-Da . . .

*pretends to think of something
not racist to say . . . and fails*

Mo'Betta:

😂😂😂 I can't w/you rn

Rah-Rah:

Remember when Ms. Hopkins
called me RahSEEda the entire
year? Like there's an actual H
there, pronounce it!!!

Mo'Betta:

But you let her tho.

Rah-Rah:

Cause I'm really gonna break on
my English teacher? 😟

Mo'Betta:

💀 anybody can get it!

Rah-Rah:

Remember when Tai went off on
Mr. Berk for telling her she owed it
to herself to learn more about her
Korean heritage? Lawd! 🙄

Rah-Rah:

She almost got suspended for
that. Thas exactly why I wasn't

> about to do all that w/ Ms.
> Hopkins. RahSEEda close enough.
>
> Lolz
>
> **Rah-Rah:**
> Where'd you go?
>
> **Rah-Rah:**
> Wow 😬

Mo had stopped texting because the door leading to the bathroom creaked open. "You didn't lock the door," she whispered, gauging whether she could shut it on the person before they popped in.

"I forgot." Mila stared at the door, too, erect on her bed like she was ready to bolt depending on who walked through.

Mo put her phone down. "Hello?" she said with bass in her voice.

The face of her suitemate filled the narrow opening. "Hi. I'm Brenna. Can we come in?"

Mo wasn't sure she was going to say no, but she wasn't sure she was going to say yes, either. Mila answered, relieved smile on her face, with a cheerful, "Hey. Yeah."

Mo sized up her new roommates. Brenna had a face full of freckles and straight ashy brown hair to her shoulders. She was about Mo's height, but both her legs equaled one of Mo's.

The other one, Katie, had thick and wavy auburn hair that stopped at the middle of her long neck. Her face had some color to it, like the sun had kissed it then ran. Her brown eyes took in everything, including Mo and Mila, unapologetically. She towered a good four or five inches over Brenna.

"What you guys up to?" Brenna asked. "I mean, obviously you're not guys. But saying gals feels weird. What? Are we in a production of *Oklahoma*?"

"Chilling," Mo said, thinking it would stop Brenna's nervous flow and that they'd see nothing was going on and go back to their side of the bathroom. But Brenna held up two pairs of pointe shoes.

"Anybody else need to sew? It's so much easier when I do it with other people." She frowned at Katie. "Ms. Perfect has already sewn all her shoes. I hate her."

In between Brenna's mother's eleventy million questions she kept saying, practically praying, that she hoped Brenna and Katie would be compatible roommates. Mo knew Brenna was joking about hating Katie, but still, how are you gonna joke like that with somebody you didn't know?

Katie didn't seem bothered by the comment. She trailed behind Brenna. What else was she going to do when she didn't know anybody else but her roommate? It made Mo even happier that she had Mila.

Next thing Mo knew, Katie and Brenna were on the floor, Katie with her long giraffe legs stretched out, leaned back on her hands. Her eyes scanned their desks, under their tall beds, even their walls, taking inventory of their stuff. Brenna sat cross-legged with thread, ribbons, and shoes scattered around her. Mila took a pair of her own shoes out, deciding to join Brenna. They exchanged tips on the best stitch, and Brenna showed her battle wounds from sticking herself—something Mo never did because she sewed so incredibly slow.

When the sewing lesson was done, there was silence.

Nobody seemed to know how to break it.

Right before it got awkward, Brenna said, "Sorry about earlier. My mom's such a 'copter parent."

"A what?" Mo asked, then, feeling her face was twisted, she softened it to what she hoped was just confusion and asked again, "What's a 'copter parent?"

"Like helicopter," Brenna said. She hopped up and ran around in a small circle, arms out, making deep humming sounds, then burst out laughing.

"That's more of an airplane, though," Mo said, eyeing Mila for confirmation that Brenna was a little wacky.

Brenna thought about it, laughed, and plopped back down on the floor next to her stack of pointe shoes. "True. Just saying my mom is a little overprotective. Also, this is my first time going to a residential intensive. Her biggest fear was that I'd end up with suitemates that were going to be a bad influence . . . whatever that means."

Katie's head bobbed in agreement. "My mom is worried I'm going to come back with an eating disorder."

Brenna rolled her eyes. "Forever conversation in our house."

"You already pretty thin," Mo said talking to Brenna, but meaning both of them. All three of them, really. Her and her muscular legs were the odd girl out.

The one thing she'd loved about watching Ailey dancers was how strong they were. If there was one thing she knew she was better at than Mila, it was jumps. Ms. Noelle had even tapped her thighs one day and said, "Such lovely strength."

How many meals would she have to miss to shrink her thighs? She didn't even want to know.

"Yeah, and it's just my natural size. But let me say I'm not hungry and my mom is all 'Bren, you've got to eat. How are you going to have the energy to dance if you don't eat?'" Brenna's fingers expertly moved the needle through the shoe's canvas as she talked. "I mean, God, can I not be hungry sometimes?"

"We're all going to lose weight, though. The food here is gross," Katie said.

Mo could already tell Katie was going to be the know-it-all. She had a way of talking like everything she said was word. But Mo actually cared about the food. "Gross how?" she asked.

"Just like junky food. Dinner is always hot dogs or hamburgers and pasta." Katie's mouth turned up like she'd just named rat tails and roach legs.

"I like those things," Mila said.

Mo happily cosigned. "I mean, for real, so do I."

"But not every night," Katie said, with a hard shrug of her shoulders like it should have been obvious what she meant.

"Well, if it's all that bad, why is a dance program serving it?" Mo asked. She sat back against the wall on her bed cross-legged, liking that she towered over the girls on the floor.

"Because the food at the Ballet America café is different. Healthier. We eat breakfast and lunch there and dinner here at the college. So for dinner we eat whatever the college dining hall fixes, and it's always fast foodish," Katie said.

Mo had forgotten that the older dancers stayed at the Ballet America studios, in their dorms. They ate healthier, huh? That was code for no taste, far as Mo was concerned. And they could have that. She'd take the hot dogs and burgers. Every day, too.

"So who all is interested in BA's pre-pro program?" Brenna asked, intently eyeing each of them.

Mo squinted, confused. "Pre-pro?"

"The pre-professional program?" Katie said, like she didn't get why Mo didn't understand.

"Their all-year program?" Mo said.

"Yes," Katie said.

Mo's eyes rolled. "I just didn't know it was called a pre-pro."

"I'm def interested," Mila said, when she saw Mo's eyebrows raising. "But I heard it's really competitive to get in." There was nervousness in her laugh. "I read up *a lot* before coming."

"Same," Brenna said. Words rushing like she'd been waiting on this conversation. "BA has one of the best pre-pro's on the East Coast. Congrats to all of us getting into the Summer Experience. We're halfway there."

"I don't know about halfway," Katie said, eyebrows knitted. "But yeah, I'm interested, too. My mom wouldn't let me audition for anything more than three hours from home."

The conversation raced on with ballet schools Mo had never heard of dropped left and right. She hadn't looked at other schools. Hadn't thought about how competitive it was going to be to make it into BA's pre-pro until that moment. She figured if they were all good enough to get into the summer, then they were good enough for the whole year.

There wasn't any way to hide how much she didn't know about ballet or being at an intensive. But, for real, Katie had one more time to talk with that unsaid "obviously" in her voice. After that, Mo wasn't responsible for how she was going to get her put in her place. Sweet mate or not.

RASHEEDA

Sheeda lay still, eyes closed, letting the sun warm then burn her forehead. It was official. This was summer. The house quiet, because Auntie D had already left for work. Getting to feel the sun instead of being up and dressed before it rose. Having the whole day ahead of her to . . . do what?

The day stretched out long and lonely.

The only good thing was Lennie had hit her up before she went to bed. The messages had been innocent:

DatBoyEll:

the house gonna be mad quiet

tomorrow

Rah-Rah:

aww u gonna miss Mo too

DatBoyEll:

dang why that emoji tho? I mean yeah
imma miss her. Thas my baby sis. But
c'mon man u clowning. lol

Rah-Rah:

DatBoyEll:

naw I hope she do her thing tho. I can't
hate on her grind. How come u ain't
going to this dance thing?

Rah-Rah:

I didn't get in TAG so I guess Ms. N
didn't think I was right for it.

DatBoyEll:

u dance tho right?

Rah-Rah:

At church yeah

DatBoyEll:

Oh u one of them people thas church
good? LMAO

Rah-Rah:

ok bye

DatBoyEll:

I'm teasing shawty. But u know how
people be good singers in church but
then u hear 'em try tear up a song from
the radio and be like 😨 ay maybe this
ain't ur thing

Rah-Rah:

😄 fax

DatBoyEll:

I ain't trying take ur shine. I seen u
dance at the rec. u got the goods

Rah-Rah:

👑 thanx!! Me and Tai the only
ones from the original La May
group that didn't make it into
TAG.

DatBoyEll:

kind of messed up

Rah-Rah:

big fax

She had settled good into the conversation, then her
bedroom door swung open. Her eyes, already dripping

with guilt, raised to meet Auntie D's inquiring face. With her clear brown-sugar skin, hair coiffed to the gods, Auntie D was what people called cute. It was the two deep dents in her cheeks, dimples that showed up when she smiled or frowned. Not that a lot of people saw her smile. Unless she was in church talking to the pastor, deacon, or one of her fellow sisters in Christ, her face stayed frozen—right eyebrow arched, lips perpetually pressed together like she was worried somebody was going to force-feed her, dimples popping in displeasure. Her aunt was quick to judge and quicker to put you in your place—in the most godly way possible, of course.

Sheeda had stood up, properly respectful, her arms to her side so her phone's screen warmed her legs. "Ma'am?"

Auntie D's right eyebrow peaked. "Do you know what time it is?"

"Eleven thirty," Sheeda said.

"Exactly. Obviously you forgot that I get notifications when you text after eleven p.m. I'm ready to go to bed, I don't need this thing pinging me this late." With laser-pointed interest, she stared at Sheeda's phone. "It's summer, but that doesn't mean you need to be up texting all hours of the night. Who in the world are you talking to this late?"

As she lied, Sheeda prayed her aunt wouldn't ask to see the phone. "Just talking to Mo."

Auntie D folded her arms. "The number I have for her isn't this one." She peered at her own phone, then back at Sheeda's.

It wasn't anything for Auntie D to go through her stuff. The only reason she didn't go through Sheeda's phone was because she didn't have to. Thanks to notifications, she knew if Sheeda was texting at school or at night and had access to her social media. Also, she knew every one of her friend's phone numbers so when she looked at the phone bill, she would know who Sheeda was texting.

What Auntie D didn't know was that Sheeda used the social media her aunt checked just enough to make it look legit—mostly random pics of her and the squad. The social media she used regularly was under a fake name. It wasn't anything bad on her social media accounts. Not to her. But Auntie D tripped over anything, even if somebody else put up a photo wearing something she disapproved of, Sheeda caught the sermon. The fake account was easier.

She cursed herself for slipping. She'd been too caught up to remember the stupid late-night notifications.

The thought of her aunt seeing that she was talking to

a boy had made Sheeda's legs wobbly, but it didn't stop her from continuing the lie.

"Mo and her brother switched phones because hers got broken and her mother didn't want her going away without one."

"I tell you what. You better not go breaking or losing your phone. I bet I won't be jumping through hoops to get you another one." She shook her head. "I know she's gone and y'all probably catching up, but it's late. Time to cut it."

"Yes, ma'am," Sheeda said, holding in her sigh of relief until her aunt's footsteps disappeared.

The day she'd made the fake FriendMe account, she was so nauseous Auntie D made her drink ginger ale and eat soup for dinner, thinking she was coming down with something. That was the biggest lie she'd never told.

This time, determined to have at least one fun thing for herself, she'd slid into new territory by agreeing with Lennie to only talk through the chat app. Only this time, instead of nausea, she was dizzy with the adrenaline—lighter, like her head could pop right off her body and float to the ceiling. She usually did what she was told and probably always would. But Auntie D made everything a reason to head to the altar and ask for forgiveness. Her and Lennie were only talking. It wasn't a big deal.

It had been a close call, though. That's when she'd decided she'd go ahead to the carnival with Yola and Kita. Lennie seemed to like only hitting her up at night. There was seriously nothing else for her to do.

Lying there in the bed, instead of the excitement for what the day could bring, there was only emptiness in her chest. Some of it was already missing Mo. But that wasn't all of it. Summer reminded her of home. Home before the Cove was home. Thinking about it made her stomach bubbly.

Summer had been when her and her five cousins ran the big, mostly dirt-packed front yard of a small house with the paint so chipped you couldn't tell if it was white or an ashen gray. Once school let out, there was nobody to tease them and call them funky or laugh at how their clothes were frayed and tattered. It's why she'd loved summer back then.

Summer was safe.

Summer was also one of the few times that she thought about her mother. She realized that she hadn't thought about her old house, or for that matter, her mother, in a long time.

She took inventory of her tidy box of a room. There

wasn't a sock on the floor, a shoe peeking from under the bed, or even a stray hanger waiting to be hung. Auntie D demanded clean spaces. Sheeda wasn't even allowed to hang anything on the walls. Just because they lived in a low-income row house didn't mean it was going to be unkempt and cluttered, from the Book of Auntie D, first chapter, first verse.

Sheeda didn't see how a poster of Mack Boy Oh was going to clutter up the bare wall, but Auntie D's house, Auntie D's rules. So, it stayed rolled up in a tube in her closet.

The house she shared with her aunt wasn't just clean, it was vanilla and totally empty of anything that made it unique. Compared to her friends' houses that always smelled like some type of food cooking and every corner had evidence that people lived there, their row smelled like cleaning spray and looked like a movie set pretending to be somebody's house. A long time ago, Sheeda had loved how clean it was. How much space there was for only two people. The row had felt like a mansion compared to the tiny, always-on-the-verge-of-collapsing house she'd shared with her mother, Uncle Dewayne, Aunt Rhonda, and their five kids in North Carolina.

Down South, her and her mother shared a room.

Her five cousins shared another, and her aunt and uncle had their own room. Nine people in a house meant there were always people everywhere. There was always stuff everywhere, too, like trash, food, and roaches.

Five-year-olds didn't think much about bills or house repairs. Or how not one of the three adults in the house ever got up and went to a job. At least, she hadn't thought about it until that day the White dude visited and told her mother that the way they were living wasn't sanitary and he might have to recommend taking Sheeda away until Desiree Tate could find better conditions.

Conditions. Sheeda remembered that word, clearly, because she hadn't understood it.

No one ever explained it to her. All she knew was, her Aunt Deandra came to visit, soon after, dressed in a pale pink linen dress that Sheeda kept touching because it was so clean and bright. Her mother said she was going to stay with Auntie D for a while, or at least until she could find her own place. And when Sheeda arrived in the Cove and saw her aunt's spotless house and realized she had her own room, "a while" was fine with her.

Sheeda didn't know anything about guardianship then. All she knew was her mother never did get another place. And, at first, Auntie D would send her to visit her mom each summer. The first summer Sheeda had been glad to be back with her cousins. The second she'd spent most of the summer cringing from the cockroaches and praying none crawled in her bag. By the third Auntie D announced, "Your mother is trifling, no sense in me making you stay in that pigsty just so she can still claim she your mother."

Sheeda had put up a small fuss, too ashamed to admit she'd been relieved. It was the first time she'd ever been thankful for her aunt's many rules.

After that, Sheeda and her mother only talked by phone. There were always promises of her mom coming up to visit. But it seemed like before every visit, her and Auntie D got into it about something and then her mother would cancel in a huff and mutter about how Deandra needed to remember who was Sheeda's mother.

She and her mother still talked. If you could call it that.

Sheeda's first summer without visiting her mother was the year "the schedule" was born. The year, she and Mo became certified best friends. They'd followed the schedule ever since:

- Sleep in late

- Have a bowl of cereal in front of the TV

- Call or text as they watched their favorite shows

- Meet at the bleachers to watch dudes run ball on the basketball court unless it was Tuesday or Thursday, then you hit the rec for arts and crafts

- Chill at the rec to play games in the evening

The schedule was so ingrained that Sheeda looked over at her phone, momentarily panicked that she'd missed a message from Mo fussing that she was watching one of their shows alone.

This summer, the whole squad had decided they'd watch *Straight and Narrow*, a reality show about these girls in a juvenile detention center. Sheeda and Mila always felt sorry for the girls. Mo usually played color commentary, pointing out how if that was her . . . , then following it with what somebody wouldn't say to her. Tai hate-watched it, wondering, every single time, why they'd pick *this* show.

Sheeda was surprised to see a bunch of messages. Apparently everybody except her was already up. Mo, Tai, and Yola had hit her phone. Her eyes scrolled up and down her chat screen until she was positive Lennie hadn't sent her any new messages. He hadn't. And what was she going to say to him? Hey . . . what you doing?

Dumb.

He was doing the same thing she was doing this summer. Boo squat.

She'd wait until he made a move.

She sat up in the bed, knees to her chest, anxious to see what Mo was up to, then decided she'd save those messages for last.

The fact that Mo was over two hundred miles away and still thinking about her filled Sheeda with love so fierce she had to scroll away from Mo's messages, fast, in order to read the others first.

DatGirlTai:

You up? 👀

DatGirlTai:

Hello?! My God, are you gonna sleep all day? 💀

DatGirlTai:

We going with the rec to the zoo right?
Nona already signed my slip. They due today!

The plans were the closest Tai would probably ever come to being openly pressed about something or saying she was lonely. Sheeda didn't really feel like spending a whole day in the hot zoo with her. But Mila was Tai's best friend and Mo hers—they were best-friendless together. She left Tai hanging a little longer, unsure how to tell her she definitely couldn't go to the zoo. She planned to leave out that she'd never bothered to ask for permission. She opened the Bap Girls Do chat.

Yo-La:

What did your aunt say?

Rah-Rah:

I can go

Yo-La:

Ayyy 😁

Rah-Rah:

🙂

Yo-La:

Gonna be litt-y 😍

With that done, Sheeda raced through brushing her teeth, slowly poured milk over a bowl of Honey Toasted O's, then propped her phone up against the sugar bowl. Her fingers delicately scrolled to Mo's messages. She snorted at the first.

Mo'Betta:

You probably up eating ur toasty O's 😁 meanwhile only cereal here is seeds and granola clusters and skim milk. Seriously? Skim?! Oh but also yogurt and fruit. I repeat yogurt and fruit. I can't. 😞

Mo'Betta:

not loving how early we gotta get up.

It's literally like getting up for school.

WTF?

Mo'Betta:

wench when are u getting up?! ••

Mo'Betta:

we gotta take a class so they can put us

in our right level. 🎧 I thought we was

just in class w/whoever was our age. 😕

Wish me luck.

Sheeda read Mo's last message three times. When they tried out for TAG and were waiting for the results, Mo had gone between frustration and annoyance, but she never seemed worried. Maybe she wasn't now, but seeing "wish me luck" in writing made Sheeda nervous for her best friend. She texted her fingers off sending the best wishes she could:

Level 10 lets go! You got this! Good

luck!! 🖤 🖤 🖤 🖤 😉 💨

MoBetta:

Thaanxxx! Sleeping in huh? Lucky!

She was excited and scared for Mo, but something else, too. Envious. When she got back, spilling over with all the new things she did, Sheeda would only be able to do what she always did, listen.

Nobody ever cared what happened at First Bap. Sheeda barely did. It didn't totally stop her from talking about her church stuff. What else was she gonna talk about? But this time, her same old felt even more inadequate compared to the summer Mo had ahead. She couldn't help pitying herself as she texted Mo:

> Shoot, don't have nothing else to do
> but sleep in. I know ur nervous but I bet
> its still more fun than I'm having. 🙄

Mo'Betta:

I bet this three weeks fly though.

> **Rah-Rah:**
>
> I hope so. I mean not trying rush it
> for you. I know u and Mila excited.

Mo'Betta:

If u get bored hit Lennie up. He ain't
doing boo but playing video games all
summer. 😆

Sheeda sat up at the mention of Lennie, but tread carefully.

> **Rah-Rah:**
>
> He only hit me up at night when
> he bored.

Mo'Betta:

Umph don't let him play you like that.

Then again, wait . . . I'm not in it! 😐

Rah-Rah:

Nothing to be in, for real. Not like

we talk much.

Mo'Betta:

Good cause I don't feel like playing

match maker for y'all.

Rah-Rah:

Didn't ask you to. 😐

Mo'Betta:

Salty much? I was just kidding. But do

you. 😐

Rah-Rah:

My bad wasn't being salty. 🙂 You

not in class yet?

Mo'Betta:

On the bus heading to the studios. Mila

asking what u and Tai doing today? 😄

Rah-Rah:

Bye! 👋

Mo'Betta:

Definite salt that time 😂

Rah-Rah:

Mos def! 😆

Sheeda read over the messages, especially what Mo had said about Lennie. Mo had been right, Sheeda was salty when she responded. It had just slipped out. It didn't seem like Mo cared if her and Lennie talked, but Sheeda wasn't totally convinced and it seemed better to not care. But it came off defensive and backfired on her. She wasn't good at clapping back or being fast on her feet with sarcasm.

She needed to get it together. If Lennie was her only distraction this summer, she was in trouble.

She said a prayer of forgiveness for the lies she was about to text to Tai.

Hey, girl. My Aunt making me hang out

w/my church friends. I can't do the zoo.

😐 I hit you up when I'm free.

She probably wasn't going to hear the end of it for leaving her hanging.

She ignored the messages from Tai that came in after—it was too early to argue—and settled in to binge a few eps of *Straight and Narrow*.

Her and the girls in juvvie were in lockdown together.

MONIQUE

The only place Mo had seen like Ballet America's studio was the Players' Cultural Arts Center back home. Its massive size. The way it stuck out next to the buildings beside it like it knew what happened behind its walls was better than whatever went on at the other businesses.

Since TAG, she'd been in the Players' more than she had her whole life: once for TAG auditions, another time to see a play, and then to watch a modern dance company that wasn't Ailey but was still amazing.

Players' was an auditorium and a maze of music and dance rooms and studios. If it was artsy, it went down at the Players'. That explained its size. BA's building could probably hold a whole cul-de-sac of row houses and was only used for a bunch of dancers. Check that. A bunch of ballet dancers. Not even like a troop of ballet, modern, jazz, tap, and hip-hop. One type of dancer. And somewhere in there were dorm rooms where people her age got to live every day.

With its all-glass front, it took Mo's breath away. From the street she saw people filtering into the studios and wondered how people walking by didn't stop and enjoy the dance classes like they were shows.

She snapped a photo and texted it to Sheeda:

This place big fancy!!! 😱

Once inside, her tennis shoes squeaked against the shiny ultra-white tiles on the floor. That's when she noticed that most everyone else was wearing either flats with their tights pulled up over their ankles or these things that looked like soft snow boots. Their feet didn't make noise.

"How come everybody got those bootie things on?" she asked Mila, focused on picking up her feet so they wouldn't squeal against the floor. She followed the crowd and signs pointing them up a flight of stairs.

Mo swore Mila sounded almost like their suitemate Katie when she said, "They're to keep your feet warm."

But then it was gone as she added, "Aren't they cute? But they're, like, fifty dollars."

"Oh, naw. Fifty for slippers?" Mo side-eyed the shoes surrounding her. Her mother had to work OT to get her a second pair of pointe shoes. She couldn't see paying that much for something just to keep her feet warm. Hello, just wear socks.

She felt out of uniform in her tennis shoes. At least she did have on the same type of warm-ups as most everybody. Ms. Noelle had given her and Mila a pair of black nylon trash bag pants, as gifts. Mo had thanked her, but after doubted out loud to Mila if she'd ever wear the pants that made swishing noise when she walked. It was like wearing a jacket on your legs. Turned out that was the point, to help warm up your legs. They were working, too. Mo's legs were toasty enough to sweat.

If anybody else felt like stripping down, they hid it. They all filtered into the studio. The glass let the outside in and made the packed room of dancers explode with brightness. The rec and TAG's narrow, windowless studios were nothing like this. When it was time to dance across the floor, only two of them could go at a time or somebody would get elbowed or kicked as they leaped and turned. And all they had was the usual fake lighting that buzzed a little until the bulbs warmed up.

There were probably a hundred dancers gathered, and even though they had plenty of space, Mo stayed close to Mila, their arms touching enough so Mo was sure she was still there. That her blackness was still there. It had been one thing to not see other Black people, back at the dorm; now she was literally drowning in pale faces, every one one of them with a bun glued tightly to the back of their heads (and booties on their feet. Don't forget the booties).

She couldn't tell one dancer from the other, even when she was looking right at them. If she hadn't known for sure that Katie and Brenna were beside her, if they turned their heads they could have been anybody.

She lost herself in a text to Sheeda, needing to feel close to somebody:

Yo, everybody here is a ballerina barbie
doll. It's wild.

She chuckled at Sheeda's response:

And you and Mila the only two
Black ones? Oops, factory sent the
wrong dolls. 😂

Funny thing was, she hadn't lost hope that there would be other Black girls at the intensive until they had gotten to dinner the night before. By that time, she begrudgingly added anybody who wasn't White to her count and even then the number only reached six—three were Asian and one looked like she might have been Latina.

From her spot in the back, against the wall—for extra support in case Mila decided to inch away—the brown faces bobbed in and out of the sea of white like buoys bouncing on waves that were too far apart to swim from one to the other safely.

Mo wondered if the other brown girls felt as alien as she did. It didn't seem like it. Their chatter was a steady hum of a comfortable language she didn't understand.

"Parkwood's SI is good but you only partner if you're in six or higher."

"The sample schedule totally lied. We didn't do any Balanchine last year."

"I heard that Mr. Val already knows who he wants to dance the Pas this year."

SI? Balanchine? Pah?

Her stomach growled, reminding her that it usually had two bowls of cereal and maybe even a slice of toast by now, thank you very much. Instead, breakfast had been an apple and juice. Katie hadn't been wrong; the food was gross. At least breakfast was. Mo couldn't bring herself to try the dry-looking egg-white sandwich. The yogurt, white and slimy, looked more like lotion than something to eat. And the cereal was basically seeds. She prayed that lunch would be better. They weren't fitting to starve her no matter how nasty the food was. She hoped.

"I'm so nervous," Mila said.

The confession pushed away some of the cold fear snapping at Mo's insides. She ignored her phone and pressed tighter against Mila to steady the tremor making her shiver. She whispered so their suitemates couldn't hear, "I've never been around this many White people in my whole life."

Mila's chirping laugh was a little bit of home in the studio.

Mo shifted, trying to give the dancers in front of her their own space while still claiming a piece of floor for herself. There was more than enough room in the cavernous studio. But everyone was herded together. Maybe they were as nervous as she was even if it wasn't for the same reason.

The thought that maybe she had something in common with some of these girls, after all, calmed her.

She peeked through the bodies at the glass wall that looked out onto the busy city street below. Cars drove by, their engines and horns silenced by the dancers' growing banter. Sun reflected off a wall of mirrors, making the room feel never-ending. It was pretty.

She was really here. She was really going to do this.

She found enough courage to ask the question that had been on her mind since she'd seen the words *placement class* on their schedule. "What if we're not in the same level?"

Mila answered without hesitation. "We will be. Mademoiselle said that mostly everyone our age is at a similar stage."

Mo took a closer look at the robot ballerinas surrounding her. Their height, each of them erect as a soldier standing at attention. The way nearly everyone stood with their ankles together, feet splayed in first position like they could dance on command. Even Mila stood that way. "These girls been doing this every summer. No way they're not better than us."

Than me. She forbade the confession from spilling out.

Mila squeezed her hand. "Mademoiselle said that the dancers that are super strong or super weak will get moved up or down accordingly. Everybody else will stay put. We'll be together."

Mo hoped so. She was horrified at the heat she felt in

her eyes. She couldn't cry. Not here in front of all these White girls.

Katie nudged her arm. "Are you okay?"

Mo wanted to say something sarcastic. The look of genuine concern on her suitemate's face threw off her words. She only nodded, releasing the grip she had on Mila's hand.

"It's kind of scary always being judged, but trust me, BA isn't as hard-core as some of the others," Katie said. "I did Pavlov's last summer and figured out that the Russian schools aren't my thing."

"One of the girls from my studio went there last year. Our director said they forced her turnout," Brenna said.

Katie nodded knowingly. Mila was listening intently. She didn't nod, but she also didn't ask what Mo wanted to know—how could somebody force a turnout? She knew what a turnout was. Ms. Noelle spent every class, their first year, teaching them the proper way to turn their hips outward. How could somebody force that?

She left it alone. She wasn't going to keep asking a million questions.

Maybe Mo was just too nervous and her ears weren't working the same, but Katie didn't sound as know-it-all as she had back at the room. Feeling lost, Mo wouldn't have cared if she had been. She needed some of Katie's confidence right about now.

Like they had made a pact that Brenna would be the talker at the dorm and Katie would take over at the studio, Katie probed, asking where they danced "year-round," reminding them that the last week was the week they'd be under the microscope for the BA pre-pro, and giving them inside tips like always try to stand near the front or go in the first group when it was time to go across the floor to draw the adjudicator's eye.

Since listening and being able to act on corrections was one of Mo's strengths, she soaked it all in, deciding to fake it until she could make it. She pieced together that adjudicators were the instructors who would be watching them during placement class.

Even though she hadn't known it was called a pre-pro, thanks to the brochure she had already known the instructors would be watching them the entire intensive and inviting the strongest dancers to join the school. (So take that, Katie.) *Strong* was definitely her. Somebody at BA must have thought so. She'd gotten a whole scholarship. She just needed to get through these placement classes.

If Ms. Noelle was right and they were looking for dancers with potential, she had that all day. She wasn't sure if she could really go to a school where she was the only Black girl, but it wasn't about that. She was going to show she belonged here.

A petite woman with a large, beaklike nose called out in a voice louder than her small body should have been able to muster, "Good morning, everyone. I'm Sharon McCord, the director here at Ballet America."

The dancers applauded. Mo looked around thinking someone had walked in. But they were clapping for the director lady. Mila was clapping beside her as the woman talked on.

"BA has a proud tradition of training some of today's most well-known professional ballet dancers."

She listed off examples, each one getting a bit more applause and awed admiration. Mo hadn't heard of them. She waited to hear their dance teacher's name. She'd gone to BA and she'd danced professionally for a while. But the director lady—Ms. Sharon, she forced herself to remember—went on without uttering Ms. Noelle's name.

"You will be exhausted after your days and nights here. If you're not, ask yourself, did you do your work?"

Mo couldn't tell if she were joking or not since her face didn't crack a smile. Apparently, nobody else could tell, either. There was nervous laughter.

Ms. Sharon wasn't a big woman. Her silver hair was in a neat bun. Mo imagined that it stayed that way without bobby pins since it looked like she'd been doing it that way forever. She was mad styling in a pair of wide-leg pants that stopped above her ankles and black leather ballet slippers. She didn't seem mean, but something about how she talked made Mo want to pay attention and get it right.

"All right. We're going to divide you into three groups. Group A will go into studio one, group B will remain here, and group C will go to studio three."

The names were called off quickly. If you missed yours, oh, well.

Mo's breath caught as she got called for group B.

"Kathrine Jensen," the adjudicator hollered.

Katie's eyes rolled. "Why do they ask what you prefer to be called if they're just going to call you by your name anyway? Cool that we're in the same group, though."

Mo concentrated on each name. She blocked out the noise of people gathering their dance bags, of feet tipping softly across the floor, of whispered conversations as people left their comfortable circle then melded into new groups—and prayed Mila's name would be called for B.

Ms. Sharon closed the book of names. "If I haven't called your name already, you're in group C and I'll meet you down the hall."

"Mila, we're groupies together," Brenna said, her smile all teeth.

Mila put her hand up and Brenna happily high-fived it. She smiled Mo's way. "Kill it."

Mo forced the words, "You, too."

High-fives were corny, but she sort of wished Mila had given her one.

"*Merde* you guys," Katie said.

Brenna sang it back over her shoulder as they walked out.

Mo stared after them. The question slipped out before she could stop it. "What's *mared*?"

"Are you serious?" Katie asked.

Mo was ready to snap on her, but Katie seemed more curious than ready to clown.

Katie sat down and pulled out ballet slippers. She slipped them on her feet. "Do you guys go to a ballet school, dance studio, or what?"

"Neither for real," Mo said, listening close. If Katie said something to the left she was going in, suitemate or not. "Our studio is a program at the recreation center in our nabe. And we both in a talented and gifted dance program at school."

"Ohh. Okay." Katie nodded.

"I mean, you ain't need say it like that." Mo backed her butt against the wall, putting her shoe on while standing. "Like—oh, that explains why she don't know boo."

"I didn't mean anything by it." Katie's face never flinched. And what she said wasn't an apology. "A lot of this seems new to you. I can see why. That's all." She was unbothered by the frown on Mo's face. "*Merde* is, like, good luck."

"Then say *good luck*," Mo said in a huff.

Katie shrugged. "It's a ballet thing."

"It must also be a ballet thing to not recognize talent," Mo said, snapping her other ballet slipper on. "Me and Mila are in the same level at home."

Katie smiled. "You know these groups are just in alpha order by last name, right? These aren't our placements."

The realization dawned on Mo slowly at first, then like a cool splash of water awakening her. She played it off with a hasty, "I know."

"You totally didn't know."

She and Katie stared at each other, each of them waiting for the other to make a move to decide if this was going to be an argument or funny.

Katie looked confident, like she'd seen all of the cards in Mo's hand and knew she had nothing.

Mo wanted to bluff and couldn't. She confessed, "No lies told. I didn't know."

"So obvs," Katie said, with a smile.

Mo put her fist out. Katie bumped it with her own.

"*Merde*," Katie said.

"Time to kill it," Mo said.

No translation required.

RASHEEDA

The ride to the carnival was torture. As close as Makita and Yola seemed at church, things were shaky from the start. Yola sat up front, on her phone—no doubt, texting Jalen—leaving Sheeda and Makita hostage to Ms. Carla's questions.

Sheeda was tempted to pull out her phone to see what Mo was doing, but Sister Carla hadn't stopped talking since they'd gotten into the car. Her questions and demands streamed out behind each other as she peeped into her rearview, smiling as if to make sure Kita and Sheeda hadn't escaped.

"I'm so glad you three are finally getting together. I

know Deandra says you stay busy, Rasheeda, but the girls would love to spend more time with their sister in Christ." Peep in the rearview. Smile. Eyes back on the road. Then, before Sheeda could answer, "It's going to be a lot of traffic with everybody picking up at once, so make sure you all meet by the PHC Volunteer of the Month parking sign. Okay?" Peep in the rearview. Sort of smile but mostly eyebrows knitted to make sure they knew she meant it.

Sheeda wanted to make a face at Makita and somehow mentally scream—*oh my goodness, will she ever stop talking?* But for all Sheeda knew, Yola checking out and her friends having to answer umpteen questions was normal.

"Reverend Weems's youth day sermon was a good one. I hope you girls were listening." Her laugh was light before she dove into a full lesson. "I mean, obviously Miss Yolanda wasn't since she hasn't taken her face out of that screen. But I'm glad to see you two girls have enough manners. Must mean you heard the pastor loud and clear about not letting the world distract you to the point where you let it come before what you know is right."

Right up to that point, Sheeda had played along and answered when she could:

"Yes, it is a little harder to get together because of TAG."

"Yes, ma'am, we'll meet you there, nine sharp."

But the second church came up, she gave Makita a slide glance. Makita's face was tight as she stared straight ahead at Yola's head, so Sheeda offered, "Oh, I didn't hear that part of the sermon," then bowed out completely.

As Mo would say—I can't.

Even though obviously the pastor and Sister Carla thought phones were low-key evil, mini machines eating up their minds, she sat hers in her lap, thanked God her brightness was low, and tapped off a quick message in the Bap Girls chat:

a little help. Your mother talking our

ears off 😶

Yola's head popped up as if she'd been pricked with a pin.

"Ma, what time do we need to meet you?"

Sheeda groaned under her breath. Way to show you didn't hear a single word, Yolanda.

By then Makita had flames coming out of her eyes. She rolled them, one hard squeeze, then all whites showing, when Yola's message popped up:

My bad. Just trying see when Jalen

gonna meet us.

Sheeda scrambled out of the car, away from the last-minute and final reminder about what time to meet. The sights and sounds of the carnival swirled around, inviting her to join.

The first thing she noticed was it was like the Lake Hill carnival in reverse. They were outnumbered by White people. Other than that, it pretty much had the same rides, same food. So a carnival was just a carnival. Instead of proclaiming her obvious discovery aloud, she sniffed at the thick smell of oil for French fries, funnel cake, fried Snickers, and anything else the vendors could dunk in it.

Screams of joy and fear pierced through the *boomp pah boomp pah* sounds of the kiddie rides. Faint strains of a hip-hop song came from one of the rides near the back, luring the older kids. She leaned her head toward it, trying to catch which song it was, when Yola and Makita's bickering reached her.

"Can't Jalen just text you when he's here?" Makita's light brown eyes never veered away from the long line at the ticket booths. There was tightness to her voice like she'd lost patience one sentence ago but was fighting to hide it. "We can stand in line while we decide if we're getting wristbands or single tickets."

Yola squinted. "I mean, how many rides are we really going to get on for real?"

Makita's head swiveled as she took inventory of potential rides. "It doesn't matter. Most of the rides need at least four or five tickets. Even if we get on . . ."

Determined to throw a kink in the plans, Yola said, "But it's three of us. How we gonna do the rides that are only two seaters?"

She was shorter than Sheeda by at least three inches, tiny. Not just thin but small like she'd fit into somebody's backpack. Light skin, more yellow banana than golden, with a small nose and wide dark brown eyes that were now looking up directly at Sheeda. Her arms were folded tightly, like she was holding back what she really wanted to say as she waited.

Makita was Sheeda's height. She was what Sheeda thought of it as Hershey Bar–toned and had thick hips that made all her shorts too tight. Long box braids framed her face. Her wide nose was flared with the effort to stay calm. She popped her eyes at Sheeda as if to say *Well?*

Sheeda's first thought was, I don't know, I mean y'all invited me. Nobody in her squad would have ever expected her to be the one to decide. She couldn't not answer. That would leave them standing all night going in circles.

Yola obviously didn't want to get on many rides. In a plot twist that surprised no one—she and Makita were only a loose cover so Yola could meet Jalen. Since they'd gotten out of the car, her neck had been straining, looking over and through rides for him. Makita, on the other hand, had talked nonstop about the Tasmanian Devil and Tilt-A-Whirl in the chat. Now they wanted Sheeda to be the tiebreaker.

Wait for Jalen or start their fun?

She tugged at one of her twists, feeling the rough texture between her fingers as she wondered how to please the two girls, who up until now she'd only ever been with when she had to. Somebody was going to be mad, and it would be her fault.

Everyone around them was enjoying themselves. The carnival grounds with its swirling lights and jangling music had made their troubles disappear. She wanted to feel the same way. The sun had gone down and the summer air had a chill that felt good on her skin. It was the perfect night to be out. She didn't want to waste it fussing. The answer floated out of her mouth, "Let's get the wristbands. When Jalen gets here, that's on him if he wants to do rides."

Makita smiled huge. She went on about the rides she loved and hated. Without taking a breath, she pointed out the funnel cake place to avoid: "It's like eating crunchy oil bites."

Sheeda tried to ignore how Yola sidled over to the line with them, head still checking for Jalen, not saying a word. She stayed looking down at her phone, cradled in her folded arms, or craning to see through the bulging crowd.

The few hours they spent together at rehearsals didn't leave a lot of time for arguments. The tension from Yola was unbearable. Sheeda wanted to change her mind and suggest they text Jalen, ask where he wanted them to post up and wait on him—maybe make the circle friends again.

It would probably make Kita mad, but . . .

A colony of bees were in her chest frantically looking for a way out through her throat. She swallowed against them, answering just enough to keep Makita's constant flow of conversation going through the long line and getting the wristbands. Right as the buzzing reached her head, Jalen appeared out of the crowd. He wore khaki cargo shorts and a fresh, white pocket T-shirt, looking every bit the part of a Park Heights carnival goer.

Relieved, she yelled his name and waved him over, happy to shrink out of the lead.

He nodded at Sheeda, smiling big at Yola. "What's up?"

Yola's voice was a high-pitched squeal. "Hey, Jay."

Makita's head bobbed as she looked over Jalen's

shoulder and off to his side. "I thought you was bringing some friends."

"Couldn't find anybody to roll with me." He shrugged. "Why you got mad attitude about it?"

"Because you always frontin'," Kita said.

Sheeda wanted to cosign. It was hard to explain. Sometimes Jalen was all right. But most times Jalen was irritating. Always bragging about things and people that Sheeda had a feeling weren't real. But how would they know? They usually only hung out at church. Did he even have friends outside of First Bap? She stayed quiet, a spectator once again in the circle, as Jalen defended himself.

"Ain't nobody frontin', Kita. Nobody could come." He raised his hands in a so what?

"Did you get a wristband already?" Yola asked, her eyes never leaving his face.

"Naw. Y'all?"

Makita got loud. "Of course we did. We been here almost a half hour already."

"Come on. I go with you to the line," Yola said.

They were barely a few feet away when Makita went off. "I knew he wasn't bringing anybody. That's why I wasn't trying to wait all night for him." She watched as the crowd swallowed Yola and Jalen. Sheeda recognized the hurt in her eyes and tried joking it off.

"At least we know who riding with who."

Makita snorted. "Right." She pointed to a ride. "Want to get on that one?"

"You don't want to wait for Yola?"

Makita headed to the ride, no longer interested in Sheeda's permission. While they waited in line, she stayed facing the ticket booth where Yola and Jalen were meshed together like conjoined twins. Her lips twisted into a pout. "No. 'Cause if Jalen doesn't want to get on the ride then neither will she, and I'm not going to spend all night doing what he wants."

Yola couldn't have run off any faster than if somebody had shouted, *one, two, three, go* and popped one of those track guns. And yet, watching Yola snuggle up to Jalen made Sheeda think about Lennie. She wanted to feel the same buzzy friction jumping off Lennie's skin while she looked up at him, grinning all wide. No way she'd say that to Kita, though. She played the middle.

"Jalen can get on my nerves, but it wouldn't matter as much if he had brought some of his invisible friends, for real, for real."

"Not his invisible friends, though." Makita laughed, all along nodding in agreement. "But, yeah, true."

"Yola did sort of dump us," Sheeda said, then regretted speaking her mind.

"Not even sort of." Makita looked like she'd bit into a sour candy. "Sis straight dipped."

Sheeda played along. "Ghosted us to our face."

Makita yelled toward the black sky, "Curbed us, lovely."

Their cackling was lost in the piercing music of the ride. By the time they'd strapped in, Sheeda was genuinely glad she'd come. Three rides later she wasn't so sure anymore.

Catching Up

Rah-Rah:

whatchu doing? ●●)

Mo'Betta:

not a thing. Lights out at 10:45.

Rah-Rah:

umph they tell ya'll what time to

go to bed?!

Mo'Betta:

I mean fr fr we just gotta be in our

room at that time. I'm tired so not even

mad.

Rah-Rah:

were u sleep?

Mo'Betta:

No. Me and Mila was just talking. We
got our class placements and we not in
the same level. 🙃

Rah-Rah:

Tell her I said hey. Wait. Y'all not in
same level?!

Mo'Betta:

She said hey back. And no 😤 Her and
our sweetmate Brenna in same class
and me and Katie in same class.

Rah-Rah:

That's good that you know
somebody though. Right? 🤔

Mo'Betta:

I guess. You have a good time w/your
Jesus friends at carnival? 🙂

Rah-Rah:

SMH some parts of it was cool.
But good time? 😐 Are u cool that
y'all not in same class?

Mo'Betta:

TBH naw I'm not cool w/it. I can't take
nothin from her. I know she a good
ballet dancer. I get it. But peep this—I'm
in level 2x and she in 3x. There's a level
3, so she TWO levels ahead of me. That
ish is mad dunk.
😠

Rah-Rah:

Oh no. wow. 😱 😶 Whenever I see
u and Mila dance together you be
hanging right there w/her, tho.

Mo'Betta:

IKR exactly—I CAN hang w/Mila! But
the instructors don't think so. They so
irky. 😒 Katie said sometimes they do
move people up tho. 🙏

Rah-Rah:

🙏 I promised Tai we'd kick it at the
rec. So, um 🙏for me to please!

Mo'Betta:

sending prayers up—dear lord give
Sheeda the strength to ignore Tai's
shade, the courage to put Tai in her

place and the wisdom to know when
to do which one. Amen and halleluryah

Rah-Rah:

Amen Amen and AMEN

Mo'Betta:

Lemme go on bed. Mila knocked
already. Good luck w/Taizzles.

Rah-Rah:

And I just screenshot that to
show her. There will be immediate
hate of the nickname

Mo'Betta:

I kno u kno better than to evah
screenshot me, sis. Nite girl.

Rah-Rah:

Nite!

MONIQUE

After only a few days, the faint stink of feet had made itself at home in their room. The bad news was, they couldn't get rid of the smell. They sprayed the freshener when they left and the funk was waiting when they got back. The good news was, Katie and Brenna's room smelled just as bad (maybe worse), and after a few minutes she'd be nose blind.

Her arms throbbed and her legs were spaghetti. All she wanted was a shower and to lie her head on a soft pillow. Her leotard was stuck to her. It was like wearing a swimsuit, only worse. The leos were so tight they dug into her leg.

Mila was on her bed, in a robe, chilling. Mo perked up, suspicious. Mila and Brenna had been back in the room for a good thirty minutes already. Mila should have been finished with her shower. The schedule said so.

Mo was the only one who didn't think they needed a schedule for who took a shower first. It was four of them. Call first and let it rock from there.

"Why you not in the shower?" she asked like it didn't matter. But even as Mila answered, "Bren got into the shower first. I'll go next," the blood raced, pushing the words out of her mouth at the same speed that it pulsed through her body.

"Mila, we did a whole schedule. What's the point if everybody can shotgun their way in? You need to let her know not to do that again." Her voice went from fierce whisper to purposely loud so Brenna could hear. "It's your turn, period. Period, it's your turn."

The tiny crimp of her lip, like a hook lifted the corner, was Mila's weak attempt at a smile. "It's fine. For real."

Mo knew the tone and look of Mila's calm-down vibe from the many times Mila stepped in between her and Tai's epic disagreements. At home, Mo usually backed down. She needed to do that now. Let Mila go ahead and sit there all sweaty and sticky, funking up her own comforter. But something about hearing the water running, knowing Mila was supposed to be in the shower, made Mo's blood run hot.

She stormed into the bathroom, ignoring Mila's pleas of "It's not a big deal," and stood outside the shower stall, yelling to be heard over the water.

"Brenna, you can't be getting in the shower anytime you want. It was Mila's turn."

Brenna stuck her head out, full of shampoo. "What?"

The word raked against Mo's nerves. If her and Lennie ever said "What?" to their mother, she shot off like a cannon about how rude it was. Now Mo saw why. The word was irritating. She lit into Breanna. "Why are you in the shower?"

Brenna squinted through the water dripping down her face. "Um, to get clean."

"Okay, yup, that's cute." Mo stepped back to avoid the water dripping out of the stall. "It's Mila's turn to be in the shower first. You can't just jump in whenever you want. Weren't you the one who had the great idea of a schedule in the first place?"

Finally Brenna caught the anger in Mo's voice. She stuck herself back into the stall, put her head under the water. Tiny tides of water hit the floor as she rinsed, quickly. She talked over the noise. "Sorry. I just jumped in. I didn't mean to—" She turned off the water, still shouting to be heard. Her towel slid off the shower door. She came out, wrapped up, dripping everywhere. "My bad, Monique."

Her suitemates stayed calling people by their full name. It annoyed her. It was like always talking to a teacher who refused to call you by anything else. She corrected her, "Mo."

Brenna's eyes lifted to the left, wondering what she'd said wrong. "My bad . . . Mo. I was so gross after class, I just jumped in."

"We all gross after class." Mo pointed to the handwritten schedule taped to the back of her and Mila's door. "But the schedule is big as day."

"No. You're right. I didn't even look." Brenna stepped past her, tipping lightly so as not to slip. She was already apologizing as she entered their room. "Jamila . . . I mean, Mila, I'm sorry."

Mila's eyes slid away from Mo's, but not before Mo saw the embarrassment.

"It's okay," Mila said, her smile at Brenna all but screaming *please ignore my ghetto roommate*. She grabbed her towel. "I was texting my dad anyway. I think he's missing me."

"Aww that's cute. My dad is probably glad for the break." Brenna laughed and her hair sprinkled the floor with droplets. "But, anyways, big promise, I'll actually read the schedule now."

It wasn't enough for Mo. She'd lost thirty minutes of her life while they put the stupid schedule together—so durn right, they were gonna follow it. Why couldn't Mila at least back her up on that? "How you not following a schedule you started?" she asked.

Mila's exasperated sigh made it clear that Mo could stop talking at any time now. Mo threw her hands up. Fine. She was done. She sat down, hard, at her desk, refusing to sit her sweaty body on her comforter, just wanting Brenna to go back to her side of the bathroom.

Mo knew her suitemate was a little afraid of her. For one, the way she almost always directed what she said to Mila first. It annoyed Mo how she was always hugging or touching Mila, like they'd already known each other for months.

Mo knew her face was a little twisted sometimes. Only because any thought Mo had that she and Mila would catch up once in the room was always shattered by Brenna coming in. Even after a full day of being together, she made herself at home on Mila's bed talking, wanting to play card games, or dragging Mila to somebody else's room to "see something."

Everything was "we," like the four of them had to be together 24-7. Thankfully, Katie wasn't the same. She'd come over sometimes, usually by Brenna's invitation. It wasn't that they didn't have a good time talking about things that had gone on in class, comparing notes on what the teachers were saying to them about their technique and stuff—Mo just didn't want to do it every day.

Everyone was getting close too fast.

Maybe she was the one tripping.

She didn't want the girl scared of her, just follow your own stupid schedule. It was obvious her loud voice made Brenna nervous. She probably shouldn't have based on her.

Once at dinner Mo had asked, loudly, how the cafeteria had run out of brownies. Brenna shoved hers over with the quickness. "You can have mine."

Mo appreciated the offer, but she'd only asked a question. She wasn't going to start a riot over the thing. Brenna, Katie, even Mila had looked at her like they were holding their breath, waiting for her to kirk over a daggone brownie. She couldn't help that she talked loud. Or that she spoke up when somebody was being done wrong.

Just as she thought that, Brenna, damp body and all, came over and wrapped her arms around Mo's shoulders. Her stringy wet hair plastered itself to Mo, some of it tickling her face.

Brenna playfully pleaded, "Don't be mad. I'm not used to sharing a bathroom with anybody. Only-child probs." She crossed her fingers. "Last time I forget."

Mo wasn't sure whether to be irked by how touchy-feely she was or glad that her goofiness was always nearby. She almost wanted to apologize, so Brenna knew they were cool. But an apology would mean she was wrong. And she hadn't been.

She wasn't going to apologize for standing up for herself and for people she cared about. It wasn't something she could turn off.

Neither Brenna or Katie came back over that night. At first Mo was glad. Her ears didn't mind the break from Brenna's nonstop talking. And her and Katie were in classes together all day; they didn't need to be together at night, too. She used the quiet to catch up with Sheeda.

Sharing a bathroom with three other people ain't the move.

Rah-Rah:

LOL but it gotta be better than

sharing w/your brothers

Mo'Betta:

oh true. Still. LoL I gotta lock the door

cuz if I don't Brenna just bust in there

talking like its normal to be talking

about how much her feet hurt while I'm

butter butt balled nekkid in the shower.

Rah-Rah:

😂 space, it's a good thing

Mo'Betta:

Bruh, all good!! 😂

She laughed to herself reading about the wack time Sheeda had at the carnival. For some reason, Mo could never keep up with who was who of Sheeda's friends. Sheeda had probably told her their names a million times, and every time Mo wanted to ask, "Who?" She didn't this time, letting Sheeda vent about the two girls she was stuck with and reminding her the time was already going by kind of fast. And speaking of time, it wasn't until the RA knocked on the door, then stepped in to confirm both her and Mila were in the room, that it hit her that maybe Brenna had warned Katie away from their side of the bathroom.

Mo put her phone down, not sure how to feel about the new silence.

Mila had earbuds in and was reading a book. Mo wondered if she was mad. But didn't want to know bad enough to ask. All she had been doing was trying to make sure nobody thought they could roll over them. It hurt her that Mila had seemed embarrassed.

Mo wanted to remind her that Mila never minded Mo sticking up for her when Tai got on everybody's nerves or when Simp said something stupid like how Mila was skinny enough to hide behind the streetlight. But she didn't.

If Mila was fine with suitemates that never knocked, the stupid shower schedule and people not following it, that was on her. Mo couldn't roll with things that easily.

After a while, Mila nodded off. Mo listened to her soft breaths. She could never drift right off. No matter how tired Mo was, it always took her body a little while to realize it was finally time to stop turning and leaping across the floor. Then another few minutes to remember she wasn't home. Then more time still to get used to how dark and quiet it was.

There was a safety light behind her row house to keep people from dealing drugs in the woods. The only thing it succeeded in doing was filtering into Mo's room enough for her to read the poster she had on her door, a gift from Sheeda's Auntie D when they all joined La May that had a dancer in a flowing white Praise skirt, mid-leap and read: *Let them praise His name with dancing.*

Mo had never slept in a totally dark room until now and was glad for the block of light from the hall creeping under their door.

She lay in the dark room, her mind processing like a software program, going over things she'd heard during the day. Things she'd said or did. Katie was the only person she knew in her class. For real, she didn't want to know anybody else. They were there to dance. She didn't let herself think about what she'd do when Katie made other friends.

When, because it was going to happen. She needed to be ready to have nobody to talk to.

The silence in the room helped her imagine going all day without talking to anybody.

The only noises were Mila's breathing, murmurs from across the bathroom as Brenna talked Katie to sleep—because she thought whispering was basically not shouting, and the RA's heavy footsteps as they walked down the hall doing room checks. Eventually, when those sounds stopped, there was nothing else. Mo popped in her earbuds and let the darkness overtake her until the music lulled her to sleep.

RASHEEDA

Sheeda wasn't in the best mood. The carnival had been a disaster. She'd held back complaining too much to Mo. Sounded like she was already dealing with too much at the intensive. So Sheeda had only told her that it hadn't been as much fun as when they all went to the carnival.

Truth was, things were a mess.

When Kita had refused to answer Yola in the group chat, Yola had gotten angry. She'd even threatened to call her mother to tell her they'd left her. Never mind that she was the one who had dipped on them. Still, the claim had made Sheeda nervous—Auntie D would never let her do anything if she couldn't go out without drama with her church friends. Then Kita had rolled her eyes and said, "Let her tell her then." All Sheeda could do was roll with the flow.

At one point, Yola had walked by where they were eating. Sheeda waited for Kita to call out to her. When she didn't, Sheeda had stayed quiet, too. When Yola walked past a second time, she'd finally seen them. She came over, short legs pumping, asking why nobody had answered her. As the two of them bickered, Jalen and Sheeda had stood there, awkward bystanders.

Sheeda hoped they would smooth it out once they got to Yola's, but Kita had called her mother, saying her stomach hurt and asking to be picked up. Yola had been hot and kept saying Kita was just jealous. She ragged on her for the longest time, then proceeded to ignore Sheeda the rest of the night as she texted Jalen.

Sheeda hadn't taken anybody's side but still caught Yola's heat.

And now, she was taking plenty of her own heat from Tai.

Sitting on Sheeda's front stoop, words tumbled out of Tai's mouth like she'd been saving them up for this one moment. They were a gnat in Sheeda's ear as she texted the talking head emoji and the eye-rolling emoji to Mo. She waited for Mo to answer. Ten minutes later, still nothing. No doubt, she was in class.

The neighborhood pulsed with people. It always did near Sheeda's row house that stood beside the main road of the hood—the rec center to their front, the basketball courts to their back. Sheeda could clock half the nabe coming and going. She loved people watching, especially today. It gave her something to do while Tai laid her out.

A car rolled by, slow, music thumping so loud the car beat like a heart. A few little boys chased after it, shouting the lyrics blasting from the car's window. A group of little girls were chalking the sidewalk. From where Sheeda sat, their drawing was a series of fat bubbly shapes. Each girl was covered in chalk dust, accumulating more when they scooted down across their work to a new patch of naked sidewalk. Sometimes they'd all laugh at something. Other times Sheeda caught a few bursts of disagreement.

"Nuh-uh, a gingerbread house wouldn't look like that."

"How you know? Gingerbread houses not even real."

Sheeda chuckled under her breath at the wrong time. Tai's side-eye was severe.

"I don't know what's so funny, Sheeda. I mean, I ain't even gonna waste my time fussing about Mo and Bean not jumping into the chat. Everybody act like they so busy they can't even drop into the chat."

"I really think they be dancing all day." Sheeda knew better than to confess that she and Mo still texted. Had in fact just texted her. "They're probably tired."

Tai wasn't having it. "Okay. But you right here and hard igging me."

Sheeda hugged her knees to her chest, still watching the little girls as she answered.

"I wasn't igging you. I told you, my aunt . . . "

"Made you go. Shoot, I woulda told her I didn't feel good. You the one who always talk about how you get tired of being around them girls from your church."

Sheeda was glad the door was shut so Auntie D couldn't hear. Tai stayed being loud.

"So that's how it's gonna be the next few weeks?" Tai's face twisted deeper into a frown. It made her eyes practically disappear. "You gon' keep leaving me for your Jesus friends?"

Sheeda stretched her legs out, picked at a piece of lint that wasn't there on her capris, then folded her arms. "Can you not call 'em my Jesus friends, please?"

When Mo did it, it was her way of joking. Coming from Tai it felt like an insult.

Tai peered at Sheeda like either she'd heard her wrong or didn't know who Sheeda was. Sheeda played with one of her twists, wanting to apologize. She felt naked without Mo there to defend her or Mila to make peace. She clamped her mouth, trapping the apology inside.

After a few seconds, Tai chuckled. "My bad. Just saying, I don't feel like spending the next two weeks in the house doing nothing." She swatted at Sheeda's legs. "Ooh, Cove Days next week. Don't forget I'm working the cotton candy booth and my dance team performing. You coming to help me, right?"

"Help you dance?" Sheeda asked confused.

"Yeah, Sheeda. Help me dance." Tai sighed toward the sky. "Help work the booth with me. It'll be fun. H3 saw how good your girl was and wanted to check out who else around here got them moves. They're recruiting, so they're doing a cotton candy booth, a dance contest, and then blue and red levels performing, hoping to sign up some dancers. I'm psyched."

Tai's excitement gave Sheeda another little burst of envy. Tai hadn't gotten into TAG dance, either, and she hadn't stopped being salty about it until Hip-Hop Heads, a local hip-hop dance company, had given her a tuition scholarship.

Everybody was doing their thing. Too bad her only "thing" this summer was church. Odds of Auntie D letting her go to Cove Days was about zero. Vacation Bible School at First Bap was always that same exact week as the week-long community fair.

She didn't want to ruin Tai's mood by reminding her of that. "I'll ask if I can go."

Tai brightened up. "That's right. We stuck with each other, girl."

Sheeda kept her voice low, in case her aunt was listening at the upstairs window. "True. But my aunt was happy that I went to the carnival with Yola and Kita. She probably gonna try to get me together with them again."

There was a wooden feeling of resignation thinking about it. Hanging with Kita she could probably deal with. Maybe. But the Bap Girls Do chat had been silent since the carnival. At praise dance, the three of them hadn't talked, unless you counted Yola wondering too loudly in Kita's general direction "Oh, but I thought your stomach hurt?"

Kita hadn't answered, just stood in her spot and waited on direction from their advisor.

It was just her luck that the summer without Mo, the First Bap Pack was falling apart around her.

Voice projecting loud as can be, Tai ignored her cue to

shush. "We almost fourteen. Your aunt can't be making playdates for you. Like, just be honest with her that you don't mess with them like that."

Sheeda stood up abruptly. "Come on, the rec finally open."

"Besides," Tai went on. "You went to the carnival with them, so you owe me. She gotta let you do Cove Days."

"Please, please come at my aunt by telling her she gotta let me do Cove Days." Sheeda laughed, genuinely amused at the thought.

A small horde of kids were already pouring into the rec, talking over one another, calling out the games they were going to play. Her and Tai took their time. The older kids owned the table games. It was a given.

Tai wiped her butt of the stoop's grit. "Whatever, man. I know your aunt strict and all, but I hope she know that just 'cause you in church all the time don't mean you not wylin' out."

"Hello, that's exactly why she tries to keep me in church all the time."

"So girls who go to church don't end up pregnant?" Tai's eyebrow flicked. "Or suspended from school or whatever?"

"I didn't say all of that. But it's fact that if I'm in

rehearsal every hour of the night, then I'm not really out there to get pregnant." Sheeda hated that she was basically reciting from the Book of Auntie D, second chapter, third verse. But wasn't it true?

"Well, you can't be in church twenty-four-twenty-four," Tai said with an indifferent pop of her shoulder.

"It's twenty-four-seven," Sheeda said, sure not to laugh. Tai got mad too easily.

"You knew what I meant, though," Tai said. She stopped at the door to the rec. "Your aunt be acting like just because me, Bean, and Mo don't go to y'all church that we the ones that might be a bad influence on you." Her mouth turned down like she'd just sucked a lemon. "It's like she be finding reasons to keep you in church. Did you tell her how your lil' friend pressed about that dude Jason? Is she cool with that?"

"It's Jalen. And, no, I didn't tell her," Sheeda admitted. She'd only told Tai because neither of them did anything all day. Now Tai was using the information against her.

"Exactly," Tai said.

Sheeda trailed behind her as they walked in. "Exactly what?"

"That they ain't no angels. You didn't say nothing to your aunt about how what's-her-name was texting him and in his face all night. So, she still thinking ice don't melt in their mouth. Why you letting her think we got you out here wylin' like they never would?" She gave Sheeda one last questioning look before walking into the game room and calling back over her shoulder, "Ping-Pong table or foosball?"

Kids, most of them younger, streamed into the rec past Sheeda. The two times a week the rec was open late, it stayed crowded. Even though the board games were usually missing pieces, the card decks, too, the rec was still the best escape from the muggy summer nights.

Tai staked out the Ping-Pong table without Sheeda's input. She kept the paddles and the ball in her hand while she talked to Marcel, one of the tenth graders who used to tease them years ago. If Marcel remembered her bullying, she didn't act like it. Her and Tai talked like old friends.

A hand touched Sheeda's shoulder. She turned, and Lennie's grinning face was inches from hers.

Kids nudged them aside as they squeezed through the door without saying "excuse me."

"No red shorts today?" he asked.

Sheeda shook her head, unable to find words.

He eyed her capris, light blue linen pants that made her H-shaped body look even blockier. Why had she picked these?

"It's cool. You can wear 'em for me next time," he said.

Next time?

Every time she and Lennie talked, she figured it would be the last time. That either whatever bet he'd made with his boys that she'd jump at talking to him was finally over or that he'd move on to somebody more interesting. Hearing him confirm that they'd talk or meet again made butterflies take flight in her belly.

She angled her chin up like Yola did with Jalen. She wasn't as short as Yola and her and Lennie were almost the same height. Still, it felt flirty. "What you doing here?"

"Your last post said you was gon' be here." He smiled down at her, proud to be stalking her social media. "I just rolled by to see what was up before heading to D-Rock's. We got some Crown Battle business to take care of."

She couldn't dial her smile back. "Y'all stay gaming."

"'Cause it be too hot to ball outside." He nodded toward the gym, where a whistle blew and sneakers screeched across the court. "And Mr. Andrews let the shorties play first. So, yeah, Ioun be coming to the rec a lot. Like I said, I just swung by to holler at you."

Unsure what else to say, Sheeda blurted, "Yeah. Mo be back home in ten days."

His teeth glinted as he grinned. "Do I make you

nervous? You hugged up against the door like I'm gonna bite you."

Sheeda shook her head in denial, but her laugh tremored like a hiccup—ha-ha-ha.

She forced herself to be normal. It was Lennie. She'd known him forever. Still, now that they were talking in person, she didn't seem to have anything to talk about except . . .

"I can't lie, it's really weird chilling here without Mo and the squad."

She looked past his shoulder around the empty lobby like everyone was hiding from her.

Lennie sucked his lips in, then let them go with a loud smack. "Naw, I know. The house dumb quiet since my moms be at work most of the time. And when she home she sleep, so—"

Sheeda rushed to cheer him up. "At least it sound like Mo doing good at the intensive thingie. She don't know no other way but to kill it." Her head cocked in thought. "Wouldn't it be wild if she ended up liking it up there?"

"What?" His eyes widened. "Like it to stay? Pish, man, please. I can't see that."

"I can," Sheeda said, sad in advance.

"You think Mo could really live at some White school

just to do ballet?" He snickered. "Naw. That's not her."

Sheeda didn't bust his bubble. If anybody knew how super competitive Mo was, it should have been Lennie. The rest of the girls up there better had been bringing it, because Mo definitely would be. But Sheeda didn't like the idea of her best friend going away for good any more than he did. She let it go.

"Remember when hanging out at the rec was, like, the best part of the day?" She jabbed the rectangle of glass of the game room door in the direction of the little girls that had chalked the sidewalk. Their three heads were together over one mic singing lyrics as they rolled across the TV screen. "I bet they feel so grown right now. No adult telling them what game to play or whatever. Being able to stay here until ten."

Lennie shifted his body, so he was standing right behind her, close. He peered over her shoulder at the girls. His breath tickled her ear. "For real, that age? Naw, I don't. I remember middle school and coming here 'cause that's where all the girls were." His head leaned closer to her ear. The bass in his voice vibrated against her back. "That's the only reason Simp, Chris, and them other hardheads roll with y'all so deep. Trust."

He smelled like washed laundry. She inhaled it, liking

the freshness. His body wasn't touching hers, but their body heat filled the small space between them.

She spoke carefully, afraid to move. "Maybe that's why Simp hang with us. He's definitely pressed for Tai." A tiny laugh fluttered out of her dry throat. "But nobody else in the squad checking for each other like that."

"Nobody checking for you?" he asked. The surprise in his voice made her giddy.

The truth was, Rollie wasn't around anymore, and Simp and Chris didn't get along. Anytime the two of them were in the same room, an argument broke out. It was an all-girls squad now. There really was nobody to check for her. She liked that Lennie thought so.

Her twists wriggled against his chest as she confirmed no.

"That's what's up," he said.

The cool air where his body had been pulled Sheeda from her daze. By the time she turned her head, he was at the exit, then gone.

There was no time to wonder if it had really happened. Tai's voice called from inside, over the little girls' karaoke.

"Sheeda, are we playing or naw?"

Rasheeda pushed through the door, striding to the table. "Sorry. You was talking to Marcel so . . . "

"I been stopped talking to Marcel." Tai's eyebrows rose up her forehead. "Lennie was so far up in your spot, you didn't notice. What. Is up. With that?"

"Nothing." Sheeda grabbed a paddle from Tai harder than she meant, to steady her shaking hands. "We was talking about Mo, mostly."

"Oh my God, you like him?" Tai said. She lowered her voice. "Does Mo know?"

"There isn't anything to know, Metai," Sheeda said with more force than she knew she could muster. She held her paddle up. "Are we playing?"

Tai's paddle clattered to the Ping-Pong table. "Nope." She grabbed Sheeda's wrist and led her out to the quiet lobby. She sank down against the wall onto the floor, pulling Sheeda with her. "Wow, you really are out here wylin' out. When did all this happen?"

Sheeda frowned at her. "No, I'm not."

She didn't like that just talking to Lennie was bad.

A few sixth-grade girls walked past, talking extra loud. It was what sixth-grade girls did. Sheeda remembered being the same way. Feeling like you knew everything there was to know just because you had finished elementary school. Summer made you forget that you were starting over from scratch once school started again. But in those few weeks, before it hit, you wanted the world to know you weren't a little kid anymore.

Their voices carried until they were deep into the gym, and even then Sheeda could hear them laugh when sneakers weren't squeaking. Sixth grade had been uncomplicated. Her aunt wasn't as annoyed all the time. She had Mo all summer. She'd even liked church more.

Now having a crush on somebody was wylin' out. It was like walking out of a dream and into a life that looked like hers but wasn't.

She told Tai everything. About when Lennie first hit her up. Even how she'd lied to her aunt about his number. Tai had dapped her up for that, and it made Sheeda feel strangely proud.

She was the one everyone usually scolded for asking too many questions or snickered at for not being fast enough at getting a joke. Having Tai, of all people, give her credit for something was nice.

Tai listened, every few seconds asking questions—do y'all talk in person or only on the phone (tonight had been the first face-to-face); does he know she's a church girl (yep); was he the one who suggested they talk via DM or Sheeda (him).

Every answer, Tai seemed to calculate into some

formula, and when Sheeda was done she talked like a judge reading a verdict. "I mean, it do sound like he feeling you. You and Lennie. I didn't see that coming, for real." Her nose wrinkled. "No shade, but Lennie not all that cute to me."

Sheeda rolled her eyes. "And Simp is?"

Tai sounded ready for combat. "What Simp gotta do with this?"

Only everything as far as Sheeda was concerned. Simp had liked Tai since they were in fifth grade. For the longest time Tai was mean to him because she liked Rollie. But once Rollie was gone, you would have had to been blind not to see how close her and Simp had gotten.

Sheeda didn't know why she kept pretending. It was the squad's worst-kept secret. And since she'd told Tai one, at least Tai could 'fess up.

"Everybody has peeped how y'all be tripping off each other in the chat," Sheeda said.

Tai's eyes rolled. "I laugh at his stupid jokes so now we a couple?"

"I'm just saying—"

Tai interrupted. "Okay. Okay. I didn't mean no harm. Lennie not ugly, just saying he not cute." She shrugged like Sheeda was the one at fault for the rude comment.

She scooted closer, to be heard over the growing sounds echoing out of the gym. "I always had a crush on Mila's brother, JJ. And if he tried to holler, I can't say I wouldn't want to let him. But, for real, me and Mila already been there, done that beefing." She stared past Sheeda at the exit door so long, Sheeda almost turned to see what was there until Tai continued, suddenly. "How Mo gonna feel about this?"

Sheeda sat back against the wall. "There's not really any *this*. We just talk is all."

"Well, is it a summer fling or you think he gonna be your boyfriend or something?" Tai asked.

She wanted to say something witty, play it all off, but wasn't fast on her feet with sarcasm and didn't have much to back it up if she had been. Nothing came to her. She threw her hands up. "For real, it's just like you with JJ. It's a crush. I mean, that's all it can be anyway."

Tai chuckled. "You want it to be more, though. Right?"

"Is that wrong?"

"For real, you can't help who you like," Tai said.

It was a Tai Sheeda had never seen. Thinking before saying the first bossy thing that came out of her mouth. Sheeda couldn't help herself. "'Cause that's how you feel about Simp?"

"Oh my God, stop." Tai flicked her hand at Sheeda as if she were shooing her away.

"Nobody cares if you like Simp, Tai." Sheeda squeezed her knee. "I mean, we care. But it's cool if you like him."

Tai leaned away, like Sheeda's touch burned. "A, I don't need y'all permission. And B, me and Simp just friends. Like you and Simp. Or Mila and Simp. And I'm just saying, we talking about you, right now." Tai did a bad job of mean mugging. "Just be careful. You and Mo been tight for a long time. Much as she get on my nerves, I wouldn't want see y'all beefing if things didn't go right with you and Lennie." She shrugged. "If y'all just flirting or whatever, though, then have fun." She shrugged again. "I flirt with JJ all the time with his cute self."

"But does he flirt back?" Sheeda asked, biting back a smile.

"Oh, you got jokes." Tai tried to look mad but ended up bursting out laughing. "For your information, yeah, he do flirt back. At least his version of flirting."

"It's only a crush with me and Lennie. And I like talking to him."

Tai laughed at that. "Lennie is fun to talk to? Who knew?"

"You know what? Let me tell Mo how you dogging her brother," Sheeda said.

Tai let out a high-pitched *ha*. "Okay and let me tell Mo you trying get with her brother."

"You wrong for that." Sheeda stood up, put her hands out, and helped Tai up from the floor. "Guess we have a few secrets that have to stay in this rec."

"Not agreeing that I do. But you know, I'll keep your little thing thing a secret," Tai said, shaking Sheeda's hand, pumping it, sealing their deal. "Wanna see if we can get one game in before we have to be home?"

They headed back to the game room, Tai in the lead. She glanced over her shoulder, "Lennie, huh?"

"It's just a crush," Sheeda hollered after her, hoping that saying it enough would make it true.

CATCHING UP
ON THE LOW

DatBoyEll:

you up? ●●

Rah-Rah:

yep

DatBoyEll:

so for real none of them cats that be
rollin wit ur crew tryin holla?

Rah-Rah:

lollll nope. Its complicated, fr fr.
Tai liked Rollie. Simp liked Tai.
Chrissy liked Simp. Rollie liked
Mila. Mila liked Chris . . . I think.

😠 I'm spilling all the tea. Don't
tell anybody I told you all that. 😁

DatBoyEll:

Who I'm telling? U wasn't down wit da
love triangle, huh?

Rah-Rah:

😆 wasn't nobody left to love 😆.

DatBoyEll:

Big facts! U musta been waiting on me
to push up then

DatBoyEll:

cold left me hanging 😕

Rah-Rah:

FR I'm still confused b/c you
started talking to me out of the
blue

DatBoyEll:

we always talked when u came see my
sister

Rah-Rah:

not like this though .

DatBoyEll:

so I was s'posed to holla at u when u
was 12? I ain't petey the pedo

Rah-Rah:

We only 2 years apart
#thatsnothowitworks

DatBoyEll:

Itz different now that u ready come
over to Sam-Well high. But if u not cool
w/me trying holla ain't nothing. We
still cool ✌️

Rah-Rah:

I didn't say that. Making sure u
not playing me. 😊

DatBoyEll:

Jus shooting my shot. If it roll around
the rim and don't go in, IIWII

Rah-Rah:

IIWII?

DatBoyEll:

it is whut it is

Rah-Rah:

😁 no I'm glad u stepped to me.

DatBoyEll:

U coming thru Cove days?

> **Rah-Rah:**
>
> I want to.

DatBoyEll:

😕 But?

> **Rah-Rah:**
>
> Same week as vacation bible
>
> school at First Bap

DatBoyEll:

Ayne u a good girl for real. LoL So u
can't go?

> **Rah-Rah:**
>
> I want to try and roll thru. But not
>
> sure yet.

DatBoyEll:

for real u not missing much. dollar
store prizes and halfway thru most
people be leaving their booth cause
they get tired of standing lmao

> **Rah-Rah:**
>
> wow that's the worst commercial
>
> ever but sounds about right 😂

DatBoyEll:

😄 it's real tho. Its fun cause of who u
there wit not what u do there

                                       Rah-Rah:

                  yeah the squad make it sound like
                                        mad fun

DatBoyEll:

It can be. So holler if u gonna roll thru

                                       Rah-Rah:

                                    😄 I will

DatBoyEll:

alright well I know ur auntie 'bout them
rulez so I hit u later

                                       Rah-Rah:

                                    ok ttyl

MONIQUE

She had the game figured out.

Every day they had a technique class, a pointe class, variations (which were different parts of these classical ballets, some Mo had seen and some she had never even heard of), then either jazz or modern. They only had Ms. Sharon for technique and pointe. So, technique and pointe were what Mo cared about most.

If Ms. Sharon said the words "Very good" to somebody two classes in a row, they got moved up a level. Was it that simple? Maybe not. But it had happened to three dancers so far.

She had no idea how their teacher watched all of them.

There were thirty-six, well thirty-four now, in the class. But Mo had eyes and saw that she was as good. So she approached every Ms. Sharon class like she'd get sent home if she didn't stretch her muscles until they were screaming or go across the floor like her life depended on it.

Thankfully, the shower argument had passed. Mo had been ready for Katie to igg her, but the next morning she'd complained about how Mila and Brenna got to sleep in and how they always got stuck with the early class. Things were fine. Mo was relieved. It made it easier to focus on class.

There was a large reddish-brown piano in the corner of the studio. It still tripped Mo out that they were dancing to live music instead of from an app on a tablet. Sometimes she found herself staring at the pianist, a short, round woman with a bob cut that quivered at her chin the harder she struck the keys, wondering how playing piano for a bunch of dancers was a real job. The pianist sat at attention, her plumpness spilling all over the small bench, until Ms. Sharon gave a slight nod.

Immediately music floated from the piano and every dancer's limbs moved, like they were all attached to the melody.

Mo felt more than saw their unified movement. Some

classes she couldn't help gazing in the mirror, watching them all move together. She'd forget she was one of them and nearly stop dancing. Other times, like now, she felt the power of the class behind her, and it was like she moved with them by magic.

Dancers were spread out in the gigantic classroom, the same two and half feet between them at the barre. Katie stood at the head of the barre that was across from the mirror, Mo behind her. As far as she was concerned, these were their spots. A few people always rushed to pop their ballet slippers on to get there first. None ever made it.

In the beginning, she'd thought everybody wanted that spot because it let them see themselves in the mirror. Then Katie hipped her. The lead person had to know the combinations because a lot of times the other dancers were following her. Mo hadn't seen it happen, didn't even know it was a thing, but Katie said some teachers would make you move if they didn't trust your memory to get the combos right. Katie hadn't been dismissed yet, so she was obviously doing good.

Mo liked that Katie always walked to the spot, swiftly but without rushing, like her name was on the floor reserving it. Nobody had beat them to class early enough to snag it. Their secret? Scarfing breakfast, maybe sometimes skipping it altogether, in order to stake their places. Like they'd done this morning. She was always starving by lunch. But granola and milk wasn't much of a breakfast anyway.

She wasn't ready to lead, yet. But from her spot, she always knew where Ms. Sharon was. She often peeked at herself, fixing her arms, legs, or feet when they were off before the teacher ever noticed.

She bent and bowed to the tinkling of the music. Her body lifted to the ceiling, muscles stretching, making her feel like a rubber band. Her mind hovered above her and translated Ms. Sharon's instructions into soft whispers. There was a tiny delay, almost a tic as Mo obeyed. When her mind couldn't translate fast enough, she mimicked the way Katie held her body until they were ebony and ivory twins.

Her eyes stayed glued to Katie's shoulder blades as Ms. Sharon padded softly down the line, inspecting her corps of mechanical dolls. Mo's muscles tightened a little too much. She overcorrected, then placed her leg just right as the woman that smelled like the lemon crème cookies Mo loved came up behind her. Her stomach rumbled— memories of the buttery cookies and nerves—as Ms. Sharon stood by her side.

Mo willed her body to follow Katie's languid movement. Soon she was flying gracefully in place, arms moving from first to fifth position.

She held her breath, refusing to make any noise or throw off her lines until Ms. Sharon moved on. Her chest burned.

Very good, Mo chanted to herself. Say it. Say *very good*.

Ms. Sharon stepped closer. Mo's mouth popped open. If she didn't breathe she was going to pass out. Her muscles strained. Ms. Sharon's hand, soft as dough, touched Mo's lower back.

"Tuck in your bottom, Monique," she said, in that low but loud voice.

Mo froze in place, judging herself against Katie's form. They were the same. Arms. Head. Legs. Everything.

Tuck my bottom?

She exploded when they sat to eat lunch. "I don't get it. Is tucking your butt some ballet trick only White people know?" She didn't bother to keep her voice down. The cafeteria was the studio's lobby full of tables and chairs that disappeared once every level ate. For now, nearly every chair was occupied by a hungry dancer. Everyone was talking loud, glad for the small break. She and Katie were alone at the table. Mo stabbed at the bland, colorless baked fish on her plate and stuffed a piece in her mouth. It had zero taste. But she was too hungry to complain. She talked after she gulped the tasteless seafood. "None of my dance teachers have ever said that before."

Never mind that she'd only ever had two teachers, both Black. Neither of them had ever said that to her.

Katie munched on an apple. She talked in between crunches. "I don't have much of a butt so—" She chewed quietly until Mo's glare settled into a shifty side-eye, then answered in her know-it-all way, "Are you sure your butt wasn't sticking out?"

"My butt doesn't stick out." She tapped her rear. "I just have one. It's not my fault nobody else in the class does."

Katie laughed and apple spittle dotted the table.

"That's nasty," Mo said, only half annoyed.

Every day she'd waited for Katie to make new friends and get ghost. Every day that Katie hadn't, Mo was grateful. It was selfish. Especially since some evenings she wished Katie didn't live right across the bathroom. Everybody needed a break from somebody they saw all day, didn't they?

Not that it mattered, since most nights they were

together whether she wanted her suitemates there or not. She'd almost gotten used to it.

Almost.

Katie swiped at the apple spit with a napkin. "Your butt isn't that big. That's why I'm saying it's probably just that you were poking it out."

Mo raised an eyebrow. "I haven't heard her say that to anybody else, though. I'm the only one poking my butt out?"

"Dude, I don't know. I'm just saying you can't take what teachers say personally." Katie's tiny shoulder shrugged. The word *bony* popped into Mo's head. But maybe Katie was right. Mo wanted to be wrong about what she was feeling.

"How I'm not gonna take something about me personally?" She chomped two more bites of the fish, saw she'd finished it off, and reluctantly tossed a floret of undercooked broccoli into her mouth.

Ugh. Whoever cooked this food had never been introduced to a salt shaker. And none was anywhere to be found. She'd looked on the first day.

"I didn't say it was easy. But you're here to get better, right?" Katie eyeballed her over what was left of the apple, a few pieces of raggedy flesh on the browning core.

"Yeah," Mo said, letting it hang like a question because it was Katie and advice was going to follow in three, two, one . . .

"Just saying that they're giving you notes to help you do that. If you're going to get all mad about it, then—" Her bony shoulder hitched again. "Don't take this wrong. But it's kind of a waste of time to come to an intensive if you're going to be upset at them correcting you."

"I'm down for getting better. And I'm not mad at taking notes," Mo said, emphasizing the last word to try it on for size. Even though telling somebody their butt is big felt like criticism. "It ain't too helpful if I can't do anything about it. That's all I'm saying."

Katie nodded. "I get it. But I really don't think that's it. Ms. Sharon seems nice. I don't think she cares that you're Black."

Mo pressed her lips together. She wasn't mad and didn't want Katie to think she was. But she disagreed.

Two more girls from their class took seats at their table. Sandy and Amanda, she thought, but honestly didn't know. Samanda?

In her head, all the girls in her class were either Susan or Karen. A joke she'd only ever share with Mila.

She didn't want to talk about this with anybody else

around and was about to move on when Katie said, "Have you asked Jamila whether she's gotten that note? I feel like if she did, then maybe you're not wrong." Her eyes narrowed. "That would suck if it was. I like Ms. Sharon. I hope she's not racist."

Samanda One's eyes were wide and questioning as she looked from Katie to Mo. "Ms. Sharon is racist?"

"Oh my God, Adrian. No." Katie's head shook vigorously. "Seriously, that's how rumors get started."

Adrian. Huh. Mo would have never guessed that. She sat back from the table, hoping Katie stopped talking. This was between them.

"Who's racist?" Samanda Two asked, less interested than Adrian but curious.

"Okay. Nobody," Katie said in her best parental voice. "We were talking about notes from class."

"I don't know about any of the teachers being racist, but Mr. Zaran keeps saying I'm sickling." Adrian looked at Mo, like she had the answer. Mo had no idea what sickling was. "It's my stupid shoes. I'm scared to say anything, though."

"What type of shoes do you wear?" Katie asked.

Like that was the signal she'd been waiting for, Adrian swooped in, face turned to Katie, and started babbling.

The names of pointe shoemakers, shank, and vamp sizes fluttered like so many snowflakes until the three girls were lost in a blizzard of comparisons about what fit, what didn't work, sore toes, and blisters. If it had just been her and Katie, Mo would have been fine. But it was still too weird how much information everyone shared about their aches and pains. Like they couldn't wait to show somebody their ugly toes with nails falling off. She wasn't about that life. Not with total strangers, anyway.

She fell out of the conversation and sipped on an apple juice, which really was one of the worst juices. Sweet enough to fool you into drinking it before leaving a little bitterness on the tongue. Why couldn't they have grape or that berry juice her mother sometimes got? How could even the juice be nasty?

They really had worked overtime to find the most flavorless foods on earth.

The sugar from the juice coursed through her, filling in the gaps that the fish and broccoli hadn't. She welcomed that feeling, her mind already wanting to think about dinner.

She usually woke up thinking about dinner. It was always her best meal. She loved the burgers, hot dogs, and pizza that were displayed in big steamer pans every day.

Sometimes the burger buns were soggy; sometimes they were hard around the edges. But it still beat the breakfast and lunch at Ballet America's café.

She forced her mind away, needing her stomach to believe the bland meal had been satisfying. Instead, she thought about what Katie said about asking Mila. It had crossed her mind but only for a second. Mila was flat chested and small butted. What did she have to tuck?

Besides, Ms. Sharon had made the comment and smooth kept on walking, like it was something she said all the time, even though Mo hadn't heard her say it to anyone else. It was simple to Mo, either she'd said it because Mo was Black or because Mo was fat.

CHITCHAT

Mo'Betta:

Am I fat?

Mo'Betta:

😣 which "ministry" you at tonight? 🙄

Rah-Rah:

Bible study! Sorry. But okay, yes,

Phat ✔

Mo'Betta:

ha naw for real fat, run around the
gym until my thighs burn because they
rubbing fat?

Rah-Rah:

🙃 Did you fall and bump your head?

Mo'Betta:

😐 nevermind. What u up to?

Rah-Rah:

jus saying I'm the biggest out of all of us & I don't think I'm fat. A lil thick maybe. so how could u be fat? 💀 At least u got curves and not shaped like the letter H 😊

Rah-Rah:

Chilling now. My friend from church Yola not talking to me or Kita. 😐

Mo'Betta:

And u worried why? People be showing their real colors, forget her. 😤

Mo'Betta:

Neither one of us fat aight? We just thickalicious. Lolz but remember dat time we wuz doing donkey kicks in gym

and Martin kept singing "make that
azz clap" b/c our thighs was smacking
together

Rah-Rah:

yeah but Martin was ignorant 😐
and he was trying holla - so pretty
sure he LIKED talking about your
butt

Mo'Betta:

FAX. I had to put him and his crew in
their place cuz they thought they was
gonna hand clap every time I walked by.
Namp!

Rah-Rah:

umph yeah. u think u was fat
then?

Mo'Betta:

Nope. something happened today
made me think about it, thas all

Rah-Rah:

??? well?

Rah-Rah:

What happened?

Mo'Betta:

Nothing.

> **Rah-Rah:**
>
> You would look like a straight up
> bobble head if you were as skinny
> as Mila. 😆

Mo'Betta:

😆 😆 Big FAX!

> **Rah-Rah:**
>
> Did somebody say u were fat? One
> of the sweet mates? 🤭.

Mo'Betta:

If somebody had called me fat u woulda
seen me on the news by now cause I
woulda had put paws on 'em 😐

> **Rah-Rah:**
>
> I know thas right

RASHEEDA

Sheeda hated picking sides. It made her uncomfortable to have people mad at her. Little arguments turned into big fights all the time just because somebody said one thing that made another person mad. Saying nothing was easier.

But time wasn't moving. She would have sworn ten minutes had gone past while she laid on her bed deciding if there was a show she could watch by herself. Then she'd looked up and it had been two whole minutes. Two.

She scrolled through the endless lists of shows. Comedy. Drama. Too many choices. Her aunt had just started unblocking certain things she could watch. So Sheeda didn't want to go crazy picking out something too wild that would put the lock back on most everything.

Auntie D was against *Straight and Narrow* until she'd watched an episode with Sheeda and saw that it was about the girls' road to getting back into a regular high school outside of lockup. Only thing was the girls cursed. A lot. Auntie D's face had gone from "Oh" shock to deep frowned disapproval.

"Why in the world are the guards letting these little girls cuss at them?" she'd said, arms folded like she would have snatched one of the girls up if they weren't.

"Auntie, they're literally in jail for teenagers for stuff like robbery and assault. I don't think the guards care about curse words."

Her aunt had looked at her like she was seeing Sheeda for the first time. She'd stood up and proclaimed, "If watching this reminds you what trouble can get you, then fine. But they all need Jesus," before walking out, no longer interested in the curse words assaulting her ears.

Nobody had posted anything in the chat about *Straight and Narrow* in a while. Either nobody but her was watching it (probably) or they didn't feel like talking about it. She dropped a message into each chat, trying to get a conversation started.

Into Bap Girls Do chat:

Dumb question but what
do people do all day over the
summer? I'm sooo bored. BTW do
y'all watch Straight & Narrow?
That's my show.

Into the Squaaad chat:

Anybody wanna watch S&N
w/me? Only if you already up
to season 3

Into the Caping for da Cove chat:

Are we even using this chat
anymore? Hello, Chrissy? Chris?
Simp?

She wanted to DM Lennie. So far every time they talked, he'd hit her up first. She didn't want to jinx it. Plus, she had no idea what to talk about. But what if he were waiting on her? Sort of like a test. Did boys do that?

Real nice having friends to ask. Not. She rolled her eyes at the empty chats.

She pulled out a pen and small notepad in the shape of a round kitty face, and laid across her bed on her stomach.

She wrote out: *Things to Talk About with L.*

She'd almost written out his name. She would throw

the list away. Still, she couldn't be too careful.

The blank paper beckoned her to write something.

She wrote: Us.

Scratched it out. Then wrote:

What's your favorite color?

What's your favorite food?

How come you don't hang out at the rec? (wait, did I already ask him that?!)

How come you like me?

She scooped her phone up, excited when a few soft dings chimed.

We have a winner.

Bap Girls Do.

Yo-la:

I'm over my grandmothers down at the lake w/my cousins. They coming to the retreat this year.

Rah-Rah:

You not gonna be at praise dance tonight?

Yo-la:

I be there. My grandmother just down the street from First Bap. So what u usually do?

Rah-Rah:

Field trips and hang out at the rec

Yo-la:

So do that. 💀

Rah-Rah:

nobody to hang w/this year

Yo-la:

Ask Kita. She not doing nothing

Yikes. Yola and Kita were still seriously beefing. She dropped the phone like Yola's shade was hot, glad when a new message popped in.

It was Lennie.

What up?

Rah-Rah:

Bored.To.Death. 😑

DatBoyEll:

Come see me.

Rah-Rah:

Umm. See you see you?

DatBoyEll:

😄 Hit me w/da double see you. Yeah like, at my house see me.

Rah-Rah:

I can't.

DatBoyEll:

Your aunt home?

Rah-Rah:

No. But I'm the world's worst liar.
She'd see it on my face that I did
something. LoL I be all at praise
dance tonight needing to pray

DatBoyEll:

LoL wow. Ok.

Rah-Rah:

Sorry 😭

DatBoyEll:

Nah u good. U ever ask ur aunt bout
letting u kick it at Cove Days? 👀

Rah-Rah:

Not yet.

DatBoyEll:

All she can say is no.

Rah-Rah:

I know. I gotta time it tho. Imma
ask.

DatBoyEll:

Kind of wack if I gotta wait til my sister
get home see u tho.

Rah-Rah:

I'll def be at the Cove Days
basketball tournament. Will you
be there?

DatBoyEll:

I will now

Rah-Rah:

😁

DatBoyEll:

So like what y'all be doing at church
that u there every day?

Rah-Rah:

lol I sing and dance. And then u
know like bible study and youth.

DatBoyEll:

Oh u double threat? You good?

Rah-Rah:

Church good 😆

DatBoyEll:

I haven't been to church since I was
little

Rah-Rah:

Mo be going w/me sometimes

DatBoyEll:

I know.

> **Rah-Rah:**
>
> You should come w/us one time.

DatBoyEll:

I'm good. lol

> **Rah-Rah:**
>
> Right. I don't blame u. We have
> fun sometimes though.

DatBoyEll:

Still good over here.

> **Rah-Rah:**
>
> 😄 just wrong

DatBoyEll:

If I go church that mean ur aunt let me
holler at you?

> **Rah-Rah:**
>
> Nope.

DatBoyEll:

Oh. Yeah I'm way good over here 😄

> **Rah-Rah:**
>
> Speaking of needing permission
> tho I feel like Mo would be mad
> if she knew we was . . . talking. I

mean she know we've talked but
still talking. Like you know. 😑

DatBoyEll:

She be alright

Sheeda didn't push it. She didn't agree, either. Lennie veered off into talk about how he and his cousin, Quan, were trying to earn enough money to get into a Crown Battle tournament. How they went to gaming arcades and played people for money. It was how he'd paid for Mo's pointe shoes. She was twirling on a cloud when he revealed even Mo didn't know how he'd earned the money.

It felt right to tell him a secret, too. But why would he care about the drama between Kita and Yola? And that was all she had since he was her only secret worth keeping.

She didn't realize she'd spent the entire day chatting with him, while watching her show and throwing her praise dance practice leggings in the wash (thank goodness she remembered), until her aunt's keys jingled in the door.

OMGoodness It's already 5?! I GTG
my aunt home.

She ripped the leggings out of the dryer and was regretting putting them on fresh, the cotton scorching her legs, when her aunt stood in her doorway.

"Ready for dance, Luvvie?" she asked.

Sheeda perked up at the nickname. Auntie D was in a good mood. She smiled, like her legs weren't burning and she'd been dressed for hours. "Yes, ma'am."

"Let me change and then I'm ready," her aunt said.

Sheeda texted Lennie quickly:

call 911 I think I got 3rd degree burn from putting on these leggings straight from the dryer! 😣

DatBoyEll:

LMAO I do want see u in leggings doe

Not knowing how to respond, Sheeda left it. She read the message several times before meeting her aunt in the car, enjoying how it made her feel. Nobody had ever wanted to see her in anything specific. And it was only recently that her dresses didn't cover every inch of her body anyway. Auntie D read Sheeda's good mood.

"Praise His name. Somebody happy to be going to praise dance tonight."

Sheeda couldn't help the smile on her lips. She told the thing closest to the truth. "I'm in a good mood today."

"Understandable. You ready to dance for the Lord."

Sheeda changed the subject to avoid the guilt that would settle in if she had to keep pretending she was happy because she was heading to rehearsal. "I hope Yola and Kita make up soon."

Auntie D's forehead furrowed. "Make up from what?"

"They're just not getting along," Sheeda said, refusing to snitch details.

"Lord. What now?" Her aunt's eyes rolled. "Don't you get in the middle of any nonsense, please."

Sheeda felt like saying, *How can I not when we're always together now?* Before the conversation could suck the joy out of her, she nodded her obedience and changed subjects once more. "What age is right to date?"

Asking the question was like seeing how close to the edge of a cliff you could stand before your foot dangled over nothing but air. She was shocked when her aunt smiled and hit her with a witty, "For you, no years old."

After a few minutes, Auntie D pressed on. "Which one of these little boys you call yourself liking?"

Sheeda stopped herself from laughing aloud. Hello, none of them First Bap boys, for sure.

"Nobody. But Yo—" She was really about to talk about Yola and Jalen. She eased away without hesitation. "You used to say when I was eighteen. That was a joke, right?"

"Mostly a joke. Yes." Her aunt's easy laugh was

something Sheeda knew existed but rarely saw these days. It disappeared as quickly as it came, and a thin edge of concern frosted her words—not quite a sermon but close. "I guess you think going into high school means you're grown. Trust me, you're not even close. You have plenty time for dating, Rasheeda. Focus on your ministries for now."

The question that was on the edge of her tongue— *Why can't I focus on my ministries* and *like somebody?*— she knew better than to ask. Especially since Auntie D had gone from Luvvie back to using her real name, which was the period at the end of her sentence like Sheeda wouldn't know who the words were meant for without her name attached. It was best to let Auntie D believe that being at church or in church somehow was a shield that stopped her from liking a boy.

Instead, she texted Mo:

> One week down! Miss you like
> chocolate miss peanut butter 😊

Her heart leaped when Mo hit her back:

help! These white girls got me watching
some movie about a dog trying find his
way back home. 😳

> **Rah-Rah:**
> did somebody die yet? Somebody

> always die in movies with a dog.
>
> Lol

Mo:

Ugh ew. You right! 😆

Sheeda let Mo narrate the movie and was only tempted once to ask for her advice about Lennie. Luckily, by the time her fingers almost slipped to text, she was in church. Saved by the cross.

MONIQUE

"We gon' have a par-tee," Mo sang at the top of her lungs.

"We gon' get it pop-inn," Mila sang in return.

Right on cue, they belted out, "We ain't gotta do SSSHHHHH," two junior librarians shutting down their own jam. It was more fun to make the explosive shushing sound than it was to use the lyric's curse word.

The song played on without their assistance as they tried to out shush each other. The joke never got old.

Mo sang along again under her breath, "That's my jam."

Without a pause, the song started over.

"Ayyy," they said in unison, like somebody besides

Mila had rewarded them with the replay.

In celebration of having free time, their room was festive. The music pumped life into the space, bass beating like a heart. They laughed at everything. Just happy to be in the room together after a week of being two trains passing and tooting at each other.

It was finally Sunday. They were going to see a special production of *Giselle*. Mo hadn't ever watched a classical ballet; now, she'd seen five. Once a month they watched and then discussed a different ballet or modern dance production at TAG sessions. She still wasn't totally used to how they didn't talk in a ballet. She had fallen asleep on *Romeo and Juliet*. Couldn't understand why a story about kids committing suicide was even a thing, much less a whole ballet.

Eventually she began to understand how the story was told through the dancing. Some of the ballets were still kind of boring. But she was hyped for *Giselle*. Who wouldn't be down for a love story where a bunch of bitter chicks come back from the dead to haunt a dude for his dirt?

At this point, she didn't care where they were going as long as her feet got a break. It was a welcome change in the routine. By Friday she'd felt like she was carrying bricks on her shoulders. It had gotten harder and harder to get up every day and keep it pushing. Not to mention every part of her body was sore. Anytime your pinky toe ached, you know it's bad.

She had almost faked sick to skip Saturday's class. The screaming in her thighs was only part of it. Every day she felt a little less sure of herself. Doubt crept in so deep she'd waited until Mila fell asleep Saturday night and texted her mother.

Moodles:

Hey mommy. You at work? ●●

Mom-E:

Yeah Boo. Caught me on my break though. Isn't it lights out? Everything okay?

Moodles:

As long as we in our room by curfew nobody really be making sure our lights out.

Mom-E:

Oh okay. How's my baby girl?

Moodles:

Mom-E:

Uh-oh. What's wrong? You homesick, babe?

Moodles:

No. A little bit. 😐 Not sure I like ballet
as much as I thought.

Mom-E:

Why? B/c it's hard? Lol

Moodles:

Yeah that. lol I be feeling so out of
place here. Even Bean fit in better
than me.

Mom-E:

Because . . .

Moodles:

She just do, ma. 🙄

Mom-E:

I can't help if you don't say what
you mean, Monique. Why does she
fit in better?

Moodles:

She catch on faster. She a stronger
dancer than me. I mean IDK. all
that. I thought dance was just dance
but everybody here love ballet. It's
different.

Mom-E:

Wishing they had hip-hop or jazz?

Moodles:

We do a little jazz. But its white jazz 🙄

Mom-E:

What's white jazz, babe?

Moodles:

Like broadway play music. It's wack.
It's not that tho. I wanna do good but
everybody know more than me. Even
Bean.

Mom-E:

You have to stop comparing
yourself. I've seen yall two
dance side by side. You're just
as beautiful a dancer, baby girl.
The whole point of this was for
you to work on things that need
work and come out the other side
stronger. You can't come in and
slay everything. 🙂

Moodles:

I guess

Mom-E:

And I KNOW 😏

Moodles:

LOL naw, you right

Mom-E:

As always

Moodles:

You tripping, Ma

Mom-E:

If it was easy everybody would do it. Enjoy this experience. Don't beat yourself up over not being the best dancer there. Okay?

Moodles:

Okay

Mom-E:

Love you 🖤

Moodles:

Love you too 🖤

By the end of the conversation, Mo's pillow was drenched from tears. She'd sniffled quietly, not wanting to wake up Mila. She couldn't take being consoled. It would have broken her. Her mother's words had cooled the growing anxiety gnawing at her heart.

She felt brand-new today. Tired, for sure. But whole again.

Every day felt like two at Ballet America. If anybody had told her that she would have already exchanged socials and phone numbers with a tall skinny girl from Jersey and a petite shorty from Connecticut, she would have laughed right in their face.

But there she was on Brenna's FriendMe page, Brenna hugging her waist and Mo's face frozen in a smile, eyes cast down looking at the human clinging to her—Brenna had squeezed like she'd float away if she loosened her grip. The caption was already their inside joke: Mo like woah wake me up b4 u go go.

The other day, she hadn't heard Katie and Mila say they were heading to dinner or their instructions for her to wait on Brenna. Bathroom time was her own, and Mo always made it last. All she knew was when she came out, Mila and Katie were gone. Panicking, she'd thrown on shorts and booked it. Her heart had pounded as she walk-ran to the cafeteria like somebody was chasing her. When she arrived at the table, out of breath, Mila looked up and around her, confused.

"Where's Brenna?"

"I know this why?" Mo had asked, gulping air.

"Because when we left, we told you to wait for her," Katie said, her *duh* left unsaid.

Brenna showed up ten minutes later looking as harried as Mo. There were jokes about Mo looking like the White Rabbit from Alice in Wonderland in between Brenna's "Dude, why'd you leave me?"

Mo took it. She knew she'd been shook, for real, because when she thought they'd all left her behind, instead of being angry, she'd been scared. The cafeteria was a five-minute walk from their dorm, on a sidewalk that was lined with full trees and usually with people—college students there for the summer. It was probably one of the safest places in the world. But the trees and quiet always closed in on her. Even when she was walking with other people, she couldn't help looking over her shoulder making sure nobody popped out from behind a bush. When they teased her a minute too long, she finally admitted she felt safer in the hood than she did there on campus.

Mila had nodded. If not understanding, at least not questioning. Katie and Brenna had looked at each other, probably wanting but not knowing how to ask how that could be. Good, because she didn't have an answer. Instead, Brenna had tackled her with a big hug and Katie had got the shot. The post was born and had gotten fifteen likes from Brenna's followers.

Mo had started to repost it. Then didn't. Brenna was cool. She didn't want her followers to go there with White girl–this or White girl–that jokes.

What happened at Ballet America would just stay there.

She eyed the time. Mila was ready in a white sundress with yellow and green flowers, looking fresh and cool. She sat primly at her desk, legs crossed, foot swinging along to the music as she texted. Every now and then she'd laugh, then report something Tai or her brother JJ had said.

Mo rolled an iron over her outfit, a black romper with silver stars. The wrinkles and creases of the crinkly rayon material ignored the iron like the thing wasn't on.

"I don't know why I'm doing this." She pressed harder over a stubborn crinkle.

"I honestly think it's supposed to be wrinkled," Mila said, not bothering to look up.

"I do, too, but the wrinkles irk me so bad."

Mila teased. "I'm pretty sure that's their goal in life . . . to irk you."

"Probably." Mo pressed down harder, going over one spot for a full twenty seconds. It was personal, at this point. The iron hissed quietly. She propped it up abruptly.

"Should I wear the orange romper instead?"

She pulled a deep tangerine romper out of her closet. It was off the shoulder with filmy angel sleeves made of chiffon. There was also chiffon over the short bottoms, making it look almost like a skirt. She'd gotten it because orange looked good against her brown skin. And she liked how the chiffon made it looked like she was floating. Of the two rompers it was the dressier one, for sure. But these were her only two choices for the intensive's two dressy outings. She couldn't rerun an outfit and have people thinking she only had one decent outfit.

She placed the romper under her chin. "What say you?"

Mila sized it up. "Either one of them is cute."

"But should I be dressier for the ballet or the dinner?"

She envied how the white dress with its spaghetti straps against Mila's chocolate skin made her look put together, almost grown up. Maybe it was the effect of finally seeing people in regular clothes, but Mo suddenly wished she liked dresses.

She never knew how to sit in a dress. Legs crossed made the dress rise too much. Sitting with her ankles crossed made her thighs wing out. Her style was rompers, gauchos, even palazzo pants.

Mila assured her. "The black romper is fine. Especially

once you beat the wrinkles out."

"Oh, you real funny," Mo said. She put the orange one away and gave up on ironing. "It is what it is."

She put the black romper on a hanger, turned to go into the bathroom, and bumped into Katie, who was wearing a floor-length sundress. She even had on heels, which made her about six feet tall. Katie laser beamed the outfit in Mo's hands, a small frown on her face.

"Is that what you're wearing?"

Mo snapped, "Yeah, why?"

Katie shrugged. "We're going to the ballet."

"It's just like wearing a skirt, though," Mila said, ever helpful. She was at the mirror on her closet door, pulling her many braids into something like a manageable ponytail.

"I guess." Katie slid past Mo and sat on the edge of Mila's desk. "How do you get all of it in a bun?"

"Lots of bobby pins," Mila said.

Annoyance enflamed Mo's entire body. She hadn't asked for Katie's advice. Worse, now she doubted her choice more than before. People stayed not minding their business.

She raised her voice to be heard. "First of all, I left my mother back home in the DRB. Second of all, if you gonna come for somebody, come all the way. Not halfway."

Katie looked to Mila for help. When Mila kept her eyes on the mirror, Katie's chest sunk visibly as she sighed.

"I didn't mean anything by it, Monique. I just asked . . . "

"Nope." Mo's temples pounded. She couldn't let Katie carry her. "If you didn't mean anything by it, then why ask 'Is that what you wearing?'" Her imitation of Katie was high-pitched and nasally. "If you feel some kind of way about my outfit, at least say it to my face."

Katie stood up too quickly and wobbled in her heels. She held on to the desk chair, to steady herself.

"Rompers are just really short. That's all." There was resignation but no surrender in her tone. "Seriously, I didn't mean to judge. You take everything so personally, Monique."

Mo's body stiffened. "And stop using my government name. It's disrespectful."

Katie's mouth dropped open. "Your government name?" Her voice had the slightest quiver. "What does that even mean? How is me calling you your name disrespectful?"

Now, you can stop now, Mo told herself. All she had to do was wear the orange romper instead. It was the nicer romper. She knew it. But pride wouldn't let her do it. Every time she thought she fit in, she was reminded she didn't.

"It's whatever." She closed the bathroom door on Katie's last words, only catching "How is tha—"

She stood in the middle of the bathroom, her anger slipping into hurt. She wanted to stay mad. Forget Katie. She was always so nosy. Her and Brenna, both, always barging in without knocking. Her and Mila could be butter-butt balled naked and they'd walk in and carry on a conversation like it was nothing. Mo wasn't down with that. Her and Mila had seen each other without clothes plenty between gym and dance. That was different.

If Katie had knocked, for once, Mo could have told her she was getting dressed. She could have had the black romper on and been fine with her decision. Now she was worried the romper wouldn't work. She'd probably be the only person not wearing a dress.

She sat on the floor. The cold tiles felt good against her skin, still flaming from her anger. They all knew by now not to mess with her when she was in the bathroom. She was the only one that dressed in the bathroom with both doors locked so nobody could bust in. It drove Brenna crazy. But Mo needed that privacy. Sometimes the few minutes alone was like being on low battery and getting enough charge to keep going.

She started a text to Sheeda three times:

Remember that romper I got from the
mall

I wish I had brought a dress. LOL I
shoulda borrowed one from you ☺

How come it seem like nobody ever pay
attention to me unless they tryin point
out something wack?

She deleted that one, too. Sheeda was probably out having fun with her Jesus friends. At least one of 'em was having a good time. She didn't want to ruin it.

After a few minutes, the quiet of the bathroom was like a light frost on her hot mood.

The bathroom was nearly as big as her room back home. The shower had its own room. The toilet was in its own cubby. The space between the two rooms was wide enough for at least two people to stand with their arms out. A pink rug around the toilet and their damp, musty towels were the only decoration. A full-length mirror hung from Katie and Brenna's door. Mo slipped on the romper and stared at herself, letting the cold tile of the floor ice her toes.

The romper's stars, dull blobs with points at the end,

could have been polka dots or starfish. Their dull shimmer broke up the crinkly rayon. Strapless, it tied in front and zipped up in the back.

It was Mo's idea of dressy. Or had been until Katie came in dressed like she was heading to some Cinderella ball.

She looked at every angle, battling silently with her reflection.

Maybe it wasn't the dressiest outfit, but she looked good in it. She'd always liked her curves. Liked that her clothes fit her like they loved them, too.

Her shoulders were toned and shiny with cocoa butter. Her tummy was mostly flat—food babies didn't count—they'd just had lunch. Her thick wedges made her taller. With her hair piled high on her head in a "messy" bun that had taken thirty minutes to get perfectly messy, she actually looked like all the other ballerinas. Her version of them.

Her thighs were thick and solid like a Thanksgiving ham. She rose on her toes and the two hams clenched. A line formed where her chiseled quads dipped into the hump of her knee. She turned, looked at her muscular behind. It was tight and hard. The romper came down a few inches over her butt. Plenty enough so her cheeks weren't peeking out. Bending over was out of the question. But, hello, why would she be doing all that?

It was a good look. If she had been home, Tai would have said "She bangin'." Anybody could look "cute" or "good" in an outfit. But you had to look good, know you looked good, and feel good about looking good to get a she bangin'.

This look was her. Her style. Her flavor.

Just because she didn't look, dance, or dress like everybody else didn't change that. Let all of them figure it out on their own. She'd picked the romper out because people dressed up in black when they were trying to flex. So, bloop. She had this.

She snapped a picture of herself, adjusted the light until the blobs on her romper actually looked like stars, tapped in a caption: *They not ready*—and posted it just as a knock came at the bathroom door.

"Dude, come on," Brenna whined.

Brenna's hand was still in mid-knock when Mo pulled the door open. She pursed her lips, working hard to sound genuinely annoyed.

"Did I rush anybody else when they were in the bathroom?"

Brenna didn't fall for her act. She teased, "No. But

nobody else takes as long as you." She kept step with Mo as they exited through Mo and Mila's room. "Cute romper."

"Thanks," Mo said, touched by the compliment.

Katie and Mila's whispered conversation stopped as they entered.

"Well, finally," Katie muttered, but in a softer tone than usual. She went to the door, her chin up in the air, like she expected more blows from Mo. She had one foot out in the hallway, then looked back to make sure they were following. "We're ready, right?"

Katie hadn't said anything Mo wouldn't have said herself, if she felt some kind of way about somebody's outfit. Mo felt bad for kirking on her. The apology she knew she owed Katie was stuck in her throat. She looked Katie in the eye, swished her hips. "Too short or naw?"

A smile lit up Katie's face. "Or naw?"

Mo cracked up. "Or naw, question mark?"

Katie laughed. "Definitely or naw."

Mila gave her a thumbs-up. "She bangin'."

Mo twirled then posed, twirled again, and clomped toward the door in a runway walk. "Coming to a ballet school near you, that new-look ballet chick."

Brenna linked arms and joined her on their imaginary

catwalk. They sashayed past Katie.

She yelled after them, "So, I guess I'm locking up the room . . . or naw?"

The hallway filled with their laughter.

RASHEEDA

It was now or never.

It was Vacation Bible School week. She had to ride Auntie D's good mood. Something about seeing all the children of the church gathered to play and learn the Bible, one coloring activity at a time, filled her aunt. Their kitchen counters and table overflowed with boxes of hot dogs, packs of spaghetti, bottles of sauce, long swords of French bread, burger and dog rolls, and a supersized duo of ketchup and mustard designed for the world's largest cookout. Auntie D sang, "Grateful, grateful, grateful" absently as she packed it all into cardboard boxes.

Sheeda made small grabbable stacks of the spaghetti

that her aunt scooped and placed into the box.

"Thanks, Luvvie." Auntie D surveyed their kitchen. It was the only time of year clutter was allowed. She smiled at the harvest of quick-cook foods. "My job really comes through with these donations. I need to make sure that Pastor Weems pays a visit to my supervisor this year." She thumbed toward the fridge. "Still not sure how we're going to get all that ice cream there without it melting."

Sheeda filled a smaller box with utensils, napkins, and paper plates, then peeked inside the freezer. Boxes of chocolate-covered drumsticks, her favorite, blotted out other food. "I'll take one for the team and eat a few boxes if we can't fit them all in the cooler."

Auntie D patted her slim hips. "If we ate all that, we'll end up looking like a drumstick."

Sheeda knew that by "we" her aunt meant her. Auntie D was tall with rail-thin legs and no hips. She could probably eat a whole box of drumsticks and be fine. If Sheeda spent a weekend eating fast food, pimples sprouted and her belly jiggled. And she had Tate hips. To keep them from spreading, her aunt didn't keep sweets in the house. So "they" wouldn't be tempted.

The frigid air from the freezer cooled her neck and face. As the door closed with a soft *whump*, she asked, "Is there any way that I could miss Vacation Bible School this year? Please?"

Auntie D spoke over the clacking of the bottles she was sorting. "You know I don't like when you talk in that tiny baby voice. What did you say?" Her arms were everywhere, grabbing and stacking, adjusting and moving items.

Sheeda pronounced each word like she was in a spelling bee. "Could I miss Vacation Bible School this year? Please."

Momentary joy filled her heart when her aunt said, "Yes, Rasheeda. Of course." Then Auntie D's lips pressed together. When they opened, the cold edge of a sermon came out. "Yes. I'm going to let you miss the one church event that I'm in charge of. Because that makes sense, right?" She turned Sheeda's way, her eyes two hard, brown marbles. "I run the children's ministries because I have a child that I want involved. I make sure there's things to keep you all busy and happy. I spend half my nights e-mailing people reminding them to bring their kids to this event or that activity. So, tell me, how does it look that I do all this and then my niece doesn't bother to show up?"

Sheeda's mind knew this was the signal for her to give in and apologize for daring to ask. Unfortunately, her tongue had other business to handle. She leaned against the fridge, sure to keep her arms at her sides. She cocked one foot over the other with an ease she didn't really feel.

"It's just, this is the week of Cove Days and—"

"And," her aunt said, her voice a stop sign. "The two events are always the same week. *And* you've always missed it."

Sheeda pushed past the anxiety crawling through her skin. "Usually everybody goes except me, though. This year, Tai is by herself. She doesn't have anyone to go with."

And Lennie. Don't forget, Lennie is hoping you'll be there. A flutter of pleasure stirred through her as she weathered the storm of emotion going through her aunt's face.

"The day I let some child get in the way of my mission to create a safe and happy environment for the church's kids, so she won't have to go to a fair by herself, then you need to go ahead and call your mother and let her know I'm no longer capable of caring for you."

"I just feel bad that Tai is by herself, Auntie D," Sheeda said. "I'm trying to be a good friend." She added weakly, "'Love thy neighbor,' right?"

Auntie D stopped her packing. Her eyes lit with challenge. "Oh, okay. You want to convince me with Scripture?" Her hands flew to her nonexistent hips. "What book is it from?" She was amused and Sheeda smelled the trap too late. "If you get it right, book, chapter, and verse, I'll think about letting you go to Cove Days."

Wow, think about it? She had to quote Scripture right and still not be guaranteed the reward? It didn't matter. She had no idea which book of the Bible it came from, much less the verse. As much as she was in church, she'd never been down with memorizing Scripture. Auntie D gave her plenty grief for it. She took a try anyway. "James . . . "

"Nope. Matthew twenty-two, verse thirty-nine." Auntie D's head shook more in disappointment than anger. "Um-hm. Somebody might need to study Scripture a little better if they really want to convince me. But okay, invite Tai to Vacation Bible School." She practically sang the verse, "'And do not forget to do good and share with others, for with such sacrifice God is pleased.'" Her eyebrow raised in victory. "Hebrews thirteen, verse sixteen." Seeing Sheeda didn't appreciate the lesson, she went back to work, her point made. "I have no problem bringing Tai with us. Your friends need to take you up on an invite now and then."

Her friends had come to plenty of her First Bap jamborees, revivals, and evening praise dance services. Of course, to her aunt, some isn't all. Defeat was in the air, but she continued to plead Tai's case.

"She can't do VBS, she's volunteering at the cotton candy booth. That's the other reason she wants me to go. She asked if I could help her. We might even be able to count it toward our community service hours, when school starts."

Her aunt waved away the bothersome olive branch. "Please. You'll get your hours just fine." Her packing built to a frenzy as she jammed things into the overstocked box. "Your time is always committed for Vacation Bible School this week of summer. Handing out free cotton candy is nice, but not as important as helping the kindergarten class grow in Christ."

How much were five-year-olds learning by coloring pictures of Jesus and then having a snack? The emotion in Sheeda's throat was the size of a golf ball. She crossed her arms tight against her chest to hold it all in.

"Rasheeda, you're one of the church's first kids." The tenderness in her aunt's voice jolted her. "You may not like the burden, but you're an example to the younger children." She came over to Sheeda. "Can you make a better case for missing Vacation Bible School than helping to give out candy?"

Sheeda's mouth opened but no words came out. She hadn't expected a chance to really fight for what she wanted. It had been silly to ask. Nothing ever truly came before church.

"I know you get tired of being at church so much." Her aunt chuckled at Sheeda's surprised eye pop. "I can't say I know how that feels. I've always loved church. When I was your age, we were poor and the people we went to school with looked at our worn-out clothes like it was a disease they could catch from us. At our little church, everybody was like me. When I moved up here, I kept trying to find a church that was like back home, and it took a long time. I helped to build First Baptist." She gently untangled Sheeda's arms and took Sheeda's hand in hers. "And so did you. I wish you were more proud of the work you've done there."

"I haven't really done any work," Sheeda mumbled. The soft pressure of her aunt's touch made her eyes well. She wanted to stay angry but couldn't. It had been too long since they'd been on the same side. She wanted to throw herself into her aunt's arms. Feel the closeness they'd had when she'd first moved in.

"Singing in the choir, dancing beautifully, and taking part in discussions at Bible study is your work, Rasheeda." Auntie D led her to the table. The open boxes made a small fort around their chairs. "Can you at least remember one Scripture for me?"

She waited for Sheeda's nod of consent before going on. "'Every good and perfect gift is from above, coming down from the Father of Heavenly lights.' That's James chapter one, verse seventeen. You give your talents at church and that's your work." She rubbed Sheeda's knee, easing the blow of her denial. "It wouldn't be a big deal to let you miss one year of VBS. I'm not going to, though." She let that sink in, giving Sheeda a chance to object. When she didn't, "All school year I work with your schedule. But it's summer, and you have no reason to miss this or anything else. More importantly, you have two more weeks before Monique gets back. Use this time to get involved at the church without the chip on your shoulder."

Sheeda was pricked by the truth. "I don't have a chip on my shoulder."

"Yes, you do." Her aunt's laugh was surprisingly light. "And only you can fix your heart about that, Luv. I'm saying that God has given you a few weeks without your best friend. I bet she's using the time to enjoy herself. You should do the same." She was back on task at her box. "Tell Tai you'll see her at the basketball games this weekend."

It was a weak second prize. She'd always been allowed to go to the basketball tournaments held at the end of

Cove Days, mainly because VBS wore her aunt so much she was too tired to control Sheeda's schedule that day.

Without thinking, she sighed, "Okay."

Thankfully, Auntie D ignored it. "Come on. We've got to get there early and get this food put away."

They made quick work of the packing and were at the church before anyone else. It always made Sheeda feel weird to pull up and see no cars at the church, like maybe they'd shown up on the wrong day. She could tell her aunt loved it. Anytime they went into the church after or before hours, she made a production of it—jangling the church keys more than necessary and signing her name in the logbook in huge cursive letters that took up more than one log-in space. No way to miss she'd been there, and that was the point.

Her aunt was kitchen manager and head of the children's ministries. Sometimes, if someone forgot to lock up, they'd call her and she'd have to come turn on the security system. She always grumbled like it made her mad, but Sheeda knew she enjoyed it. Only five people had keys and the church's security code. Better believe Auntie D being one of them was a big deal.

She ran the kitchen like she ran her household—everything had its place, and a terse memo went out anytime that little policy was violated. Sheeda had seen the e-mails and wondered how her aunt kept friends in the church. Mo would have said, she was irky. And Sheeda kind of agreed. But, she loved the church kitchen as much as her aunt did . . . how big it was, how it always felt warm and inviting, no matter the season.

The only thing fancy about the church's kitchen was the humongous shiny metal hood that sucked and blew out smoke. It hung over the stove like a giant vacuum and came in handy during fish frys. Kids weren't allowed in the kitchen much, but when they ventured in, looking into the mouth of the hood was a main attraction. Otherwise, the kitchen was a big pantry and an oversized space, large enough so the whole five crew kitchen ministry could be inside cooking and prepping at once.

Sheeda lost herself inside the pantry, stocking the shelves with the donated food, neatly stacking the canned corn and green beans. Having each can of corn face the exact same direction on the shelf was key to them tasting good.

Next, she cut nice even chunks of the French bread for that night's spaghetti dinner— didn't matter what else was on the menu, spaghetti and garlic bread were always night one of VBS. Past memories of the melted butter and tangy garlic made her stomach grumble.

As the kitchen ministry staff trickled in, Auntie D's voice greeting and instructing echoed in the empty multipurpose room next door. It wouldn't be empty long. The multipurpose room was the heart of Vacation Bible School. Soon a small table would be set up at the door to make sure no students snuck over and took crafts or had snack before their scheduled time. God forbid. Raisin boxes and mini bags of pretzels would be on a long table against one wall, waiting for the teenage teacher assistants to scoop up and deliver to their classrooms. Half the room would be tables for each class's dinner. The rest of the room would be set up for arts and crafts.

The stage, at the back of the room, would be temptingly empty, luring everyone to step up on it to clown only to be told to get down. The VBS teachers shooed people away from the stage as if they were protecting it for a Broadway play or something. The more they warned the kids away, the more everybody wanted to step on it. The stage would only be used on the last day, when every class presented some sort of skit on what they'd learned.

Auntie D breezed into the kitchen. She was in Sister Tate mode, ready to tend to business. "I appreciate you putting the food away, Luv." She flooded the room with light, grabbed an apron, and nicely dismissed Sheeda. "I think Sister Simmons is ready for help getting the classroom together. I'll see you when you bring your class in for dinner."

Sheeda didn't mind being excused. As bad as she'd wanted to attend Cove Days, she didn't hate Vacation Bible School. Especially now that she helped instead of listening to lessons. And she liked Sister Simmons, who was probably the same age as Auntie D but acted way younger.

Sister Simmons was what her aunt called a transplant because she wasn't an original First Bap member. And even though Auntie D denied it, a lot of times the other members totally shaded Sister Simmons. Then had the nerve to act as if Sister Simmons couldn't see them being shady. But Sheeda had seen her oh-no-you-didn't face the time one of the elders told her that maybe she needed to sit back and watch how things were done before getting too involved. Ever since then Sister Simmons had gotten involved triple time. The way she spoke her mind and did what she wanted reminded Sheeda of a grown-up version of Tai—if Tai ever got any kind of chill whatsoever.

She took her time walking the quiet hall that held five classrooms and the pastor's office. A big corkboard dominated one wall. Flyers promoting dinners, members selling things, and upcoming events plastered every inch.

One big poster sat in the middle of the paper chaos. She stared at her own smiling face on the flyer reminding everyone time had run out to sign up for the retreat. On it, the First Bap Pack, Mo, and a couple others were all crispy from too much sun and swimming. Sheeda's twists were frizzy from daily dips in the pool. Stray hair haloed around her face. Those close enough to Jalen were mid-laugh, perfectly conveying just how great the Beat the Heat Teen Retreat was.

Except, not exactly. Right before the pic had been taken, Jalen had whispered, "Everybody say big boo-tayyy." It had only been funny because Brother Patterson, the photographer, working too hard to be down, had said, "I'm not going to make y'all say *cheese* or nothing corny. What do the kids want to say these days?"

"*Cheese* is fine, Brotha Pat," Jalen had announced, speaking for all of them and doing his kiss-up-to-adults act. Then in the very next breath, he'd said the bootie thing while still looking all innocent. For real, Sheeda was mainly laughing at Brother Patterson because he'd puffed up, so pleased, like getting a bunch of teenagers to smile had been the highlight of the retreat.

Next to VBS, the retreat was the only event she looked forward to. She invited the squad to plenty of First Bap events. And sometimes they came. But the retreat was different. She only ever invited Mo to the retreat. And even though Mo was always Mo, realer than real with everyone, she seemed to take a tiny step back during the retreat—happy to let Sheeda take the lead. Sheeda would be lying to say it didn't feel good to have Mo in her territory.

Even though her First Bap friends were a little awkward, they'd ended up having way more fun together than Sheeda expected. Jalen had a crush on Mo from word go and had tried to holler until he figured out real quick that Mo was 100 percent time enough for him. He wasn't used to being called out for being corny or kissing up. Something Mo did a lot during the retreat. Not in a mean way, but enough that he stayed in his lane. That's where he and Yola's little crush thing started in the first place. This year would be real interesting.

The second she walked into the classroom, Sister Simmons wrapped Sheeda in a bear hug. The oils in her locs shoved itself up Sheeda's nose. It was like having her face smashed into a bouquet of flowers.

"How are you, baby gurla? You ready for these little hellions?"

Sister Simmons laughed at Sheeda's openmouthed shock.

"That's right, I said it. Everybody know how hard it is to keep a five-year-old's attention." She pressed her hands to her hips as she mock whined. "Every year I've asked your aunt to give me the fourth graders because I do better with older kids. But here we are." She handed Sheeda a stack of paper, then busied herself on the other side of the room. Her voice carried and Sheeda had no doubt it was floating down the hallway for the other teachers to hear. "You go right on and cut those up for me. All that work and five minutes into it they're gonna be asking when can they go play kickball. 'Cause . . . kindergartners." She squinted over at the schedule—black marker on a bright yellow poster board. "At least we get the first outside time slot. We only have to keep them busy for thirty minutes before we ship 'em off to Brother Patterson. You in it with me?"

"Yes, ma'am," Sheeda said, charged by the challenge.

"My girl." Sister Simmons teeth flashed in a grin. "At least Deandra did assign me two assistants this year. That'll be a big help."

Sheeda was about to ask who when Kita walked in, church-appropriate in a pair of jeans (no holes or rips) and a yellow round-neck T-shirt that would only be in danger of showing cleavage if you DIY'ed it. She and Sheeda were practically outfit twins, except Sheeda's jeans were capris and her shirt was last year's retreat T with all the participants' names on the back. She wouldn't dare wear a good T-shirt to VBS. Kindergartners had no idea how to paint without spilling.

"There she goes." Sister Simmons rushed to wrap Kita in her arms. "Now that the brain trust is here, I need to go get the lesson plan out of my car. When I get back, we'll talk about how we're going to survive this week."

She was out of the door and loudly greeting the pastor.

Kita looked shell-shocked. "Survive? Are we doing boot camp or Bible lessons?"

"Right?" Sheeda handed half the packet to Kita. "Grab some scissors."

Sheeda's hands memorized the route of what was supposed to have been a replica of their church building. She cut automatically. "Which class is Yola helping with this year? The chat been a little . . . where they at doe, lately."

Her and Kita's eyes met, an understanding there that they weren't going to be ratchet and gossip in church. At least not today. Kita looked back down, concentrating on her cutout.

"She with the second graders, I think." Kita chuckled. "I like that—where they at doe? Yeah, it's def been a little quiet."

"Are y'all two okay?" Sheeda couldn't help asking, even though she didn't want to get in the middle.

"We fine." Kita held up one of her pretend First Baptist cutouts. "At least the paper white enough so you can actually color it in. Remember that year the copies came out so dark you could barely see what you was coloring?"

"And Sister Williams's niece started crying because none of her colors showed up," Sheeda said, shaking her head. "It was like, girl, no one actually cares about this. We're trying to get to the real arts and crafts in the multi room."

Kita cracked up. "I know, right?"

Sheeda reminisced on. "These kids got it good. We didn't even get outside time when the church was at the Legion."

"Oh my Go—" Kita slapped her hand over her mouth. Her head swiveled to the door. "Oops. I mean, for real, though. Then we only got, like, maybe two years here before your aunt made us start TAing. I'm not mad though. I like helping."

"Me, too," Sheeda said, realizing she meant it. "Sister Simmons called the kindergartners 'hellions.'"

"She never lied, though," Kita said. "I hope little Matty

not in our class. He bad as I don't know what."

They laughed in a hoarse whisper, eyes periodically checking the door for anybody that might be lurking in the hallway to catch them talking stuff.

"Is your friend Mo coming to the retreat again?" Kita asked.

"Yeah. Right now, she away at a ballet intensive for three weeks," Sheeda said, bursting with pride that ballooned at the impressed look on Kita's face.

"Three weeks? Oh, she serious, serious."

"Well, yeah, when you say it twice, that's the real deal," Sheeda joked.

"She was funny," Kita said.

They both jumped when Sheeda's phone clacked across the table as a message came in.

DatGirlTai:

Can you work the booth with me? ●●

Rah-Rah:

Sorry. No 😖

Her phone buzzed urgently. First one message, then three. Then two more.

Sheeda didn't bother to check them. The first few words of Tai's last text glowed: I don't see why—before her phone dimmed.

Kita glanced down at it. "Umph. Who blowing you up?"

"It's my friend, Tai. She mad because I can't go to a fair with her." Seeing Kita's attentive gaze, Sheeda explained. "It's, like, a community day. But five days of it. They have bands and stuff. Booths with free stuff. Basketball tournaments. I've never been, though, 'cause it's always the same week as VBS."

"Oh, right."

Sheeda cut slowly, one eye on her phone, waiting for Tai to strike again.

"You good?" Kita gathered her scraps. She crumbled the jagged handful of paper, twisting it into a tight knot.

Sheeda pulled her eyes away from the phone and gave Kita a reassuring head nod.

Kita floated her trash toward the can. It landed with a hollow thunk. "Ayy, two points." They fist-bumped. She watched as Sheeda continued cutting, then asked randomly, "It get old missing everything, huh?"

Sheeda looked toward the door, expecting her aunt to pop in with an "Aha, I knew you hated church." The hallway was quiet. Sister Simmons had likely stopped into the multi room, where the teachers and advisors gathered until things kicked off. The laughter of other TAs could be heard faintly coming from the classrooms. She wondered why Yola hadn't come by looking for them. A part of her couldn't believe they were still not talking, but she didn't want to ask Kita about her again.

"It does get old." The weight of the truth slid away. "But, honestly, I don't have nothing better to do this summer anyway. So . . ."

"That's kind of messed up," Kita said. She took a few papers from Sheeda's stack and helped. "Is it that bad kicking it with us?"

"Oh, I didn't mean it like that. I just . . ."

She stopped herself. She had meant it that way. What she wanted, she couldn't have. She would settle for hanging with Tai, but it wasn't her first choice. And she'd never be allowed to chill with Lennie. Messaging him was tricky enough. She stayed deleting their DMs. All she had left was sitting home doing nothing. Being at First Bap was at least better than that.

Kita's scissors moved smoothly around the outline of the building. Sheeda waited until she had clipped around one uneven corner before speaking.

"For real, sometimes it's that I don't fit in anywhere." Sheeda's scissors dangled from her fingers, balancing on her knuckle. She gave it a gentle push, letting the movement lull her into a full confession. "I'm here so much missing out on stuff they doing, I be feeling like I'm always trying to catch up once I'm back home. But when I'm here, I'm just the third girl that be with you and Yola."

She was grateful when Kita nodded along. Her face no longer tight.

"I have friends at school, but once summer is here I don't see them. They used to it now," Kita said. "I'm definitely closer to y'all. I mean, when I see you." Her laugh was sad. "I don't see you as just the third girl or whatever. I just figured you didn't like hanging with us."

Sheeda thought about saying that wasn't true. But it was. Time to stop lying, especially in church.

Kita politely ignored Sheeda's silence. "Meanwhile, I stay so bored at home. That's why usually I can't wait to get to rehearsal or whatever."

That part Sheeda related to. Lately, after sitting home all day, she was grateful by the time rehearsal time rolled around. As much as she'd promised herself to get out and have fun, she hadn't done it at all, at least not without wishing she were somewhere else or were with someone else.

She stacked her cutouts, patted them with satisfaction,

and asked, "Want to sleep over one day? We both have to be here all week anyway."

Kita's head pumped eagerly. "Let me ask my mother. She tired of me sitting around, so she probably say yes."

Just like that, the chip fell off Sheeda's shoulder.

MONIQUE

The rhythm of BA was a rushing wave of classes all day, then a calm flow of dinner and hanging out in the dorm room talking, playing games or streaming a movie. Unable to take any more of Brenna's movie picks, Mo had insisted they watch something that didn't involve a talking animal. They ended up watching the Royal Ballet's production of *Sleeping Beauty*, a story Mo hadn't read since she was in elementary school. She dazed out halfway through low-key regretting talking Brenna out of the talking dog movie. Some of the ballets just got so long.

Even with the talking animal movies, the rhythm had been easy to get used to.

The only real change in the schedule were night classes. They got two a week. Mo loved being in the big glassed-in studios with the sun setting or total darkness against it. And even though night classes meant eating a tasteless BA dinner—who could mess up tacos? BA—Mo looked forward to them.

The night classes also moved faster. Ms. Sharon seemed to work them harder. It made Mo imagine they were professionals preparing for a show.

The studio's bright lights blackened the glass wall. Almost made it like a mirror. In it, Mo watched her classmates take their turn going across the floor. Her legs tingled, tired but ready. It was her favorite part of class. Barre and center work were the rehearsals; going across the floor was the miniature performance. The girls who had already gone or were waiting to go watched each small group of four, like an audience.

She clocked as much as she could from the sideline—watching for people who didn't point their toes or didn't lift their leg high enough—mentally preparing her body not to make the same mistakes. The most important spectator was the instructor, of course. Even a head nod from Ms. Sharon made the sore muscles worth it. Mo was still getting used to any "notes," but believed Katie that getting a note was good. It meant the instructor was watching her.

Katie was the opener, always going in group one. Mo considered herself the closer. She chose the last group, no matter what. Her and Katie had even argued about the strategy. In the end, Mo stuck to her belief that going last gave her the chance to get her technique right.

She mouthed the technique as she watched the groups go.

She took her place at the front of her group. Right leg in front of left. Right foot facing the studio's doorway, left foot turned toward one of the glassed walls. After doing it every day for hours, her muscles no longer screamed when she turned her feet slightly more in each direction. Yay!

She positioned her head forward, neck tilted up more graceful than haughty. Her arms were held far enough from her body so if someone wanted to stuff a small sleeping bag in the open space, it might stay put.

The music ended, paused, then started again. She let it move her.

Her heart soared then eased to the beat of her jumps. She imagined it was a bouncing ball keeping time, up when she leaped, down when she landed. She ended, posed, the way she started, holding it a little longer than everyone else in the group. Milking it for a note. It didn't always work.

Ms. Sharon touched her shoulder. "Very good, Monique."

This time, it had.

Breathing hard from the effort, she flashed Katie a grin. But Katie was already in place, ready to go across the floor from the left.

Mo was giddy.

Very good.

It had taken a week, but she'd gotten one.

Ms. Sharon's compliment sent fireworks off inside her body. The last ten minutes of class were a blur as they did several more combinations across the floor. There had been no more comments or notes, but she didn't need any. The class poured into the hallway, changing out of their flat ballet slippers and into pointe shoes.

Katie barely had time to plop onto the floor to slip out of her ballet slippers before Mo gushed, "Did you hear her say 'very good'?"

"Um-hm." Katie snatched the sticky purple tape off her big toe. She tapped gently at the angry red blister, then put her hand up for a high five.

Mo wrinkled her nose. "Hard pass. I don't want to

touch your hand after it was on your stinky feet."

Katie high-fived the air. "Good job."

"No, very good," Mo said, curtseying with only her head. She slipped her feet into the hard, satin pointe shoes. Her toes were numb like someone had taken a hammer and beat them. But good news, she didn't have any blisters. "It took me a week, but I got one, K.T."

Adrian came into view, hovering above her. Since that one day, at lunch, she insisted on being everywhere Katie was. "K.T.? I thought your last name was Jensen?" she asked.

Katie laughed. "It is."

Mo's eyes rolled. She couldn't get used to people dipping into a conversation that wasn't their business.

"Oh," Adrian said. With one hand against the wall, she used the other to jam her pointe shoe on. Mo swatted near Adrian's shoe, to get it away from her head. "Sorry," Adrian said, still more focused on getting the shoe on than getting it out of Mo's face. "So, you got one of what?"

Mo scooted a few inches down. It was either that or go in on Adrian and her funky feet. She refused to let anything ruin how good she felt.

"Ms. Sharon gave her a very good," Katie said. She wound fresh purple tape on her blister, placed the cushy pink toe pads over her feet, and made fast work of getting her shoes on.

Adrian frowned. "So."

"So, you don't like to know you doing good in something?" Mo asked, her irritation rising. She wound the satin ribbons around her ankles, tied them, then carefully tucked what wasn't knotted into a corner of the ribbon. All around her everyone was doing the same. She wasn't sure when it happened, but she'd become one of the robot dolls. And she didn't hate it.

Going from one class to the other was routine now. So was lying in the hallway on her stomach while Katie tugged at her arms or pushed her legs back to stretch out while they waited for their next class. The week before conversations had been about home studios and dance schools and pointe shoe brands. Now, as they changed for pointe class—some quickly, others taking their time—there was talk about what movie they'd stream later or gossip about drama that had popped off during the weekend's trip to *Giselle*.

She could see herself living in a dorm, dancing in the middle of the day—doing this every day. She would miss her mother and Lennie, but this felt right. It took her a second to realize Adrian was still talking.

"But what's the big deal about her saying 'very good'? She says that to everybody." Adrian had switched and was now putting on the other shoe, determined to be different by standing.

Mo hated when people stood over her. It made it feel like they had the jump on you if anything popped off. She wanted to snatch Adrian down to the ground. She held her breath for two seconds before answering.

"But she doesn't, though." She got up off the floor to be eye to eye with Adrian. "Have you heard her tell every single person in class 'very good'?"

Adrian only thought for a second before shrugging. "I haven't counted. But even if she hasn't, eventually, by the time we're done, I'm sure she will have said it at least once to everyone."

Katie chuckled. "I don't know; she's pretty stingy with praise."

Mo nodded, eagerly. "And 'stingy' is being nice. She's said it to six people so far."

Adrian practically recoiled. "You've literally counted? Why?"

"You really up in my business," Mo said.

"You're," Adrian said.

"What?" Mo sneered.

"It's 'you're really up in my business,'" Adrian said, face straight.

Mo looked at Katie to verify if she was tripping or had Adrian come at her with the correction. Katie was up and pounding the toe of her pointe shoe on the floor, trying to break them in. There was no way she was missing the conversation, but she didn't look up. Mo took the hint.

"You, you're, you are." Mo's eyebrow peaked. "Pick which one you want. Either way, this was a A, B conversation, C your way out." As an afterthought she spat, "Please."

Adrian shrugged. "I'm just saying it's silly to make a big deal out of one compliment. This is the week that they start assessing who they'll invite to year-round. I think you need more than a 'very good' to get in."

"Who said I cared about getting into their little program?" Mo stuffed her ballet slippers into her dance bag and stalked off. The pointe shoes made her footsteps flat, making her dramatic exit more like a stomping duck walk. She took the front spot at the barre and looked straight ahead as she waited for the next class to begin.

Katie came in and stood at her side.

"Thanks for saving my spot."

She smiled when Mo looked at her dead faced.

"What?" Katie asked.

Mo leaned against the barre, arms folded. "You know what? Where I'm from, if somebody is dogging your friend out, you have their back."

Katie sighed explosively. The sound made Mo's face tight.

"You do a good job of having your own back, Monique." Katie slashed the air with her arm. "My bad, *Mo*. You didn't need me to step into the fight."

"Fight?" The word smacked Mo in the face. "That was hardly a fight."

"Fight. Argument, whatever," Katie said. She angrily pushed wisps of hair out of her face.

"Okay, well, there's a difference. Get the story straight. You can't go around using that word and then people be out here thinking I touched her or something."

"Okay, Mo. Okay." Katie put her hands up in surrender. "I didn't see why I had to jump in. She said what she said and you said whatever back. You get mad so easily. If I jumped in every time, all we'd do is argue with everyone."

The words cut Mo deep. She knew it. Had known, at some point, this would happen. That Katie would be on some dumb stuff, the second Mo believed they were friends. She turned abruptly, facing the glass that looked out into the darkening city. Seeing the city lit beyond the studio and the bus ride back to the dorms with her body pushed past its limit was when she enjoyed being away the most. But every time she found something to love about the program, it reminded her that it didn't love her back.

She blinked away tears, praying for her anger to dry them up. If Lennie knew how much she let these little robot ballerinas get to her, he'd clown her for days. Being angry felt better. It sucked away sadness and kept being afraid in check. She clenched her teeth, letting it fill her.

"Are you seriously going to stay in my spot?" Katie asked.

"I got here first," Mo said.

Katie stood in place. Finally, all sighed out for the night, she padded off flat-footed and took the place behind Mo.

As their teacher walked in, Katie loud-whispered, "A friend wouldn't take another friend's favorite spot."

Mo turned her head enough to be heard. "Oh, we friends now?"

Katie's tiny gasp was exactly what she wanted to hear. She closed her eyes and imagined everyone in the classroom disappearing as the piano tinkled.

RASHEEDA

Mo'Betta:

Everybody here on one! 🙈

They were in the car heading home from Vacation Bible School. Makita was hitting it off perfectly with Auntie D, telling her how Brother Patterson got hit in the 'nads during their class's kickball game. Extra points for saying "groin" instead of 'nads. Her aunt had never laughed this much or so hard with any of Sheeda's friends. The cloud of disapproval that blew in nearly anytime Sheeda had plans with them was nowhere to be found. There were nothing but clear skies. If she texted

Mo, right now, the storms would rumble in fast. She turned the phone over on her lap, waiting for a moment to text back.

"I know it's summer, but some of us still have work in the morning," Auntie D said, once they'd gotten into the house. "I don't mind you girls staying up late. Just keep it down. If I have to come in there even once to shush you, no more midweek sleep overs. Deal?"

"Deal," they chorused back.

Auntie D hummed as she went up the stairs. When she was safely out of earshot, Sheeda whispered, "Who was that?"

Kita giggled quietly. "What you mean?"

"No, you don't know. My aunt is never like . . . nice to my friends. She's mostly annoyed by them."

Kita popped an invisible collar. "Guess I got the magic touch."

When they got to Sheeda's room, she presented the space like it was a game show prize. "Welcome to my very plain space. No posters, no photos, no Post-it notes allowed on the walls."

Kita sat on the bed, examining it like a museum exhibit. She crossed her legs primly. "I think they call this design style *understated*."

Sheeda side-eyed her. "Right."

Their loud laughter was already in violation of the one rule.

"I'll get you a towel and washcloth and you can go in the shower first," Sheeda said.

She busied herself getting Kita situated—showing her how to operate the shower, which got hot really quickly if you didn't keep it on freezing and advising her to not stay in too long because her aunt was obsessed with long showers and their water bill.

Hearing the water patter and sure Kita hadn't scalded or frozen herself, she stripped out of her grimy T-shirt and capris. Brother Patterson had made her and Kita be his assistants during outside time. It wasn't their fault Jalen kept disappearing into Yola's class and Gerard hadn't shown up. It had been kind of fun helping the kids run the bases, but she smelled like old pennies and sweat. They all had afterward, and the classroom was ripe the rest of the night. Sister Simmons had to fan herself to keep the smell at bay.

Sheeda sat on the floor wrapped in a towel and texted Mo.

Is everything okay?

Five minutes later she tried again.

Hullo? ••

She texted Lennie.

You heard from Mo, today? She good?

Kita came into the room, looking worried. "Was that short enough?"

"You fine." Sheeda stood up, cinching her towel tight. "For real, she probably wouldn't be mad at you anyway. Y'all were kicking it like best friends on the ride home."

Kita made herself at home on Sheeda's bed. She was clean and smelling good in a tank top and a pair of navy blue shorts, the kind cheerleaders wore. "I like your aunt. She good peoples." She tilted her head at the look on Sheeda's face. "What? She is."

Sheeda laughed, embarrassed that Kita had caught her surprise. "I didn't say anything."

"I mean, she probably harder on you because you hers. But she's always so nice to everybody. For real, her and Sister Simmons my favorites."

"She just have mad rules," Sheeda said, leaving it at that.

Kita shrugged. "And what parent don't?"

In the shower, she thought about her aunt being somebody's favorite. The Sister Tate they saw was definitely sugary sweet. She cooed and praised all the First

Bap kids when they did well in school and heaped hugs on them during youth Sunday after they read Scripture correctly or served as the MC. They didn't live with her, though. Sheeda tried mustering annoyance for her aunt's many rules. But, nothing came.

Auntie D had been in the best mood all week. She hadn't given a single sermon. It was like when Sheeda first moved in and they'd do girls' nights—homemade facials with mayo and lemon and clear polish pedis (no colored nail polish until she was twelve).

Plus, her aunt had been right—she'd enjoyed Vacation Bible School. Sister Simmons had made her and Kita feel like they were real teachers, consulting with them on things to do with the class and going against some of the usual activities on their advice. On top of that, she and Kita had a lot of stuff in common. The dance ministry was both of their favorites, and they were both binging *Straight and Narrow*. It wasn't exactly a match made in heaven, but it had made VBS bearable, even fun.

They still hadn't talked about how Yola had stopped talking to them. Since second grade and kindergarten never crossed paths, they only had to see her if they wanted, and so far Kita hadn't done much to soothe the rift. Sheeda stayed in her lane, following Kita's lead.

If Auntie D hadn't made her go to VBS, she and Kita would have never started hanging out. She knocked on her aunt's door, giddy with gratefulness. "I just wanted to say good night."

"Come on in."

Sheeda stepped in shyly. Their bedrooms were their space. They met mostly in the kitchen, living room, and in the car on the way to First Bap.

Auntie D's room was the grown-up version of Sheeda's room. Only a few feet larger, its walls just as plain except for a small framed Scripture: "For every house is built by someone, but God is the builder of everything. Hebrews 3:4." Instead of a small twin-sized bed with petite flowers on a quilt, a large gray down comforter with what looked like purple amoebas laid over a king-sized bed that dominated every foot.

Sheeda stood at the bed's edge. "Thanks for letting Makita stay over."

Her aunt was like a tiny queen in the middle of her royal bed. She put her Bible down, a big smile on her face. "I'm glad you asked her over. You all seem to be—"

"Getting along?" Sheeda offered.

"Yes. But I was going to say compatible. That's why I assigned you both to Jackie's class." Auntie D's mouth pursed in disapproval. "I see how Yolanda has gotten herself all into Jalen. Sitting together in the pews, whispering before choir rehearsal. All up under him any chance she gets. You don't need to get yourself in the middle of that accident waiting to happen. Carla needs to handle that before it goes too far." She stopped, as if realizing she was going off. "Anyway, I'm glad you girls are having fun. Good night, Luv."

"Night," Sheeda said.

Her aunt's mild rant made everything come together like a jigsaw puzzle.

She was dazed when she returned to her room. Out of habit, she checked her phone for messages. Still no Mo. She had probably already gone to sleep. Sheeda put the phone down robotically, spacing out.

Reading her every mood, Kita peered at her. "What?"

"Nothing." Sheeda joined Kita on the bed. She spoke thoughtfully, making the words add up to the answer as she spoke. "My aunt put us both in the same class TAing because she didn't want me to hang with Yola . . . 'cause Yola and Jalen talking."

Kita didn't seem surprised. "She was on a mission, huh?"

"Right?" Sheeda held off checking her vibrating

phone. "I mean, I'm glad we're hanging. But she didn't have to go in on Yola so hard just 'cause she likes Jalen. What's so wrong about liking somebody?"

"Nothing, but Yola throwing herself at him. If your aunt see it, then you know it's bad." There was no forgiveness in Kita's voice as she went on, forehead creased down the middle. "Me and Yola been close since we was little. I told her she needed to fall back. She's too into Jalen. And she told me that I'm hating. I'm not hating. But, hey, do you, Boo."

Sheeda's stomach dove thinking about Mo looking as angry as Kita. "Are you saying y'all not friends anymore?"

Like fairy dust, the question dried up Kita's anger. "I don't know." Her shoulders sagged under the reality. "If we not, it's not my fault. I was just being honest with her. Jalen cool with me, but—" She plucked at the comforter's flowers. "Don't say anything, but she was talking about her and Jalen—" She picked furiously like the flower was a weed she couldn't pull up. Her eyes widened and she raised her eyebrows conveying a message to Sheeda.

"Her and Jalen . . ." Sheeda repeated, encouraging more.

Kita was silent a few seconds. She finally raised her

eyes to Sheeda's as she said, "She was saying her and Jalen might . . . you-know-what, if they could get away at the retreat."

Sheeda hugged her knees to her chest, rocking to keep her shock in check. This was definitely getting pulled in too deep. It reminded her too much of the summer before when the squad was almost blown apart when Mila and Tai were beefing. She couldn't do this again.

"For real, Rasheeda. Don't tell anybody," Kita begged.

"No. I won't. I promise," Sheeda said. Wanting to add, *I wish you hadn't told me.* But the relief on Kita's face stopped her.

They sat facing each other, mute. Kita was confessed out and Sheeda was glad.

A few messages buzzed into Sheeda's phone, breaking up the silence.

Kita smiled weakly. "That your friend Tai still mad that you're not at the fair this week?"

"No. Probably Mo. She hit me earlier on our way home. Let me answer her before she get hot." She grabbed her phone, thankful for the distraction.

DatBoyEll:

Naw I ain't talk to Mo. She must be
fine. My mother ain't say nothing.

DatBoyEll:

What it do shorty bop?

DatBoyEll:

U still at your VBS thing this late?

DatBoyEll:

Hit me whatever time. I be up.

> **Rah-Rah:**
>
> Hey. Nuthin. Chilling w/my friend,
> Kita.

DatBoyEll:

Who dat? What court she live on

> **Rah-Rah:**
>
> 😄 None. She a friend from
> church.

DatBoyEll:

O werd. Simp & Tai doing that official
thing now?

> **Rah-Rah:**
>
> 🤤 No. Why?

Kita's voice pulled her out of the phone. "Is that Mo? Ask her if she remember me, then tell her I said hey."

Sheeda debated telling her the truth. Half the fun of a secret crush was that it wasn't secret from your friends. But Kita was too angry with Yola right now. It didn't feel right. "I'll tell her you said what's up," she said.

DatBoyEll:

he been helping her @ the H3 booth
every night. they seem real close

> **Rah-Rah:**
>
> lol yeah. Maybe they finally ready
> to admit it's a thing.

DatBoyEll:

IIWII. never thought Tai cared whut
people thought.

> **Rah-Rah:**
>
> I care what people think. But who
> knows w/Tai.

Even though Kita waited patiently, unbothered by her texting, Sheeda ignored the allure of the incoming message.

"Mo says hey. She remembers you." Sheeda said a tiny prayer for the ongoing lie. She'd tell Kita the truth eventually. "I saw Gerard all up in your grille yesterday. Does he like you?"

"He was just telling me how he had football training camp or something. I knew he wasn't going to be there tonight." She laughed. "I didn't know Brother Pat was going to make us take his place, though."

"Oh my goodness. I knowwww," Sheeda said as she reread Lennie's message.

DatBoyEll:

why u care? People gon always want

put in they 2 cents. Don't mean u got

spend it.

"Go 'head. I know you're trying to catch up with your girl." Kita pulled her phone out of her bag.

"No. My aunt would be so mad." Sheeda put the phone down and whispered an imitation of Auntie D. "Rasheeda, stop always wanting to talk to the person who isn't here with you."

Kita nodded, laughing. "I know, right. My mother would say the same thing. They act like they've never put a friend on hold to talk to another friend back in the day."

It was good having someone understand. Her friends' parents had plenty of rules, but Auntie D's rules were always a special level of strict because you knew at some point she'd tie it to some sermon or Scripture. Nobody was trying to be rude when they answered a message. She needed to find a Scripture to back that up.

Once more, the truth of who she was texting burst at the gate of her mouth, wanting to reveal all to Kita. But what if Kita disapproved? Sheeda didn't want to ruin the mood. Kita was sitting back against the wall, her legs draped over Sheeda's, flipping through her phone. Without looking up she said, "Go 'head. I'm good."

Sheeda accepted the permission.

Rah-Rah:

😂 IDK I still care. I'm not like Mo & Tai. No shade.

DatBoyEll:

lol naw nobody like baby sis. She read u, dare u to say something back then read u again for not being real enuf to stand up for ur self. 😆 😆

Rah-Rah:

FACTS.

Rah-Rah:

speaking of being real and caring, one of us has to tell Mo b/c I don't know if she would be cool w/us crushing like this

DatBoyEll:

Crushing? U know what that mean right?

Rah-Rah:

☹️ To like somebody??

DatBoyEll:

😆 Well thas one meaning. It also mean
something else tho.

> **Rah-Rah:**
>
> 🙄 I'm talking 'bout regular
> crushing!!! OMGoodness!

DatBoyEll:

lol ok I got u. Only cuz its kinda cute
that u so nice u can't even spell out
OMG w/o adding goodness. 😄

> **Rah-Rah:**
>
> LOL habit. One time my aunt saw
> it and said, I know u not taking the
> Lord's name in vain. 🙄

DatBoyEll:

lol look tho, Mo not my mother. She
can't tell me who I can talk to. She not
urs either.

> **Rah-Rah:**
>
> she's my best friend tho. I don't
> want her mad w/me.

DatBoyEll:

yall can't still be friends if me and u
talking? Serious question

Rah-Rah:

I didn't say that. But I can't choose
talking to u over her. Sorry. 😕

DatBoyEll:

not asking u to choose. Keeping it 💯
I like u

Rah-Rah:

I like u too. Just don't think I can
keep this on the low-low much
longer

DatBoyEll:

if u want me tell her, I tell her.

Rah-Rah:

for real?

DatBoyEll:

u for real stressed over this huh? 🙁

Rah-Rah:

Yes. I am fr fr. I can't lie.

DatBoyEll:

I kno u can't. U a good girl

Rah-Rah:

🙂

DatBoyEll:

yeah for real. I hip her to it when she

get home. I mean if u really down w/
me.

Rah-Rah:

I am

DatBoyEll:

thas whas up

Rah-Rah:

can we talk later? I can't keep

leaving my friend hanging.

DatBoyEll:

no doubt. 1 more thing tho

Rah-Rah:

ok

DatBoyEll:

come see me

Rah-Rah:

don't be mad but why do u keep

wanting me to come see u. What u

think gonna happen if I do?

DatBoyEll:

Not expecting nothing to "happen,"
shawty. Just wanna see u in person.
Something wrong w/that?

Rah-Rah:

No

DatBoyEll:

u scared to come see me?

Rah-Rah:

a little 😕

DatBoyEll:

lol Bring Tai or whatever cuz I already
kno u not gon come by urself. 😆

Rah-Rah:

my aunt def not gonna be down w/that

DatBoyEll:

didn't expect u to tell her. jus say u
going over Tai's

Rah-Rah:

True. She probably still mad b/c I couldn't
work the booth. But I let u know.

DatBoyEll:

cool

Sheeda almost hadn't gotten the message typed, her hands shook so bad. Going to see Lennie was a step she still wasn't ready for. She was finally used to talking to him without getting nervous and now this. Her head felt light with excitement and fear.

She pulled her legs from under Kita's and slipped underneath the comforter.

"Oh, you finished?" Kita eyeballed the small bed. "You want me lie up there with you or we doing the feet to head thing?"

"Doesn't matter," Sheeda said. She wanted to close her eyes and not think.

Kita crawled to the head of the bed and got under the covers. "Are you okay?" She laid on her side, head on her elbow. Only inches separated them. "You ready to be knocked out on me, quick."

"It was too hot out, tonight. My stomach hasn't been right since," Sheeda said.

"I'm surprised mine doesn't hurt. Your aunt's tacos were banging. I had three," Kita said. She wriggled deeper into the cover. Her body left a small C-shaped space between them.

The mention of food made Sheeda's stomach groan in protest. She threw the covers back.

"I don't feel good."

"Should I get your aunt," Kita whisper-yelled behind her.

Sheeda hoped she saw her head shaking no. She couldn't face Auntie D now. Too much was on her heart and she wouldn't be able to stop the truth from flowing out.

She ran to the bathroom and sat on the floor, her head against the toilet seat. The lemony scent of bathroom cleaner stung her nose. She prayed silently, waiting for the urge to throw up to pass. He didn't owe her any favors, but she couldn't help asking.

Ghosted

Rah-Rah:

Hey. Things must be crazy there.
You never hit me back.

Rah-Rah:

Sorry I didn't hit u back earlier last
night. U know how A.D. get if I text
while I'm w/other people. Things
def crazy here. Yola and Jalen
getting serious. Like for real for real
really real. 😠

Rah-Rah:

I'm not even supposed to know

they planning to hook up. The
retreat is gonna be all the way wild.

Rah-Rah:

Hit me when u get a chance

MONIQUE

The second her knee twisted, she grabbed it and cried. The last few days had been the worst. She'd stopped talking, for the most part, even only answering Mila with the least amount of words possible. The tears were from loneliness, not her knee. It was more a tweak than an actual twist, for real. But she needed a reason to let them stream.

Ms. Sharon's hand went up, stopping the pianist dramatically. Mo slid down to the floor, cradling her knee, tears rolling down her face.

Everyone looked on curiously, from their spot. Katie kneeled beside her, touching the leg Mo didn't have her arms wrapped around. "Are you okay?" She stood up before Mo could answer, taking a step back when Ms. Sharon reached them. Ms. Sharon's face appeared above her, concerned.

"Monique, tell me what happened? Where does it hurt exactly?"

"My knee. It twisted," Mo managed to say. Her knee throbbed. It hurt but not bad. The tears slowed as Ms. Sharon asked Katie and another dancer, thankfully not annoying-A Adrian, to help Mo up. Once up, she hobbled to the front of the room, politely refusing Katie's offer to transfer her weight. They had her iced up with her leg raised on a chair and were back to class with the precision timing of a race car team.

Mo watched on, mesmerized, from this side of the class. Every dancer was concentrating on Ms. Sharon's instructions that connected perfectly with the piano's melodies. It was a living painting. One she'd been a part of a few minutes before. She wanted to jump back in, but knew after the tears she'd shed Ms. Sharon wouldn't allow it.

She watched the rest of the classes from the sideline, grateful that Saturday classes ended right after lunch.

"How's your knee?" Mila asked as soon as she walked into the room. Seeing Mo's questioning eyebrow raise, she smiled in apology. "Katie messaged Brenna about it. Are you good?"

Hardly limping anymore, Mo felt like a fraud but accepted the way to break the silence she'd wrapped around herself.

"I only tweaked it. It should be fine tomorrow."

She had hoped Mila would go on, but she just sang, "Okay, good," and headed through the bathroom to their suitemates. Mo swallowed the tears, refusing to cry anymore. This was what she wanted anyway, right? To not talk to anybody.

At first Katie had tried talking to her at dinner and again when they were in the room. By the next morning she'd given up. Even the thunk and tinkle of the piano hadn't covered the silence between them. Mo wanted to squash the beef. But what was the point of making up if they were just going to disagree on something else?

She wanted to finish out and go home.

When she did, she was laying Miss Sheeda straight out for taking so long to respond. By the time Sheeda texted her back, Mo's petty game was on a thousand. She hadn't bothered to answer. Let her see what it felt like to stare at the messages waiting. Besides, Mo didn't care about any of Sheeda's Jesus friends. What was she supposed to say about their drama? That was their business.

With nothing else to do, she stretched her legs out and adjusted the ice pack on her knee. Everything was a mess. She swiped through her phone looking for *Straight and Narrow*. She stared at the screen, not really absorbing anything, when Mila finally came out of the bathroom and sat on the end of Mo's bed.

"Can we talk, real quick?"

Yes, please, Mo wanted to yell. She kept it cool, lying the phone on her lap. "What's up?"

Mila twirled three thin braids around her finger. She stared at the closed bathroom door, then asked, "Can you please make up with Katie?" She put her hand up as if warding off flames. "Before you say anything—" She scooted alongside Mo's outstretched legs until their faces were only a few feet apart. "I know you're mad that Katie didn't have your back. And if I had been there, I would have cosigned. But Katie's not me. And she doesn't see it like we do." Her brown eyes begged before she cracked a smile. "For real, Katie's the White you."

Mo laughed in spite of herself. "No lies told."

Mila perked up. "I don't want to spend the time we have left with us not talking to her and Bren."

Mo winced inside. Bren. Mila and Brenna were legit

close. She didn't know if she could bring herself to feel the same way about Katie. Whether she wanted to or not.

She lifted the ice pack and rubbed at her frozen knee. "I just don't feel like pretending anymore. When I try to go along, it feel fake. When I'm myself, people out here judging and correcting me."

"Katie didn't correct you, though," Mila said.

Mo huffed. "You taking her side?"

"No. But it was the other girl that corrected you. Right?"

Mo reluctantly agreed. She barely remembered the exact conversation. All that was left was how stupid she'd felt when Adrian clowned her for getting excited about getting praise from Ms. Sharon and for thinking anyone here saw her as good. Almost like there was a whole different definition of *good* at this place.

Mila pressed on. "Katie doesn't get why you're mad. And for real, I don't know how to explain it." She sucked her lips in, pausing, then dove in. "Don't get mad for what I'm ready to say. Okay?"

Mo exploded softly, more frustrated than angry. "If you saying that, then you ready say something wild that's gonna make me mad, though."

Mila patted her leg like she was a mom. "I'm not trying to make you mad."

Mo took a breath, steeling herself, glad that Mila waited for her to get herself together. She exhaled, her mouth a big O and said, "Go 'head."

"You do get mad really easily, Mo." She patted Mo's leg faster, but more gently. "I've known you a long time and so I know you being mad don't mean any harm. But Katie and Brenna don't know that. I mean, they sort of do now. But they're still getting used to it."

Mo let the words drip into her ears and down her brain, coating it with understanding. Inside she ran through her defenses:

It's not always me being mad.

I be protecting my friends sometimes.

I'm not gonna let you say whatever you want, how you want, to me.

People act like they can say what they want but I never can.

Her head tingled. Maybe it was from fighting what she wanted to say. Maybe it was because she knew Mila wasn't wrong. She settled on, "Naw, you a little right."

Mila laughed and Mo couldn't help laughing, too.

"Even if me and Katie make up, we just gonna end up fussing again," Mo said. "Or disagreeing. I don't feel like doing all that. Maybe we not friends."

"Do you talk to anybody else in your level?" Mila's head cocked. There was no judgment in her expression.

Mo admitted that she didn't. Without Katie, there had been no one else to talk to in between classes and when they changed into pointe shoes. She'd found a corner and looked at videos during lunch rather than sit silent at the table. Sacrificing lunch saved her taste buds the humiliation of the saltless food. The other dancers went on, never making any kind of small talk with her or asking if she was okay. It made her feel like she wasn't there at all.

Mila kneeled in and hugged her. Mo sniffed to keep the tears in check, but they flowed again. She didn't want to need Katie. Didn't want to need Mila. But she did. When she was cried out, she let go of Mila and wiped at her face. The words that had been dammed up for the last two weeks waterfalled.

"I hate it here." She took a deep breath and started over. "I don't. But I do hate that I never feel like I'm doing or saying the right thing. And, for real, I feel like some of the sideways things people saying are 'cause I'm Black. But then nobody saying that kind of stuff to you. So, it's, like, well, it's just me then. But I can't be nobody but me." Her hands slapped softly at her thighs in defeat. "And, I thought I was a good dancer—"

"You are." Mila gently squeezed her wrist. "I get notes all the time in class and every time I wonder if Mademoiselle taught us wrong or something. Because I swear, I'm doing it right."

Mo's spirit danced, happy to hear that. She'd worked so hard to prove herself; it never occurred to her that Mila was doing the same. The only thing that stopped her from tagging Mila with another hug was the dull ache in her knee. She pulled the fat pillow from behind her and hugged it, listening as her friend helped bring her back to the circle.

"I was texting my father and he asked me did I think I knew everything there was to know about ballet," Mila said. "He said it wouldn't have been any point in me coming here if I did. And he's right. That's why we're here. To get better."

"My mother said the same thing," Mo said. Hope burned in her heart. She sniffed. "I just wanna do good, so bad."

"You are, though. You got Ms. Sharon's *very good*," Mila said with a cheerfulness that bordered on doing too much.

"I want more than that, though. I didn't say nothing the first time we talked about it, but I really do want to get invited to stay for the year-round program. Is that crazy?"

"Not at all," Mila said. "We all want the same thing. That's why I'm saying we need to be there for each other. The invitation letters go out soon."

With her wishes to stay at BA finally out there, all Mo wanted to do was talk about it. "Do you think your father would let you come here instead of going to regular high school?"

"Only if I get a scholarship." Mila's lips disappeared in a worried line. "Did you see how much it cost?"

Mo hadn't gotten that far. Getting in felt impossible. She didn't need one more thing to worry about. "So, I gotta apologize to Katie or something?"

"Or something," Mila agreed.

Mo planted her face into the pillow. It smelled like coconut oil, from her hair. The familiar scent fed her courage. She threw the pillow aside and hobbled off the bed.

Mila's bare feet pattered behind her as she burst through both bathroom doors.

Brenna looked up from cutting her toenails. "Oh my God." She patted her heart. "You scared the crap out of me."

Katie never moved. She was curled up on her bed,

'buds in her ears watching something on her phone. Her thin eyebrows peaked then went down just as fast, like she didn't want Mo to know she'd been startled, too.

Mo stood at the side of her bed. She folded her arms, unfolded, put her fists on her hips, then looked up at the ceiling. When she looked back down, Katie had a ghost of a smile on her lips.

Mo mustered up enough mock annoyance to say, "Never mind. You enjoying this too much."

Katie sat up, her smile maddeningly large. "I don't know if I'm going to accept your apology. But I still want to hear it."

"We all do," Brenna said. She dropped the nail clippers and pulled out her phone. "It feels like a postable moment."

"Fine." Mo walked to the middle of the room. She wagged her finger at Brenna. "Don't even think of videoing this."

Brenna dropped her phone and put her hands up.

"I'm sorry for kirking out on you. The end," Mo said, then curtsied.

Katie's mouth twisted. "If that's the best you can do—"

"It is." Mo scowled. "And now my knee hurt from bowing. Happy?"

"I'll take it," Katie said. "Are you really okay?"

"Just tweaked it. The ice is helping," Mo said.

"I now pronounce us friends again," Mila said.

Brenna sang the wedding march. "Dum, dum, dumdum."

Mo and Katie frowned at each other. "Don't they play a different song once you married?" Mo asked.

"Definitely," Katie said.

Brenna shrugged. "I don't know how that one goes." She walked over to Mo, arms open. "Group hug."

They all squeezed in together. Mila popped her arm out of the hug and took a photo with her phone.

"This, I'm posting," she said, giving Mo no choice.

Mo let go first. She felt ten pounds lighter.

She knew that she came at things hard sometimes, but it didn't mean she was wrong. Not all the way wrong, at least. She set the record straight.

"For real, though, I'm not sensitive. People keep calling me that and it's not true."

"You are a little sensitive," Katie said.

Mila and Brenna exchanged a worried look.

"We're good, y'all. But I gotta be real." Mo sat on Katie's desk. "Me and you are cool. But if we really friends, then you need to try and see why I get mad over some stuff."

Katie's mouth popped open, ready to object. She sat on her bed and motioned for Mo to continue.

"Have y'all ever been to anything where you the only White people there?" Mo looked at Katie, then Brenna. Brenna's eyes went down, answering. Katie's didn't waver. She answered, slowly, almost a question, "No-ohh?"

Mila's nodding head told Mo she was good. That it was okay to keep going. Not that she would have stopped. This had been on her chest since day one. Still, she appreciated Mila's encouragement.

"You ever have a Black teacher before? For ballet or at school?" Mo kept her hands on the desk, casually leaning back as she inquired. She wasn't going to give them a reason to say she was angry or coming at them wrong.

"My World Language teacher was Black. It was kind of weird," Brenna said.

Mila frowned. "Why?"

Brenna's cheeks turned crimson. She looked to Katie as she sputtered. "Be-because she spoke French. I had never met a Black person who—you know . . . spoke French."

"Our dance teacher is French Canadian and Black. It definitely took a little while for me to get used to her accent," Mila said.

Brenna jumped on it. "See. So you thought it was strange, too."

Seeing that she'd helped Brenna's argument, Mila mouthed "sorry" to Mo.

Mo counted to five in her head then said, calmly, "I don't care if we think it's weird. We can say that. Y'all can't."

"Why not?" Katie asked.

Mo was glad Katie only seemed curious. She was trying not to get angry. That was harder to do when Katie challenged her.

"Because y'all don't know what it feels like for it to be like some zoo exhibit when you do something or say something. Like it's not normal for Black people to be doing the same thing y'all doing."

Brenna laughed with a pitchy edginess that made Mo wince. "I don't think anybody thinks you're a zoo exhibit."

Mo rolled her eyes. "So, you know what everybody think?"

Katie came to Brenna's defense in her strongest "it's so obvious" voice. "If Bren has never seen a Black person who speaks French, it's not racist to say something is weird."

Mo wasn't having it. She caught Mila's eyes pleading with her, but went on anyway. "Y'all always around other

White people. You don't know what it's like to be me or Mila here with a bunch of White people. Period."

"But every time someone says something to you, that doesn't mean they're saying it because you're Black," Katie said.

"How do you know?" Mo asked, her voice level.

Katie thought about it, then shrugged.

"Then you don't know that it ain't because I'm Black," Mo said.

She wanted to fold her arms in triumph. Do something, to make it clear to them that she was right and they knew it. Or maybe they didn't know. Their world wasn't her world, but it didn't make their world better. She didn't know how to make them see that, but settled for how uncertain Katie was as she said, "But if you're always thinking about it, then you're always going to be mad."

"Exactly." Mo smirked. She pushed herself up from the desk's edge. "That's what it's like to be us, y'all." She headed back toward her room, stopped at the bathroom door. "See y'all in the morning."

For the first time in two weeks, she felt like herself. Better, she felt okay that she felt like herself.

Catching Up

Mo'Betta:

I forgive you. You welcome.

> **Rah-Rah:**
>
> 😁 you wuz mad huh?

Mo'Betta:

for really real yes. 😵

> **Rah-Rah:**
>
> My bad. Is everything okay, though?

Mo'Betta:

Yeah. I mean no. 😕 lonely here. It was
bad the other day. When you didn't
answer it ran me hot.

Rah-Rah:

Sorry. Kita stayed over and I was
trying to get her straight. You
lonely even w/Mila there? 😴

Mo'Betta:

It would be really bad w/o Mila here fr
fr. Got into it w/Katie and had to igg
her in class. We all good now.

Mo'Betta:

👀 Jesus friends are spending the night
now?

Rah-Rah:

you got into it with a White girl
and they ain't send you home? She
didn't go tell on you? Lol.

Rah-Rah:

Me and Kita been hanging a lot
since Yola tripping a lil bit. She
excited that you coming to the
retreat.

Mo'Betta:

FR Katie is cool. Me and her kind of
like me and Tai—she call me out
quick

Rah-Rah:

you found the white version of Tai.

I want to see that and then I don't.

LMAO A white girl calls you out?!

Mo'Betta:

Right? Which one is Kita again?

Rah-Rah:

'member the girl who had the

straight-back cornrows that went

all the way to her butt last year?

Her.

Mo'Betta:

Oh yeah. She not trying rock 'em like

that this year is she? She was looking

a lil crazy when they got all frizzy at

the top but then was straight at the

bottom. 😆

Rah-Rah:

lol Nah this year she have box

braids. They're cute.

Mo'Betta:

I'm ready come home

Rah-Rah:

did you like it there? Would you
stay if you got in?

Mo'Betta:

I loved being away on my own. No
fighting over bathroom or who has to
cook dinner. Only thing is the food is
super duper wack. But IDK. I can't see
being here w/o Mlia or even w/o Katie.
I want to get in but not 'cause I want to
go here.

Rah-Rah:

???? wait what? Lol

Mo'Betta:

😆 if I got in it's like proof I'm good.
Don't mean I'd come here tho. I can't
have my moms out here working three
jobs trying pay for ballet school.

Rah-Rah:

if u and Mila left me 🥺

Mo'Betta:

Girl these YT people not gonna let me
into this ballet school. They not ready
for this. So u good. 😊

Rah-Rah:

glad u be home soon.

Mo'Betta:

me too

RASHEEDA

It was a good day.

The one Saturday Sheeda had a morning free of errands and an evening absent of a gospel concert, play, or revival.

And . . .

After a week of wearing herself to the ground for First Baptist and its young congregants, and all the "Good job, Sister Tate," and "Girl, this was the best VBS yet," Auntie D was happily worn out.

And . . .

She was going to meet Lennie at the basketball game. She'd decided she wasn't ready to meet him at his house whether Tai was with her or not. She wanted to tell him to his face, though. She thought she'd be nervous about telling him; instead, she felt like she could walk on a cloud. Every time she thought about going to see him, her stomach fizzed with excitement. Then she thought about her aunt finding out and the fizz fell flat. Sneaking to see him wasn't worth how up and down she felt.

She looked out her bedroom window. Tai needed to hurry up. The three courts, a set of metal bleachers, and splintered picnic tables were already covered by people. Also, she didn't want to change her outfit again.

She'd changed three times already, finally deciding on a pair of blue shorts that sat high on her waist and a high-low tunic that ran all the way to the back of her knee and to the middle of her thigh in the front. She loved how the shirt made her hips look normal sized.

DatGirlTai:

I'm at the door. Come on.

Rah-Rah:

You know my aunt hates that.

Please knock and come in at least.

She ignored the frowny face Tai returned, waited for Tai's knock, then barreled down the stairs, yelling, "Tai's here, Auntie D. We ready to head to the courts."

She opened the door and couldn't help grinning at Tai's exaggerated scowl that quickly turned into a sugary smile when she heard Auntie D call out, "Hello, Metai."

"Hey, Ms. Tate," Tai sang back.

Auntie D poked her head out of her room. "You girls have fun. Be good."

Sheeda barely suppressed an eye roll as Tai waved like her and Auntie D were best friends. She pulled her arm, dragging her outside.

When they were far enough from the house, she jumped into Tai. "You so phony."

"Why?" Tai put her head in the air, indignant. "Because you made me come into the house to speak to your aunt? I would have been fine on the step. Now I'm phony?"

Sheeda cupped her hand and traced the number eight in the air, in a pageant wave. "Doing too much." She giggled. "But you know she gets hot if you don't come in to say hello."

"My grandmother the same way." Tai imitated Ms. Nona's stern tone: "Your little friends got these phones and think they don't need to come in and speak to nobody." They moved swiftly toward the crowded courts. People were on blankets watching, others leaning against the fence that blocked the ends of the court, and kids were running around.

Tai was enjoying going in on her grandmother. "One time I texted her from the bathroom at school and told her I needed to be picked up 'cause I was sick. Don't you know she made me go to the health room first? I'm, like, Nona, what if I'm in here dying, and she said then I shoulda called nine-one-one."

Their laughter was lost as a collective holler went up from the crowd.

"Is Simp playing yet?" Sheeda asked.

"They should be ready come out in a little bit," Tai said.

"Umph, you admitting you know something about Simp now?" Sheeda teased.

Tai's eyes rolled. "Let it rock, please."

Sheeda craned her neck looking for a place to sit. "I told you we should have gotten here earlier. Where we gonna sit?"

"You be so useless sometimes." Tai marched past Sheeda and headed to the bleachers. They navigated around people who sat in the area that were supposed to be stairs, toward the top.

Sheeda looked back at the bodies they'd have to go through if they had to go the way they'd came. "Where are we—" Her foot tangled on someone else's. "Sorry," she yelled over her shoulder. "Why are we going higher? There's nowhere to sit," she said to Tai's back.

They arrived at the bleacher's top bench. Dom, Simp's younger brother, and Nut, Mila's younger brother, were near the end of the long seat. They both waved. Tai sidestepped into the middle of the bleacher toward them, leaving Sheeda staring until she was beckoned impatiently.

She eased her way down the narrow aisle, pulling her butt in so it wouldn't hit people in the lower row. Most people were too focused on the court to pay attention to them squeezing in. Sheeda picked up speed as people dodged their head around her to catch the action.

She arrived in time to hear Dom say, "Where our money?"

Tai dug in her pocket and handed over some bills. Dom's and Nut's face lit up like they'd won the lottery.

"Thanks y'all," Tai said.

"You welcome," Nut said, scrambling past them to the aisle.

A girl on the bench directly below them looked over her shoulder and yelled out, "Are you gon' sit down or what?"

Sheeda's butt hit the metal seat hard in obedience. The girl looked like she was at least a senior in high school. It didn't faze Tai at all. She took her time sitting, a big smile of satisfaction on her face.

"This is why I wasn't in no rush. I had them save us seats."

"You could have just told me that," Sheeda said, willing her heart to settle. She was naked without the squad. It didn't help that they were sardined on the bench. She eyed the area they normally sat in but only saw clumps of people where the picnic tables should have been.

Tai pouted. "Can I get a thank-you, for getting us seats without us having to sit out here all morning?"

"Thank you. It's not the same without the squad, though."

Tai's forehead wrinkled. "Nona working, so it's better than sitting in the house all day."

"True." Sheeda blew down into her cleave. It was too hot to be this close to so many other people. She wasn't about to tell Tai that. She felt bad for whining. She usually loved the games—an all-day showcase of local elite rec teams' and the Cove's team, the Marauders', first official practice.

The crowd erupted in a loud "Ayyyy" as music blared from speakers at either end of the court. Tai clapped, bouncing in her seat as Simp led the Marauders out.

"Let's gooooooo," she yelled into her cupped hands.

She wasn't alone in being hyped. The Cove always represented for the Marauders. They had just won their third championship in a row and were fresh in new practice uniforms. Only the best for them. They ran onto the court and immediately busted into a drill where they ran while in a squat, half the team going right, the other left, and then coming together mixing and switching directions.

The crowd yelled and stomped, going crazy like they were professionals and not just a bunch of thirteen- and fourteen-year-olds. The tourney was only an exhibit game, nothing on the line, and the first chance for the neighborhood to see who had made the team.

"Aww, Dre is a 'Rauder now?" Sheeda pointed at Simp's brother. The two of them passed the ball back and forth to each other as they ran another drill. Simp tapped his brother on the butt then switched, throwing the ball to another teammate. Dre was taller than the last time Sheeda had seen him. He had a definite swag, like it was something they handed out once you made the team.

Lennie finally messaged her.

Where u at? I'm by court three where

the next team warming up

She typed back, vaguely hearing Tai say, "Yeah. He so

hyped for playing with his big bro. It's cute."

The people on either side of them stood, hollering encouragement at the court. Their shadows casted shade. The little bit of protection from the sun felt good. Sheeda positioned her body, leaning back, to get more of the shade on her hot arms. Tai did the same.

"Will you be mad if I go talk to Lennie, real quick?" She pointed to the court where a team in yellow and white were doing layups, everyone taking a turn shooting at the basket. "He's over there somewhere."

"Wow. You really gonna leave me hanging again?" Tai asked.

She took the tiny smirk on Tai's face as permission.

Tai clapped and shouted, "Do it, Simp," then waved Sheeda away. "I meet you down by the water fountain after this game."

Her eyes were already back on the court while Sheeda sidestepped and butt bumped her way out of the aisle. The crowd had grown impossibly thick. By the time she reached Lennie, her arms were slick with sweat. God only knew how she smelled.

The crowd thinned out the closer she got to the third court. It was only used for warm-ups, and the few people around the perimeter weren't watching. The clacking of dice and swearing peppered the air. The open space was breezy compared to the bleachers. Lennie sat on a bike balancing himself with one hand holding on to the metal fencing that helped keep the balls from rolling out onto the grass surrounding the court. He grinned as she approached him.

"Was Tai mad?" he said from atop his perch.

Sheeda shrugged. "I never know until she lay me out later."

"Y'all be on some real drama stuff." Lennie's neck stretched, head craned toward the first court as the crowd yelled out. "The game must be good. The crowd wylin'."

"I could barely see anything 'cause people kept standing up. But Dre and Simp was showing out."

"I heard little man can ball. The team gonna be good this year."

It was hard for her to get hyped for the 'Rauders since Rollie had been shot. No one ever talked about it. Rollie never removed himself from the chat they all shared. He just stopped talking in it and eventually they made a new chat without him. It was like if they didn't say anything, then it didn't happen. But it had. Yet, here everyone was pulling for the team maybe even more fiercely than before. Sheeda couldn't tell if they were mad for Rollie or mad at him, for getting out of the Cove. Goose bumps made her shiver, then disappeared as fast as they'd come. She rubbed her arms. Not knowing what else to do with them, she left them crossed.

"You cold?" Lennie seemed amused.

Sheeda shook her head. "Was just thinking about Rollie."

"Yeah, that was messed up." He looked toward the first court, somber. "I heard he doing good, though." He pedaled in place, like he was pedaling through syrup, then repeated himself, "That was messed up."

His jaw shifted back and forth, like he was grinding them to hold back more words. His silent anger comforted her.

She was getting used to not feeling like she was dreaming when they talked. They had only been in middle school together for a year. He'd been an eighth grader, and her memories were mostly of him sitting in the back of the bus loud and clowning. Sometimes teasing Mo enough to make her holler "shut up" toward the back of the bus, causing his friends to erupt in fresh laughter every time. The things boys found funny baffled her.

Had he even ever spoken to her that year? They'd be on the bus together again this school year. She tried to imagine how it would be and couldn't.

"How come you don't play basketball?" she asked. It was the Cove's official sport, yet she'd never seen him play for the Marauders or the rec team.

He pedaled backward, picking up speed. "I played when I was ten. Tez was recruiting me for the 'Rauders but my mother told him no." The bike wobbled as he shifted his hips, letting his legs rest. "Two of my brothers played for him, and she blame them being on the team for them getting into trouble. So that was a hard no for her."

"Was you mad that you couldn't play?" She had to shade her eyes against the sun to look up at him.

"At first." He was finally still, staring at whatever part of the action he could see from atop the bike. "Everybody think I'm like my brothers anyway, whether I'm on the team or not."

"That's kind of messed up," Sheeda said, her heart sinking for him.

"Not even kinda," Lennie said, then laughed. "It's whatever, though. People gon' think what they want think."

It made Sheeda angry. Her aunt judged people like that all the time. It was annoying.

"But you not like your brothers. People should be able to see that."

His face was expressionless. "They figure sooner or later Imma be like them." His shoulders popped. "Ioun even trip over it no more."

A light bulb went off in Sheeda's head. "Is that why you stay gaming?"

"I guess." He rubbed his hands together. "Trying get down with that Crown Battle tournament." His face lit up as he went on about the game. "The prize is like twenty g's."

Sheeda's eyes widened. "For playing a game?"

"Yup. Gamers can clock some mad scrilla. But my moms ain't down with entry fees and buying credits." A cloud darkened his face. "I gotta get a job next summer. So probably won't have time to keep gaming anyway." He pointed toward her house. "Your auntie got a telescope so she can see you?"

"For real, she might." The thought was funny and unsettling. She took comfort in the crowed. Even if she wanted to, there were too many people for Auntie D to pick her out. "But she watching her shows today. Maybe even taking a nap."

Lennie kicked his leg over and dismounted the bike. He leaned it against the fence.

"Cool. So she won't see if I do this?"

Next thing Sheeda knew his lips covered hers. She pooched hers back and hoped she was doing it right. Salt and spearmint mingled in her mouth. Her head was still tilted upward as Lennie stepped back.

"You still coming to see me?" he asked, looking almost shy.

No. She was supposed to say no.

She found herself promising, Tuesday.

MONIQUE

One time, when she was eight, Lennie gave her a piece of chocolate candy. It had been so good that Mo found out where he'd hidden the rest of the bar and ate another square. One more tiny square. Typical Lennie, he'd gotten mad. He'd said, "That's all right, watch. It wasn't really candy; it was one of those things that help you go bathroom." He had pointed and fell out laughing. "Ahhh, and you ate two."

A few minutes after that, her stomach had rumbled and she'd gone running to the bathroom. She was on the toilet for nearly fifteen minutes, pooping. She'd told on Lennie the second their mother got home and their mom

demanded to see the candy. When she did, she smacked
Lennie upside the head and told him to stop teasing his
sister. It had just been a plain old candy bar. Mo insisted
the candy was rotten or something because it had made her
go to the bathroom. She hadn't imagined that. Her mother
told her that the mind was powerful and could convince
you of almost anything you wanted to be convinced about.

Mo had never forgotten that. And that's why she
figured it was her imagination that her leaps were higher
and her body was longer and leaner when she danced. She
had wanted to be better so bad that she imagined she'd
gotten better. Because three weeks couldn't have changed
that.

It had changed other things, for sure. Almost like
magic. Like how she finally understood the words coming
out of everyone's mouth.

"I finally have my double."

"We have Nut auditions as soon as I get back."

A double was two pirouettes. The Nut was the
Nutcracker, one of the ballets she'd seen with TAG. The
girls at BA knew every part. Once the conversation turned
to the Nut, it went on awhile.

Once the music stopped, the class burst into hearty
applause for their pianist, for Ms. Sharon, and then

themselves. There was explosive laughter and loud talking. The weight of the unknown was gone, and all that was left was lightness.

Mo had survived.

With no other class to head to, the dancers moved fast to the hallways, anxious to get back to the dorm for last-night fun. Katie lingered by the barre, taking her time gathering her skirt and slippers.

Ms. Sharon tapped Mo on the shoulder. Her hands were a cool balm on Mo's sweaty hot skin. "Monique, you've done really good work."

Mo's chest heaved, mostly from the strenuous class— Ms. Sharon had worked them harder than ever—also from pride. She curtsied. "Thank you."

"Did your knee give you any extra trouble?"

"No." Mo added, "Ma'am. The ice helped."

"It can be a lot to go from a few hours a week to a few hours a day. Be sure to tend to it back at your home studio," Ms. Sharon said. "Good luck with your dance season. I know you'll do well."

As she walked away, Katie gave Mo a thumbs-up. "That was even better than *very good*."

"I mean, we never got moved up, but I'm not mad at it," Mo said in agreement.

She watched their teacher's back. She could have been looking at Ms. Noelle or Ms. Pat, her TAG teacher. They all had the same walk, as if a string was pulling them erect toward the ceiling. Mo didn't walk that way but had a feeling if she went to BA or any other ballet school, she might. Maybe they offered a class on how to do it. It was such a confident walk. Almost like royalty. It sounded stupid, but she wanted to walk that way, too.

She told Katie she'd catch up, then waited a few feet away, waiting for Ms. Sharon and the pianist to finish talking. The pianist was like a sidekick. Mo had a feeling if Ms. Sharon said jump, the pianist would ask how high. She wasn't trying to clown her, she'd just never seen a grown-up act that way toward another one. If Ms. Sharon knew she had that kind of control, she hid it real good. She patted the pianist on the shoulder, dismissing her with a cheerful, "Thank you," then turned right to Mo.

"Is everything okay?"

Mo's chest rattled as her heart picked up speed.

The first time she'd cared about something was TAG. Getting in had been the best thing to ever happen to her. That had only been a year ago. Now here she was, again, caring about BA. It scared her.

She stood straight up, her hands clasped together,

her right leg behind her left, pointe shoe toes down. This time she didn't have to imitate anyone. It was the way they stood when talking to the teacher, a pseudo curtsey ready to be completed with a tiny head bow and knee bend. She straightened out her eyebrows and asked, in the practiced whisper that seemed to come natural to all the other girls, "Am I gonna get a invitation to the year-round?"

Ms. Sharon's face tightened, her lips crimped a few good seconds before relaxing. She pulled the piano bench out and sat, hands on her lap. "The invitation letters have already been sent. It will be waiting for you at the dorm."

"I know." Mo's voice was loud in the silent room. She lowered it immediately. "Can't you just tell me what the letter says?"

"That's not how this works, Monique. I know it seems like we go overboard with tradition, but there are reasons for it."

If she'd gotten in, wouldn't Ms. Sharon just say it? The smile on her face felt like pity.

"How long have you been dancing?" she asked.

Mo's brows crept together. What did that have to do with anything? She pushed down the urge to talk back and answered, ballet whisper in place, "Three years."

This time Ms. Sharon's smile was the real thing. "Only

three years? I would have guessed four."

Mo snorted. "You can tell the difference between three years and four?"

"I usually can." Ms. Sharon nodded. "What's truly impressive is that most of the young ladies in this level with you have been dancing for well over six years. You should be proud of yourself for blending in so well with them." She laid her hand on Mo's. "Are you proud of that?"

"Yes," Mo said, afraid of the *but* in her teacher's voice.

"Good." She patted then lightly grasped Mo's hands guiding her closer. "I like the way you attack technique. I saw how hard you worked. And there's been a lot of improvement." Her hand fell back onto her lap. "Being ready to attend a pre-professional program takes dedication. But it takes other things as well."

Mo wished she hadn't bothered. A yes was a yes. Anytime somebody started talking about being proud just to get nominated was a no. She was prepared for Ms. Sharon to list off what other things it took. Instead, Ms. Sharon sat silent until Mo blurted, "Like what?"

She didn't really want to know. It just seemed like that was her line. She looked out to the hall. Katie was in conversation, in no hurry, for once. Mo was about to tune out completely, let Ms. Sharon finish so she could go when she said, "Like wanting to be taught."

Mo fought back. "I do want to be taught."

"I'm not sure you do." Ms. Sharon's finger went up, forbidding the flow of words she expected from Mo. "I can tell you want to do well. I see your competitive spirit. That's not the same as wanting to learn and be taught."

"Ain't it . . ." She paused, correcting herself. "Isn't it BA's job to teach me, though? I mean, teach me whatever you're saying I don't know."

"Our job is to help you master the technique of ballet." Ms. Sharon stood up. "In order to master something, you have to love learning how to master it. You can't focus so much on the prize."

Mo felt the dismissal coming. It was either going to be a shoulder pat or squeeze or a light clasp of the wrist. She stepped back, out of range, not ready to be let go. She still didn't understand. And she didn't know what to ask to help her understand.

"Isn't getting into the program just being good enough?" Mo asked.

"'Good enough' isn't how I'd describe it." Ms. Sharon took a step closer but didn't reach out. "I wish it was simple. I wish you could finish one step and be closer to the prize. But ballet doesn't work that way." She gripped her sweater, closing it against a chill Mo didn't feel and continued. "There are lots of mini prizes. Getting into our Summer Experience is one. Getting into our year-round would be considered another."

"So, I didn't win?" Mo asked, genuinely trying to understand. "Is it because I'm Black?"

"We do not take race into consideration."

Mo swayed back a step at the pained look of offense in her teacher's face. She was close to apologizing except had no idea what she'd be apologizing for.

As if to convince Mo of her sincerity, Ms. Sharon kept on, "You and Jamila both were great students. Your potential is as high as any of the other dancers."

Ms. Sharon had never been anything but nice, still, "tuck your butt" was lodged in Mo's memory. She couldn't help feeling like, in BA's eyes, she was more Black than Mila was. She was racing down a road she hadn't meant to, her tongue pushing words out past the polite ballet posture she'd learned so quickly. "Then how come me and Mila weren't in the same level? We are back at home."

Ms. Sharon's face went through one, two, then three emotions. To Mo they were:

Wait, what?

Did this child just ask me this?

and

You're the adult here; get it together.

Beneath the shaky waver of surprise, her voice was low and pleasant. But the words came out sharp, cutting. "Monique, we make our own determinations on a student's level based on what we see in the first class. Mila's technique is slightly stronger than yours."

"But she was two levels above me," Mo said, the need to fight back crawling up her throat like an itch. She inhaled and spoke again, in a calm tone. "It just seems like you think Mila is way stronger than me. And I—" Mo debated. She what? Was she going to tell a teacher she was wrong? Ms. Sharon didn't flinch, waiting, maybe even daring her to finish. So, Mo did. "I don't agree."

A bless-your-heart smile appeared on Ms. Sharon's face.

"I've taught for many years and you've danced for three," Ms. Sharon said, a tiny take-that nod along with her smile. She finally took another step forward, hot to dismiss Mo. "On this note we're going to agree to disagree."

"I don't mean I know more than you. But I feel like me and Mila were treated different. That's all," Mo said.

Ms. Sharon considered that. "Treated different because?"

"Because she looks like the rest of the dancers here, tall and thin, and I don't. Because she fits in and, I guess, I don't."

"You're different, yes. As are the other dancers from one another. None of you are as alike as you might think." Ms. Sharon's eyes wandered past Mo. She was speaking slowly. Her sentences like she was thinking then rethinking before saying them out loud. For the first time, she seemed unsure. Then, just as quickly, her face brightened as if she'd had a great idea. "I'm sorry you felt unfairly judged. Unfortunately, that's what we sign up for in ballet."

To Mo, that felt like an answer you gave when you didn't plan to change a thing. It sat in the pit of her stomach. She pushed past it. Because anything could be accomplished if you worked, right? "Am I too big?" she asked, needing to know something.

Losing weight was easy. Easier than not being Black at least.

Ms. Sharon's face had a pink tint. Her hands were white from gripping the throat of her sweater. Her voice remained surprisingly calm. "Monique, listen to what I'm saying. We're not discussing the status of your enrollment.

I'm talking about a dancer's journey in general. Success at BA or any program is a formula made up of many things. But I'd say it's about having the right combination of strength of technique and strength of mind."

"And I don't have that?" Mo asked, whispering out of defeat.

Ms. Sharon's shoulders heaved. "This is why we don't traditionally have conversations about a student's enrollment status." There was the hand, light on Mo's arm. "You're a beautiful dancer, Monique. There's promise there. *If* you haven't been accepted into the program, that doesn't mean you'll never be accepted."

"So I wasn't accep—"

The hand squeezed, just enough to interrupt.

"I cannot share that with you. You'll have to wait and see what the letter says." Her eyes stayed locked with Mo's. "A ballet dancer's journey is a marathon. Each summer is a chance to cut down on your time and get to the finish line faster."

With another affirming squeeze, she was gone.

Mo trailed behind her, head swirling. Ms. Sharon hadn't said yes. She hadn't said no, either. The rules didn't let her. The letter might still say yes. But she couldn't stop thinking about the look of hurt surprise on Ms. Sharon's face when Mo asked if being Black mattered.

If she'd been accepted, Ms. Sharon probably wanted to snatch it back.

If.

If.

Katie was already layered in a sweater and trash bag pants. Her dance bag was on her shoulder. She held out leggings to Mo. "Come on before we miss the bus. Bren texted me. Her and Mila are waiting for us to open their letters. They're already back at the dorm."

Mo dressed in a fog. She would have never been able to say what they talked about as she got dressed or while they were on the bus. Her three friends rushed her through a shower and were already eagerly sitting on her bedroom floor, envelopes in hand, as she slipped on shorts and a tee.

She joined the circle.

Brenna put up her hand to stop everyone from tearing open their envelope.

"Let's promise that if anybody gets in, we'll all be happy for them."

"Of course," Mila said. "Even if I get in, my father can't afford the tuition. So . . ."

"They have scholarships," Katie said.

Mo could see that the idea made Mila hopeful. "I

don't want to open mine in front of everybody." She got up from the floor.

"Are you going to open it in the bathroom?" Brenna asked, laughing until she saw how serious Mo was. She tugged at her shirt. "I'm kidding. It's better if we do it together." She looked around for confirmation and got a vigorous nod from Mila. "Seriously. No judgment if somebody doesn't get in. Right?"

"Definitely," Mila said.

Mo tried sending her a message with her eyes:

I can't do this. But Mila was fanning the envelope, like it was too hot to keep holding, anxious to open it.

"It's hard to get in. We're not all going to get in," Katie said in her best know-it-all voice. But Mo heard the uncertainty. It was exactly why she didn't want to open it in the group. She didn't know how she was going to react. On top of what the letter was going to say, she didn't need to worry about crying or lashing out.

"I just can't do it in front of everybody, all right?" The envelope weighed a ton in her hand. She didn't want to open it at all now. Or wished she could tell Katie and Brenna to leave. She could open it in front of Mila.

Katie squinted up from the floor. "Did Ms. Sharon already tell you whether you got in or not?"

"Not really." Mo shifted from one foot to the other. She looked above their heads as she admitted, "She said I'm not ready."

Mila's mouth was an O. Brenna gasped.

"She said that? That you're not ready?" Brenna asked.

"She may as well have," Mo scowled down at the letter. She wanted to know. Had to know for sure. She wasn't going to do it in front of the group. Period. She slipped on a pair of slides. "Look. I be back. I want to open it by myself. All right?"

She wasn't trying to be menacing, but still Brenna shrank from her. Mo couldn't deal with that right now. Her slides flapped against her feet hard, an exclamation point on her exit, as she walked out into the hallway.

An entire party was going on. Or felt like it. Music blared from different rooms. A lot of the doors were open and girls were going back and forth between them. There was singing from one room and a burst of applause. She wondered if they were celebrating being done or someone getting into the program. Brenna would probably know. She'd gotten to know everyone on their floor. Mo had never bothered to get to know anyone else. Maybe when you didn't fit in, the RAs reported that kind of stuff back to the directors. Maybe that's what Ms. Sharon meant about strength of mind.

But how was her mind not strong because she didn't feel like being Fannie Friendly with everybody?

She couldn't make sense of it.

She turned the corner, thankful that no one was in the lounge. A short beige sofa with stained cushions sat in the middle of the room. A few bucket seats surrounded it. They all faced a television that was only on when the RAs looked at it. Soda and snack machines were against the wall. A set of windows looked out onto green grass and two other buildings. A few of the college kids were throwing a Frisbee in the dwindling light.

She took a corner of the sofa, curling her legs beneath her. The noise of the hall felt miles away. Every few minutes a high-pitched yelp or giggle floated her way. It was comforting in its rhythm. She was going to miss being here.

She tucked the envelope under her knee.

Moodles:
Hey mommy. Whatchu doing?

Mom-E:
Hi baby. Sitting for a few minutes

before every patient ring their bell
at the same time. 😐

Moodles:

                          Mom-E:
My baby be home soon. 🖤 I've
missed you.

Moodles:
Miss you too.

                          Mom-E:
You ready to come home?

Moodles:
Yes and no.

                          Mom-E:
What?!!? Now see, how come I
didn't get no messages about you
suddenly liking it. I only get the
boo-boo face messages. Lol

Moodles:
Ma for real I be too tired to text. But
nah, it's been fine

                          Mom-E:
Just fine?

Moodles:

We got letters today.

Mom-E:

Letters?

Moodles:

That say if we got into their all year
ballet program.

Mom-E:

Well??

Moodles:

I'm scared to open mine. Mila and 'nem
wanted to do it together but. IDK. if I
don't get in I don't want everybody all
in my face about it, trying hug me and
stuff.

Mom-E:

SMH Something wrong w/your
friends consoling you? Or what
if you get in? You have people to
celebrate w/you. Nothing wrong
w/either.

Moodles:

I guess. But I'm in the lounge so don't
matter now.

Mom-E:

Go ahead and open it, Monique.

It's not life or death, baby girl.

Moodles:

😒 Okay, Ma. Goodness.

Mo closed her eyes. The envelope was warm from her leg. She tore it open, ignoring her phone's chime. How fast did her mother think she could read?

She took a breath, chanted:

"It's not gonna kill me no matter what the answer is.

"It's not gonna kill me no matter what the answer is"—and looked down at the bright white paper with the red and blue Ballet America logo—a pair of pointe shoes whose ribbons made up the stripes in an American flag.

She could hear Ms. Sharon's voice as she read it. She read it once, then again, picking apart words trying to see beyond what it said. In the end, the letter was clear. She took the rejection personally. But she'd already broken down once in front of everyone. It wasn't going to happen again.

She looked down at her mother's last message.

Well??

She aimed her phone at the letter, took a picture, then texted it back with:

I'm okay. TTYL

As she walked back to the room, her phone chimed softly. No doubt her mother trying to cheer her up. Normally she'd want that. But she wanted something else more. To get back to the room and talk to somebody, three somebodies who would understand how hollow she felt.

They were waiting on her when she opened the door. She couldn't read their faces. Whatever the results of their letters were, they had put it on hold for her.

She raised her arms, meaning to be sure and cool about it, but her voice cracked as she said, "I didn't get in."

The words pulled them off the floor and onto her. They huddled around her, rubbing her back and cooing things like, "You're an amazing dancer," "They're crazy for turning you down," and "BA isn't the only school out there." And she wanted all of it. All of the sappy, soothing words of comfort she'd run from, she wanted. She needed.

Dear Monique,

Thank you for your interest in Ballet America's pre-professional program. Each summer, BA attracts dancers from across the globe to its premiere intensive program. Your presence at our Summer Experience signals not only your dedication to ballet, but a level of skill that we look for in our students. We hope that you have used this time to concentrate on your technique and are confident that you are leaving with the knowledge you need for a successful dance year.

As you know, many are interested in studying at BA beyond the Summer Experience. At this time, we are unable to offer you a position within the BA pre-professional program. However, we would like to extend a scholarship to next summer's intensive. Please share the enclosed information with your parent or guardian and respond by the deadline to hold your Summer Experience slot.

We wish you the best of luck in your dance endeavors.

Sincerely,

Sharon Ruff

P.S. Have you ever considered focusing on contemporary ballet? Do your work! :-)

RASHEEDA

"So, can you come or not?"

The square where Tai's face should have been, on the phone, was a beige wall and a sliver of a pink, white, and black zebra-patterned curtains. Her voice came from the other side of the room.

"I can if you wait until tomorrow. If I don't get the clothes together to donate, then Nona won't take me school shopping."

Sheeda didn't dislike school, but she wasn't ready to go back yet, either. For once, she wanted to say something very Tai-like and go in on Ms. Nona for expecting Tai to be getting ready in July. But she was afraid to go to Lennie's by herself and couldn't just not show up now. She needed Tai.

She resorted to begging.

"I already told him I'd come today. And my aunt is only working late tonight." Tai couldn't even spare a minute to be on camera. Sometimes she was too irky for words. Sheeda's voice rose in exasperation. "And I have choir rehearsal tomorrow."

Tai's honey-colored round face burst onto the screen, frowning. "We can just go during the day while she at work. Being your relationship tutor is exhausting."

"I didn't ask you to be my tutor," Sheeda blurted. The surprise on Tai's face only emboldened her. "You always on everybody when they don't do this, that, and a third for you. I asked one favor. How come you can't be the one that lie to your grandmother this time? Tell her you forgot and will do it tomorrow."

"What I got to lie for?" Tai dug in. "I'm not the one thirsty to see some dude."

They glared at each other. Anger pulsed in Sheeda's throat, threatening to send words out of her mouth that she would usually bury deep. Like how Tai got on her nerves. How she was sick of always doing things her way. It all sat waiting to tumble out, hot and hateful.

If she let the truth free, then what? Part of her knew it

would feel good. Part of her knew she couldn't. She hated trouble. When it came calling, Mo was always there to push it back. And she'd gotten herself into this. It wasn't Tai's fault.

She needed to say bye and let it go. Arguments with Tai were never worth it. She opened her mouth to agree, that they'd just go tomorrow, when Tai walked away from the phone, saying, "If you want somebody to help do your dirt, then you gotta roll with when they can ride with you."

Sheeda hated the truth in the words. Still, Tai didn't have to put it that way. "Why it gotta be that I'm doing dirt?"

Tai never heard her mutter, "Never mind. Forget I asked." She was too busy going on, teaching to herself. Sheeda wasn't listening anymore. She'd placed the phone down on her dresser, purposely giving Tai an eyeful of her bare ceiling. She threw on Lennie's favorite red shorts, wincing as she rolled them up until they pinched her thighs. It was one roll too many, but she didn't undo them.

She sat on her bed, quiet and out of view, waiting for Tai to notice that she'd stopped talking.

"Simp wanna know if we can go skating Friday. The 'Rauders doing some kind of fundraiser." It was silent for a few seconds before Tai shouted. "Hello? Where you go?"

Sheeda exhaled silent anger and willed it toward the phone. She stayed calm, waiting until Tai confirmed she'd caught the negative vibes.

"Really? You got me looking at the ceiling, though?"

Sheeda picked up the phone, kept her face blank. "You had me looking at your wall."

"I can't with you." Tai sucked her teeth. "Can you go skating Friday or not?"

"I don't know." Anger seethed beneath Sheeda's flat voice. "Look, I gotta go."

"Wow. For real?" Tai said. "I know you all pressed, but I'm not the one, Rasheeda. I can go tomorrow. If you not good with that—" The camera wiggled with the force of Tai's shrug.

Sheeda withstood the reprimand. It kept her angry enough to stand up for herself.

"And that's fine," she said.

"So, you just gonna be mad about it?" Tai asked, astounded.

"I'm not mad," she lied. "But I gotta go."

"Fine. Bye."

She knew it was coming, had provoked it. Still, the black screen on the phone smacked the numbness out of Sheeda and reminded her why she hated arguing with people. The jittery electricity of anxiety made her want to call Tai back, say just as snappy, "Fine, we'll go tomorrow."

She texed a message to Lennie to let him know, finger hovering above the send button, and couldn't. If she went tomorrow, it would prove that she always needed somebody to hold her hand. And she didn't, starting now.

She pushed the phone into her pocket and headed out the door.

It was the hottest day of summer so far. Once the rays pulled back, the streets would be alive again. For now, the only things moving were a few cars in and out. The loud hum of people's air-conditioning was a gigantic mosquito in her ear. Two kids' arguing came from a house as she went past J Court.

In the very back of the neighborhood and surrounded by a thick forest of trees, the K was even more quiet than the other courts. In the dead of the heat, it looked like all the other cul-de-sac of row houses in the Cove. There was no proof of the fights that broke out regularly or the drug deals that took place just behind the homes.

Sheeda welcomed the peace. Inside the quiet, regret settled in. Her and Lennie weren't officially anything yet and she was already acting like Yola, wylin' on her friends. She didn't want that.

Standing up for herself was fine, but she'd never done it before and hated that the first time was because of a boy. She stopped in the shade of a large tree and texted Tai.

I was a little OD. Just nervous about

☹ everything. Sorry!!! Forgive me for

wylin'? ☺

She stuffed the phone back into her pocket. Her phone vibrated, a tiny massager against her leg as Tai messaged back. There was no time to check them.

The door to Mo and Lennie's was open, as usual. What little sound was in the court were the distant shouting and laughter of him and his friends playing games. She knocked on the screen door and called out, "Hey, it's Sheeda."

His cousin Quan appeared at the door. Sheeda only knew him from all the posts on each of their pages. He and Lennie were super close. He was tall, Sheeda guessed at least six foot, and looked like he could easily play the part of a skeleton. He had on blue jeans and a white undershirt. The jeans made his legs go on forever. He had sleepy eyes in a long face that reminded her of the Frankenstein butler on that one TV show. Not saying he was ugly, but definitely his height and that long face made him kind of funny-looking.

Sheeda stepped back. "Is Lennie in there?"

"Yeah. He playing, though." His long arms stretched the door open, leaving plenty of room for Sheeda to walk in. "Ell, your girl here, yo."

Lennie whispered-yelled back. "Come on, yo, you know my moms upstairs asleep. Stop yelling."

Sheeda let out a breath she didn't know she was holding. Ms. Linda was home. Good.

Then what Quan said hit her. His girl? That meant Lennie talked about her. She walked taller, pleased, stopping a few feet into the house. The stench of burned bacon and underarms made her snort, to rid her nose of it. She played it off by sniffing (ugh).

Two beanbag chairs were in the middle of the living room. Lennie was sunken into one and D-Rock, a short dude with the early spiked twists of locs, sat in another. It was like all of his friends had decided to grow their hair out at the same time. The spiky-haired dude club.

Another guy stood behind the beanbags whisper-shouting instructions. Every time his instructions weren't followed, the liquid contents of the glass slid dangerously close to spilling.

Quan sat on the couch, his long legs kicking up against the back of the beanbags, his arms spread across the back of nearly the entire couch.

Lennie had headgear on and was talking in it to whoever was playing the game from the other side of the television. He lifted his head in a nod. Sheeda waved, waiting for him to get up or at least tell her to sit down.

"You can sit down. He gon' be a minute," Quan said, reading her mind.

The couch had two large cushions. Quan sat in the middle, straddling both cushions. Sheeda sat on the far side, as far away from Quan's pits as she could. Minutes went by without anyone acknowledging her.

When he still hadn't interrupted his game, she cleared her throat. Quan spoke before she could. "I thought you was bringing a friend?" His lids drooped, but she could tell he was eying her.

"She couldn't come," Sheeda said. She wondered if Jalen had felt this way—squirmy inside for not delivering on a promise, but also annoyed—when Kita had asked him the same thing at the carnival. She directed her voice to the back of Lennie's head. "I can't stay. I just came to—" She paused, wondering why she'd come, other than Tai had made her mad. Quan was watching her, the only one listening. Sheeda spoke up, not even sure if Lennie heard her. "Tai couldn't come and I didn't want text you."

"Hold up . . ." Lennie's shoulders jerked as he worked

the controller. He threw his hand up, "What you know about that?" He and D-Rock bumped fists. "Got heem."

Quan's finger lifted one of her twists. "You got leave already?"

She dipped her head away. "Lennie, I gotta go."

She pressed herself against the arm of the couch. Her finger rubbed the couch's velvet, harder when Quan's finger lifted at her hair again. She eyed the steps, praying Ms. Linda would come down and fuss at the boys for being too loud. But they seemed to have mastered shouting in whispers to keep from waking her.

"Stay. I teach you how play Crown Battle." He hollered over to Lennie. "Ell, me and your girl got next."

D-Rock instinctively shushed Quan. "Come on, man, before Momma L kick us out."

"Kick y'all out, maybe. I'm fam," Quan boasted.

Sheeda squeezed so tight against the couch's arm, it bit into her ribs. She leaned her head away. "No. I'm good."

She exhaled in loud relief when Lennie came over and handed Quan his controller. "You got it, son." He put his hand out and Sheeda grabbed it, allowing him to pull her up from the couch. They walked into the kitchen. She wanted to throw herself into Lennie's arms. She gulped at the kitchen's fresher air, ignoring the acrid sting of whatever they'd burned earlier.

The kitchen door leading to the backyard was open, leaving a hot spot where the sun shone in through its screen door. The heat warmed away the goose bumps on her arm. She clenched her teeth to stop them from chattering against the winter storm swirling inside of her.

She kept her eye on the living room. Quan was still standing, talking to the other two dudes. She couldn't tell if he was playing the game or not.

"Ay, so why Tai not with you?" Lennie asked.

"Did you only want me to bring her to hook up with your cousin?" she asked.

Lennie frowned. "No. I just figured you wouldn't come by yourself."

He pulled out a chair, sat atop the back of it, his feet on the seat. Sheeda was sure Ms. Linda would fire him up for that. The thought relaxed her, and she stepped out of the doorway's heat closer to him.

"Oh. She couldn't come with me." She looked over Lennie's head to the living room, checking for Quan. Assured he was preoccupied, she relaxed. "I didn't want you to think I was playing you. I wanted to come by and let you know me and her be back by tomorrow, if that's cool."

He chuckled. "You came by to say you can't come by?"

Sheeda laughed, releasing the last of her nerves. "Pretty much."

His arm stretched toward her. He tugged her until her kneecaps crushed against the chair's seat. She bent at the waist, leaning in to keep moving forward.

"Can I at least get a kiss before you go?" he asked.

Sheeda's eyes closed. Her face floated toward his like they were magnetized. When their lips grazed, Quan's voice boomed, "I'm next, right?"

Sheeda leaped back. She looked to Lennie. Other than shaking his head in disapproval, he didn't seem bothered.

"Ignore him," he advised. He extended his arm, but Sheeda stayed planted near the door.

"I gotta go," she said in a whisper.

The front door was a long way off. Even if it wasn't, Quan stood between her and the exit. His eyes were probes. To Sheeda it felt like they were poking through her clothes, going from her face, to her chest, to her thighs, back to her face. They lingered at her chest as he smiled.

"Ell forgot to tell you that me and him fam. Family share everything."

"Man, stop being dumb," Lennie said.

Sheeda wanted him to stand up, take her hand, and guide her out. He seemed comfortable on the chair, just waiting for Tropical Storm Quan to blow through. Sheeda wanted to run, then felt silly for the prickly fear. Quan was being dumb, like Lennie said. That was all. And Ms. Linda was just above their heads. It was fine.

Boys always played too much. Though Quan wasn't really a boy, boy. He was sixteen and still pushing up on girls by tugging their braids. She kept an eye on the boys in the living room. They were in the beanbag chairs, focused on the game. She was going to walk out. Tell Lennie hit her up later. Easy.

She mapped out her path. Go between the beanbag chairs and the couch, not in front of it. If she went in front of it, she'd trip on the game's cord. She repeated it to herself, needing to be sure her legs did what her brain said. It was all good. She didn't need an exit plan; she just didn't want to look crazy tripping over the stupid wire. That was all. When she counted to ten, she was going to go. Walk right past Quan.

One.

Two.

Three.

"Man, you ain't tell your girl that big cuz gotta do a test run first?" Quan said.

Her legs went the wrong way, stepping farther back

until the kitchen door ground into her back. Was that annoyance on Lennie's face? At Quan, probably. Ready to say something to him?

Four.

Five.

"Man, ease up," Lennie said. He was leaned over, elbows on his knees like every day he had girls over that his cousin tried getting with. "You always clowning. Sheeda don't know you just playing."

Sheeda looked from Quan to Lennie. Quan's smile was stuck in the same exact position, glued to his face even as his eyes roamed her body. This time stopping at her thighs, where the shorts were practically cutting off her circulation. He put his hands up, showing her he didn't have anything to hurt her with.

"I know Tai would be time enough for him, though," Lennie said. "You wouldn't be able to handle Tai, son. She little, but that mouth big as a mug."

Lennie's mouth was moving, saying things. That was good. But Sheeda needed him to stand up. Stand up and walk her out. She was ready to keep it pushing.

Six.

Seven.

The next thing she knew, Quan was in front of her.

"I'm just tripping with you, shawty. Cuz been talking 'bout you. Just peeping his game." He put an arm around her. Her head banged against the door's edge trying to escape Quan's thick musty odor.

"Aw, man. You good?" Lennie asked. He seemed ready to laugh but was holding it back.

Quan laughed openly. "You all right?"

The hit wasn't that hard, but tears came to her eyes just the same.

Quan's arms were all over her at once. He had her in a hug, her arms pinned to her side. "My bad. I ain't mean make you hit your head, for real." She wriggled, trying to get her nose free of his stink as his hot breath talked into her ear. "We cool? Ioun want you be mad."

"We good," she said, muffled into his chest.

He squeezed. "All right, hug me back so I know we good."

Lennie sucked his teeth. "You doing the most, Yo. Just let her go."

"I can't . . ." Her voice broke. She swallowed back tears. "You got my arms pinned down."

He kept his grip, but winged his arms so hers could come up. She made a loose circle around his waist. His undershirt was damp and clammy with sweat.

"A for real hug," he said from over her head.

Sheeda closed her arms around him. The tears were going to come if she didn't get out. She squeezed. For a second they were in a tight embrace, then she felt his hands grip her butt. She pushed off, hard.

"I gotta go."

She didn't remember whether she took the right path out of the door. She raced out, blind. Quan's voice loud as he said, "She got cake for days, son."

Lennie said something back to him. She didn't know what. She didn't care.

Just as she reached the door, Ms. Linda came down the steps. Her face etched with sleepiness and confusion. "Rasheeda?" she asked, stopping on the next to the last step.

Rasheeda stood frozen as Ms. Linda eyed the room full of boys, now all tight-lipped, their eyes looking at the floor like they were afraid to look anywhere else.

"What's going on?" Ms. Linda asked, her arms crossed.

"Hey, Auntie," Quan called out cheerfully.

At the sound of his voice, Sheeda burst out the door. It remained opened after she pushed out of it. When she didn't hear it close, she thought maybe Quan was behind her, following. She walk-ran, tears running down her face, until she'd gotten home.

In her room, she ripped the red shorts off and kicked them toward her closet. Her phone fell out of her pocket with a thud. She eyed it suspiciously, like it was to blame for how icky she felt. She shuddered when she caught a whiff of Quan on her shirt.

She realized she was standing in front of her window in just a shirt and underwear. She closed her blinds on the empty basketball courts. The instant coolness calmed her some. She peeled her damp shirt off, flung it in the direction of the shorts, and changed into a pair of loose shorts and a First Bap retreat shirt.

What had happened? Had something happened?

The message light of her phone blinked blue, winking at her until, hands trembling, she picked it up from the floor.

Tai's messages, especially her last one, brought fresh tears.

U wuz a LOT OD. But we good. I guess.

Nah fr fr we good. Cuz u pressed as a mug I hurried up and threw stuff in the giveaway bags. Imma be mad if I gave away something I meant to keep. 🙈 I don't want ur thirsty butt go down to

Lennie's by urself.

I'm at your house. Answer the door.

Hello? Where u at? 👀

Are u at Mo's?!

Is everything okay? 🫠

MONIQUE

Driving into the Cove was different and the same. Everyone looked like they'd been frozen in time. Like they'd all stood in the exact spots they'd been in while she was gone and stayed there until someone pushed the start button once she rode past. Simp and his little crew were still sitting watch at the fence near the front. He threw her a salute when she came in. She waved back, feeling like a celebrity coming home after being off in Hollywood.

Different because she'd never looked at it like this. Had it always looked like the heat had dried up anything that had once been green? The entire nabe was surrounded by trees, but there was hardly any grass or green spaces for people to sit or play on. The entire neighborhood felt like it was sitting on a hot, hard stone. People were out on their brick stoops, gathered on the concrete sidewalks, or walking down the middle of the blacktop streets.

What little bit of grass surrounded the basketball courts had burned to a brittle crisp in the summer sun. It was home and she loved it, but she longed for a little color. She hadn't realized how used she'd gotten to the campus's smothering greenery.

Things were off, at home, from the start. She thought maybe it was only her. But the group chat she had with Mila, Brenna, and Katie confirmed they were all going through the same thing—feeling connected to BA and its schedule by a spiderweb that hadn't let them go yet.

She couldn't do anything without comparing it to life at the intensive. Had her room gotten smaller? Had the toilet handle needed so much jiggling before it flushed when she was home before? Her brain was slowly awaking like she had amnesia. Lennie must have sensed it. After giving her a strong hug, he had stayed scoping her out. No doubt to pounce on anything she did that she'd never done before.

She stopped herself several times making sure she

wasn't talking too proper. She was still the same old Mo. A little foggy, but still her. Then Lennie had caught her walking and called it out quick.

"Why you walking all straight like somebody stuck a stick up your back?"

Mo let her shoulders down, just a little, then threw it back to him. "Boy, I been standing like this in class everyday for, like, five hours a day. What you expect?"

She'd have to practice her royal walk away from him. Other than that, he didn't say much, like he wasn't sure how to talk to her anymore.

They had cooked one of her favorites, hamburgers and gravy. But after three weeks of flavorless food, even her tongue was confused. The meat was almost too salty. She took smaller bites, letting herself get used to the food she'd missed. It was good. Better than anything she'd had at BA. But it was still too salty.

Her mother wanted to know what the intensive looked, smelled, and felt like. Eventually, Mo eased into describing the girls she'd lived with, how huge the studio was, the precise way everybody acted like they had been given a script. Some things she'd told her mother when they texted and other things were new.

Her mom had a knowing look on her face. "Sounds

like you enjoyed it to me. What you think, Len?"

"Long as you didn't come back talking White," he said begrudgingly.

"I told you nobody was coming back brand-new." She crimped her nose at him.

"Whatever, man. You welcome for dinner. Now you can do the dishes."

"Not on her first night," their mother said.

"Ahhh, you thought it was," Mo said, laughing.

"Man," he muttered.

Their mother gave him a stern look. No words were needed. He pushed the food around on his plate and stayed quiet.

She had thought Lennie would be backed up with insults and teasing. She was kind of glad he wasn't because she felt out of practice. He could have easily won any argument.

"What's been going on around here?" She looked from Lennie to her mother. "I think I got a whole one text from Lennie the entire time."

His fork clattered against his plate. "Snitch."

Mo had no retort. She had meant it as a joke. She threw him an apology with her eyes, but he wouldn't look up from his plate.

"Leonard, settle down," their mother said, calling him by his full name just as calm as she pleased. "I'll let your brother catch you up on hood haps." She got up, kissed Mo's forehead. "I'm glad you had the experience. And even though you were disappointed about not getting into the full program, I would have missed you too much to let you go away." She jabbed a finger into Lennie's shoulder blades. "Now I just need to send your brother away so he can get some act right."

Mo waited until she heard her mother's steps on the stairs before asking, "What you do now?"

She jumped as he whipped up from the table violently, snatching his plate. The dishes left on the table, rattled. "Why it gotta be I did something, Monique?" He ran water, dropping plates and utensils in the sink as the water gushed. "Don't be coming at me with all that. Spoiled, bougie-ass self. You sitting up in the boonies somewhere dancing all day then gon' come back and ask what I did. That's wild."

His outburst had caught her sleeping. She'd spent three weeks trying not to snap on people. Now that she needed to, she couldn't muster up the heat to clap back. She wasn't trying to fight anyway. Dang, she'd just gotten back. He was a sore loser sometimes and hated if you teased him too much. But this was OD even for him.

"Why you kirkin?" she asked when the water stopped, leaving the kitchen silent except the clunk of him moving dishes around in the sink.

"You need bring me your plate if you done," he said, without turning around.

Mo didn't like how wooden he sounded. It must be bad.

Cold dread iced her chest. She mentally checked off boxes in her head, wondering what he could have done.

Drugs?

No. He wouldn't be standing here talking to her if their mother found him using. And he'd probably be in some sort of lockdown if he'd been caught dealing.

Stealing?

Doubtful. He'd stolen a bag of potato chips and a soda from the Wa once and their mother had made him walk up there to take them back. She drove and was waiting for him, at the store, to witness the transaction. Either he'd gotten really good at stealing or never did it again. Mo never knew which for sure.

There was no school to get kicked out of. He didn't go the rec that much, so probably didn't get in trouble there. She was about to give up then thought—a girl.

God, she hoped he hadn't gotten somebody pregnant. Seems like her mother would have been more mad if it was that.

She walked her plate over, sunk it carefully into the sink, and leaned against the counter. Her voice had nothing but concern in it. "What's going on, Ell?"

"Your little friend tripping," he said.

"Can you be more specific? What friend?"

"Rasheeda," he said, exasperated, like he'd already told her the whole story and was tired of retelling it.

"Y'all still chopping it up over DMs?" She shook her head in disappointment. "You ain't have nothing better to do this summer than lead my friend on? Bruh, you gotta get out more."

A tiny volcano of water erupted as he slammed his hands into the water. "Ain't nobody lead her on. Is that what she told you?"

Mo's eyes narrowed. "I didn't know there was nothing to tell. Before I left, she said you friended her. I figured you was doing some kind of stupid challenge with Quan 'nem." She faced him, hugging herself tight. She didn't want to know, but knew she had to. "What happened?"

"All right, look. It wasn't even me." His hands wiped at

a plate. It squeaked under his rubbing. He looked toward the kitchen entryway then raised his voice but not much. "She came by and—"

"Came by where?"

"You don't need get loud," he said, getting loud himself.

"I mean, obviously mommy already know," Mo said. She lowered her voice anyway. "Why did she come by? Are y'all talking or something?"

"Something like that." He glanced at her, then his eyes skittered away back down to the dishes. His hands moved faster, washing.

Mo put her face in her hands. "Why would you do that, though? You don't want me messing around with none of your hardhead friends. Why you gonna come blow up my spot with my friends?" The thought ran her hot. "Honestly, Lennie, that's drama for nothing. All these girls in the Cove, why you gotta step to one of my girls?"

"Do you want know what happened or not?" Some of the old edge was back in his voice.

"I could just ask Sheeda," she said, just as snappy.

It was an empty threat. Whatever he'd done, she'd smooth over with Sheeda. Sheeda wasn't the type of person who stayed mad at you. But Mo had to hear his side first. Lennie's mouth turned up. He pressed his lips together, calling her bluff.

Mo sucked her teeth. "Just tell me."

Her first thought when he finished, was, so it had been about a girl. Her best friend. That part blew her a little. She was relieved, though. She'd thought it was going to be much worse. She was definitely annoyed. At Lennie. At Sheeda. For sure, at Quan.

He was always on his stupid. Their mothers were first cousins, and even though they only lived ten minutes apart and had been much closer as little kids, Mo didn't mess with any of Quan's sisters the way him and Lennie hung out. They were ratchet and stayed in trouble. Their mother used to always force them on Mo—Monique, you want your cousins do a sleepover, Boo? She swore if they hung out with Mo enough, they'd get interested in something besides dudes. It wasn't until Mo admitted to her mom that she didn't like spending time with them, that her mother started making excuses for her—"Mo has dance tonight."

Sometimes it was true. A lot of times it wasn't.

Of course, Quan had gotten Lennie in this. If he wasn't dumb, he wasn't nothing.

She had been ready to help Lennie dry the dishes. She

was actually feeling bad for him because he was acting so nervous. Again when he'd said, "Now Sheeda won't talk to me," and she saw that he seemed legit sad. Instead, she punched him in the arm and said, "That's what you get for creeping," and left him.

She went upstairs, laid back on the little piece of bed that wasn't covered in duffel bags and plastic bins. She dialed up Sheeda, scowling when her friend's face popped up on screen.

"When was you gonna tell me, wench?"

"Hmm. Welcome back, I guess?" Sheeda said.

Mo hadn't planned to keep up the fake mad act long. Sheeda's serious face ended it dead. She tried again. "Why didn't you tell me you and Lennie was—" She pretended to gag. "Talking."

"I didn't want you to get mad," Sheeda said, not even cracking a smile at the joke.

Mo waved it off. "I mean, it's hella weird to think of y'all like that. But Lennie gonna do what he want anyway. I thought at least my girl woulda put me up on it, though."

"I'm sorry I didn't tell you," Sheeda said.

She'd said the words, but still looked like she didn't want to have the conversation. Mo pushed once more. "But why you ain't tell me what happened with Quan?"

Sheeda shrugged.

"He always been extra like that. It's why I don't mess with Kiera and Kelsey, his sisters." Mo kicked a duffel off the bed, to stretch her legs. "They just extra all the time. He ready be a senior in high school messing with girls our age. Just dumb." She snorted. "Hmmph. He woulda never pulled that mess if I had been home." Noticing that Sheeda hadn't said anything, Mo peered at the screen.

Sheeda was looking off to the side and down. Mo teased, "I know you not side chatting me."

"I was talking to Kita on another chat. Was telling her I'd call later." Sheeda stared full on into the phone. Her face was blank. She looked tired.

"You good, sis?" Mo asked, trying one more time.

"I'm all right," Sheeda said.

First with Lennie, now she had to play Riddle Me This with Sheeda, too? She swallowed her anger and infused so much cheer into her voice even she knew it sounded fake.

"Lennie told me that your auntie came down here and gave a sermon." Mo wasn't mad to miss that. Rasheeda's Auntie D wasn't bad, but she was OD with the Bible stuff. "Lennie punished. Did you get in trouble?"

Sheeda's twists whipped gently against her face as her head shook side to side.

"Oh whuttt?" Mo laughed. "How you sneak down here and not get in trouble? Which Scripture say, thou shalt not creep creep to a dude's house?"

Sheeda frowned. "I guess my aunt figured that almost getting raped was my punishment."

The words pulled Mo straight up at attention. "Almost raped? Okay, wait. Did Lennie forget to tell me something?"

"I don't know what he told you," Sheeda said.

"More than you did." Mo scowled.

"I don't feel like arguing about it," Sheeda said.

Her almost Katie-like sigh pushed a button deep in Mo. Quan was wrong. And Lennie should have shut him down from word go, when it was happening. But it was all squashed, now. Lennie's gaming system was off limits for the rest of summer, and their mother was looking for a job for him at the hospital. One he could do on weekends even when school started. Not having Lennie to kick it with was Quan's punishment, she guessed. Who knew?

If anybody should have been mad, it should have been her. They had her out there in the dark, first of all. And second, she'd just gotten home. Already she had to jump in and fix somebody else's mess. "Nobody arguing. But for real, what did you think was gonna happen? You was the only girl with all these dudes in the house."

Sheeda's eyebrows scrunched together.

"You think I wanted Quan to back me in a corner and grab my butt?"

Sometimes yelling at Sheeda was like kicking a puppy. If anybody else had talked to her this way, Mo would have been in their stuff, instantly. But she couldn't stop herself.

"I didn't say all that. But for real, it ain't the smartest idea to roll up by yourself. Lennie always got hardheads over here. You know that."

As she dug into her best friend, her two sides battled back and forth.

One was calm and hoped Sheeda was okay. Calm Her was saying, *Breathe. Let Sheeda get it off her chest.* The other wanted to hang up, let Sheeda handle this on her own. Let Lennie. They had got themselves into this mess. Had no business going behind her back. Now look. And hello, she had problems of her own. Sheeda hadn't even asked if she'd gotten into BA.

The two sides dueled, elbowing the other out of the way to control her mouth.

"I only went down there to tell Lennie I couldn't stay," Sheeda said.

Ragey Mo took the mic and wouldn't let it go.

"Hello, they invented this thing called TEXTING."

Mo hollered the last word. Sheeda recoiled from it, egging Mo's fury. "Lennie said he tried hitting you up to apologize. Why you ain't answer him back?"

"Because my aunt keeps my phone on lockdown, Mo."

"You ain't have to say it like I'm stupid," Mo spat.

"And you didn't have to say I wanted Quan to be up on me. Lennie didn't even jump in and stop him."

"He said you left before he could."

"I left before he—" Sheeda's eyebrows finished the sentence, going from "okay whatever" heights to "that don't even make sense" lows. "If that's how he see it, what difference does it make what I say?" The next time she spoke, it was almost a whisper. "I thought Lennie liked me, that's why I went in person."

"I mean, who wouldn't like you if he thought he could get with you like that," Mo said, instantly regretting it. She raced past it. "I'm just gonna keep it one hundred—"

"Of course you are," Sheeda said, her voice meek, but her eyebrows firmly furrowed.

"What you getting salty with me for?" Mo asked.

"Nobody is salty."

High-pitched and offended, Mo yelled, "Like I don't know what salty sound like?"

Sheeda stared, mute, before going on calmly. "I have

to go. If my aunt sees any kind of calls longer than a few minutes, she takes the phone for the whole day." Her eyes shifted as she said, "If you don't want to go on the retreat, that's cool."

"You don't want me to go?" Mo asked, hurt. Even more at Sheeda's nonchalant answer.

"Just saying you don't *have* to go."

Mo didn't care about the retreat. Long days in the sun doing arts and crafts and swatting flies by the lake while the boys chased the girls around threatening to hook them with a fishing pole that no one actually knew how to use and long nights of "revival," which as far she could tell was only permission for the pastor to give sermons longer than he gave in any church service she'd attended. She didn't necessarily want to go. But would it kill Sheeda to say she wanted her to go?

Just like that, BA's rejection washed over her, fresh. They didn't want her, either, even though she still heard the piano music and smelled the corn chip funk of wet pointe shoes— like they had become a part of her in those three weeks.

She missed a place that didn't want her. Now Sheeda was acting like she didn't care that Mo was back. Nobody wanted her.

She waited a few more seconds, hoping Sheeda would say "Of course I want you to go," and wanting to hear that she meant it. The longer Sheeda stayed quiet, the angrier Mo got. She wanted to blast her—tell Sheeda her little retreat was boring and yup, she'd pass.

Before she could, she thought about Ms. Sharon saying, "Do your work."

To Mo, that meant fighting for what she wanted. But that hadn't worked for her this summer. Besides, she was tired. There had to be another way.

Sheeda's face was expressionless—as prepared for Mo's flippant no as Mo was ready to say it. So, she did the opposite.

"I still want go," she said. The flicker of surprise in Sheeda's face spurred her on. "Unless you plan to leave me hanging for your Jesus friends while we there. If so, you can miss me with that."

"I wouldn't do that," Sheeda said. For the first time since the call started, her cheeks were plump from a smile.

Mo grinned back.

"All right. Well, let me let you go. I don't want you getting in trouble with Auntie," she said, then remembered she did have one more fight left in her. "You need me roll up on Quan for you? 'Cause you know I will."

Sheeda's tiny smile and "No, I'm good," was no

guarantee Mo wasn't going to at least light him up on socials. She didn't have to fight for everything. She couldn't. Not anymore. But standing up for a friend, she'd do every time. No apology.

RASHEEDA

She wanted her mother. Legit wanted to hear her voice and have her mother tell her that it would be okay. Wanting her mother was the only way Sheeda knew, for sure, that she was mad at her Auntie D. For a long time, she had been afraid to be mad at her aunt. Afraid that it was a sin. Wasn't everything else?

But then, one day, when the boulder on her chest made it hard to breathe, she sat in her closet and called her mother. She needed somebody who would understand that her not wanting to wear a dress that swept the floor didn't mean she was out there "running after" some little boy.

Trying to convince her aunt of that was pointless.

All she'd wanted was to hear that it was okay, normal even, to want to wear a dress shorter than one that passed her ankles.

Her mother ended up wrong from the start, answering the call, "Hey, baby girl. Tell your aunt don't be tryin' send you down here now. She call herself waiting till April to make plans for you. Well, I already got things to do this summer."

"That's not why I'm calling, Ma," Sheeda had said, trying to keep her voice down. Auntie D didn't forbid her from calling her mother. Still, it always felt wrong. Plus, the closet was the best place to hide and keep her mother's loud voice from seeping out and into the hallway. Her mother usually ranted most of the call, something Sheeda always seemed to forget until her mother started in.

"What? She still trying to say that I'm getting money for you that I'm not sending her? Tell Dee that I said—"

Sheeda stopped listening. The entire phone call was a one-sided fight. Her mother saying all the things she never got to say to Auntie D because her aunt refused to sit on the phone arguing. Every other line was, "Well, you tell Dee," or "Deandra think she know." Sheeda didn't even have to say "um-hm" or "okay." Her mother was going off that much. Sheeda couldn't remember the last time they'd had a conversation where her mother had asked how her grades were or what she liked or disliked.

The phone call always reminded her that some things were worse than Auntie D's rules. Like talking to a mother who seemed mad that you weren't with her, but then never once asked about you.

I'm fine, Ma, how you doing?

It was something Sheeda always dreamed of saying, but never once got to utter. Not in six years.

But when she was mad at Auntie D, knowing that never stopped her from wanting to talk to her mother.

The dress thing had worked out. Auntie D had relented and started letting her wear knee-length dresses the next year. Sheeda wasn't so sure things would work out that easily this time. She hadn't been punished for going down to Lennie's. But she and her aunt hadn't said more than twenty words since. And half those words were, "Give me your phone before heading to bed."

She sat in her closet, rubbing her phone screen like it would summon a genie. Maybe this time if she called, her mother would listen.

A message lit up.

Lennie:

Mo said u don't have ur phone all the

time. But if u got it right now, hit me

back. Please

Tai had been right. It was messy. And in another month, she'd have to see him every day on the bus. What if him and his friends joked about it?

Yo, chick thought she was my girlfriend.

That's wild!

Her face was hot with humiliation at the thought. She squeezed her knees to her chest, laid her head down, and cried, never hearing her aunt come in.

Auntie D peered down at her, concern but also aggravation on her face. "Rasheeda, what's wrong? Why are you in the closet?"

Sheeda wiped at her eyes. No answer would make sense. So, she gave none.

"We need to talk." Auntie D sat on the bed.

Sheeda unfolded herself and joined her. She sat on the bed's edge, her hands clasped in her lap, expecting a lecture but getting, "Are you all packed for the retreat?"

Sheeda's eyebrows rose. She ventured carefully, "Yes."

"You looking forward to it?"

Sheeda shrugged. It was her actual answer. Kita and Yola weren't talking. Mo was going, but Sheeda wondered if she really wanted to. Worse, she wasn't sure she wanted

Mo to go anymore. What was there to look forward to?

Foot tucked under her butt, her aunt faced Sheeda. Her hair was pulled back into a ponytail. Usually, no one would ever know she was the youngest of her siblings. Sister Tate mode was hair nicely done, dresses, heels, and pantyhose making her look way older. With the ponytail, she could have been Sheeda's older sister. She exhaled, and her warm breath puffed in Sheeda's face.

"You know what my biggest fear is?" Seeing Sheeda had no idea, she cracked a smile that bordered on a wince. "It's that I'll mess this up. That I'll mess you up." She wiped at a single tear. "When your mother asked me to keep you until she could get herself together, I really thought we'd only be together a few months and that I'd get to be the fun aunt, then send you back. When that didn't happen, suddenly I was Aunt Mommy and had to feed you, keep you clothed, and most importantly, make sure you turned out to be a good human being." She dabbed furiously at the tears rolling down her face. "I have rules for a reason. To protect you. And when I think about what could have happened if those boys—" Her jaw clenched, seeming to scare the tears dry. "It could have been bad, Rasheeda. Do you understand?"

Sheeda did. She'd had a few bad dreams since then,

every one of them with Quan's face close to hers, breath reeking and underarms musty, blocking her way out of the door. It scared her. But it also made her angry. At herself? Quan? Lennie? She was never sure.

"The only reason I'm letting Monique go on the retreat is because I don't want to hold her responsible for something her brother did," Auntie D said.

"He didn't do anything," Sheeda said, meaning it both ways. Lennie hadn't really done anything wrong. He also hadn't done anything right. She didn't know how to explain it to her aunt. Probably wouldn't get the chance if she could. She stared straight ahead, waiting for it.

Auntie D's voice shook with the fire of Scripture. "Exactly. Ephesians chapter five, verse eleven says, 'Take no part in the unfruitful works of darkness, but instead expose them.' Lennie should have stood up for you. Don't defend him. What he did—"

"Was wrong," Sheeda said, flat. She didn't want to fight. "I know."

"Good." Her aunt continued, a little less sure. "You don't need to be around people like that."

People like that. If Auntie D had her way, Sheeda wouldn't have a single friend, since eventually everybody was going to do or say something to be put on the list.

She stayed looking at her feet, unable to look at her aunt as the anger burned her cheeks. "All I wanted to do was tell him that me and Tai would come by later. That was it. Why is that so wrong? Why was me talking to him so bad?"

"Because you knew better." The certainty was back. A Bible quote, probably about obedience, was not far away. "Since when have I given you permission to go to a boy's house at all? Much less with no adult there?"

Sheeda didn't have the strength to quibble and remind her that Ms. Linda had been home. Didn't know if that would make it better or worse.

She closed her eyes. Quan's face and smell were burned into her brain. She wished they weren't. His face made her stomach churn and made her teeth grind. She realized she was angry at him, for sure. At herself, for going to Lennie's alone.

And, yes, she was mad at Lennie, too. It still hurt that he hadn't stepped in and stopped Quan before he clamped his sweaty body around her. But she'd seen his messages and knew he was sorry. Sheeda wanted to forgive him. She didn't know what that meant, yet. But she was going to. And that's why she was so angry with her aunt. Because, of course, her aunt who could probably tick off no less than half a dozen Scriptures about forgiveness was telling her not to forgive. Was telling her she might have to cut off the best friend she had.

Now even forgiveness was wrong?

Her eyes popped open, and the words came out before she could think to stop them.

"I never do anything right, anyway. So—" She began ugly crying, tears so hard that her words were a garbled mess. "No matter what I do, you're mad. All I did was talk to Lennie. Talk. But if I told you we talked, you would have taken my phone. The night I spent at Yola's was the worst. She spent the whole night on the phone with Jalen. But if I had told you I didn't want to hang out with her and Kita, you would have got mad about that. Then I asked could I hang with Tai, and you said no. I don't know what I'm allowed to do anymore." The words were stuck in her windpipe. She wheezed, pushing them out of her throat. "You say I knew better, but I don't know anything anymore. I get tired of being at church all the time. But I know I'm wrong for saying that. I don't want to feel so guilty all the time."

"Guilty about what?" her aunt asked quietly.

"Everything," Sheeda said, spent. It was out there, and she'd probably be punished for life.

"Look at me, please," Auntie D said. She held her palms out and Sheeda turned to her, laying her hands on top. "People feel guilt for doing something wrong. Why would you need to feel guilty?"

"Everything I do is wrong," Sheeda said, unable to meet her aunt's eyes. "Going to Lennie's was wrong. I guess that's why what happened happened."

"God doesn't work like that, Luvvie." Her aunt sighed. "Do you really believe that He punished you because you made a bad decision?" She pulled Sheeda's nodding head onto her chest. "Going to Lennie's was wrong because you didn't have permission. But what happened wasn't your fault, and it definitely wasn't a punishment from above. Do you understand?"

Auntie D stroked her forehead, letting her cry tears of relief. Sheeda had expected the sermon of all times; instead, her aunt waited while her body shook. When there were no more tears left, her temples pounded. Her eyes felt like someone had poured sand in them. Auntie D pulled Sheeda away, holding her at arm's length.

"You shouldn't feel guilty for speaking your mind. And I'm sorry that you've been feeling that way."

Sheeda forced herself to look her aunt in the eye. "I'm sorry for sneaking behind your back to talk to Lennie."

"I accept your apology. I want you to be honest with me, Rasheeda. I thought maybe having rules and a schedule would make it easier for both of us. But I guess what they say is true—too much of anything makes you an addict."

Sheeda squinted, not understanding. Her aunt laughed. "It's an old saying. I'm trying to say that the rules and schedule made me comfortable, and I got carried away making more rules and schedules." Her smile matched Sheeda's. She squeezed her shoulders, as if sealing a deal. "Maybe we can try to have more balance going forward. Pick the ministries you love most and let's see how we can make it work so you're doing the things you really enjoy at church and at home. Sound like a plan?"

"Yes," Sheeda said. "Thank you."

Her aunt kissed her forehead. "Be patient with me. I'm still figuring out this Aunt Mom stuff."

She went to leave when Sheeda called out to her.

"Yes?"

"I want to forgive Lennie." Sheeda's eyes fell at her aunt's withering gaze. She took a breath. "I'm *going* to forgive him."

Auntie D's lips pressed together. Sheeda counted to stop herself from taking it back. When Sheeda reached seven, her aunt's face relaxed. "Forgiveness is good." She took a few steps down the hall, then came back, hands on her hips. "Forgiveness is not dating, though. Am I understood?"

Sheeda's twists jiggled as she shook her head in agreement.

She texted Lennie back.

Rah-Rah:

Mo said you gotta get a job.

DatBoyEll:

Already got it. Working at the hospital
gift shop. IIWI

Rah-Rah:

Yup

DatBoyEll:

look I really ain't think Quan wuz gonna
trip like that. he always playing around
but I ain't mean for him disrespect u
like that

Rah-Rah:

I thought u liked me

DatBoyEll:

I do like u. Thas my word!

Rah-Rah:

You didn't tell him to stop or

anything, Lennie. I was scared.

DatBoyEll:

🙂 I woulda never let him hurt u tho.
I know u don't believe me but I'm for
real.

Rah-Rah:

TBH it doesn't matter. I'll be
boyfriendless a looooonnng time.

DatBoyEll:

I messed you up huh?

Rah-Rah:

I messed me up. Not trying to be
corny or anything but I wanted
you to know that I forgive you.
We're good.

DatBoyEll:

Thas solid. 👊

Rah-Rah:

👊 ttyl probably

DatBoyEll:

Be good shawty 😉

Rah-Rah:

Like I have a choice 🙂

There. It was done. She'd forgiven him. Not because she was worried he'd be mad with her if she didn't. Because the anger made her feel like she was walking underwater. Because, if she didn't forgive herself (for agreeing to meet him, for going alone, for keeping secrets), she'd drown in it.

Her eye went back to Lennie's message: "I woulda never let him hurt u tho."

"He did hurt me, though," she whispered aloud.

More than anything, she wished that day had never happened. It was like going from having your eyes squeezed shut to not being able to close them at all. She'd wanted to tell Lennie that's how she was hurt, but didn't know how to explain it. All she knew for sure was, she didn't want to walk around holding on to the hurt. Forgiveness wasn't for Lennie. It was for herself.

EPILOGUE: MONIQUE'S FALL

Mo knew exactly when things had changed.

When Mila's dad agreed to let her attend BA year-round.

Mo had assumed there was no way Mila's dad could ever afford the BA tuition. Wrong or not, it had brought her comfort knowing that for one reason or another, they'd both be locked out of BA's world. For different reasons. But, still.

Then BA had given Mila a scholarship and La May had done fundraisers in the community to raise more money. Mo had even worked one of the fundraisers, helping to sell T-shirts of Mila en pointe hugging herself, looking away from the camera, and the hashtag on the back, #CoveBallerina. When people found out what they were for, they sold out fast. Mo had never been that happy and sad at the same time.

When enough had been raised, officially, she cried like her soul hurt. It had been one thing that Mila had gotten accepted. It was another that she was going to go.

Her mother let her cry, then called her on how she felt. "Right now, you're upset because you're focused on her path and not your own."

Mo had tried arguing. But nothing she said threw her mother off course. It had been like being a book that her mother knew word for word. She pointed out that Mo had never heard of a ballet school before spring (facts), still thought most classical ballets were boring (big facts), and was acting like BA was the only place she could ever dance.

Now that, Mo had never thought about. Not really. The rejection was raw for weeks. Mo had thought about giving up dance. Didn't feel like putting her body through all that. For what?

Ms. Sharon asking her to consider contemporary ballet had felt like second prize, like a slick way of saying Mo wasn't cut out to do the classic ballets. And Mo still wasn't entirely convinced that not being accepted at BA wasn't about race. She tried to tell herself that if ballet didn't want her, then she didn't want it.

But when her mother hit her with real talk, she couldn't hide from the facts. She wanted to be accepted at BA so badly that she never admitted that it wasn't the place for her. From the start it hadn't been.

The food. Not having many Black people nearby. Explaining everything she did or said. Even the way it seemed like every White dancer stomped their way down the hall, in the dorm, were things she figured she would just have to get used to if she wanted to attend a school like BA.

Until weeks later, when her mother dropped a thick packet of paper on her bed. On top was a note that read: "Your path is your path for a reason. You just have to stay on it." And beneath it were pages and pages of photos of Black and Brown dancers. Some of them were in pointe shoes but many were barefoot or had on flat skin-toned ballet slippers. Instead of tutus, many had on unitards or flowy slip dresses. Their bodies were chocolate or tan and muscular, like they could leap off the page if they wanted. Had they ever been asked to tuck their bottoms, she wondered?

She had been mesmerized, turning the pages slowly as

if she were looking at a picture book. When the pictures ended, the last few pages were information about summer intensives at Alvin Ailey and Dance Theatre of Harlem. And on a blank page, in her mother's handwriting, was: *Can you see yourself? Then take a leap. . . .*

It was time.

EPILOGUE: SHEEDA'S FALL

Things had changed a lot.

For her ministries, Sheeda picked praise dance and helping Auntie D with Sunday church school and Vacation Bible School. She'd purposely picked ministries where she wouldn't have to do a lot of interacting with the First Bap Pack, which at this point was Jalen and Yola.

Yola had worked hard during the retreat to separate herself from them. Jalen had brought two friends and Yola had brought her cousin. The five of them had knighted themselves the alpha squad. Mo only enjoyed the retreat because she spent the whole time tripping off how they laughed the loudest, mobbed the dining hall when it was time to eat to make sure they sat together, and generally did the most to make it seem like they were having the best time, better than anybody else there.

Sheeda hadn't cared about any of it except the time Yola came over to ask if Mo wanted to play a game of chicken with them in the pool. Then when Mo said no, Yola had gotten really loud and looked over at Sister Butler as she said, "Oh, well, I asked," like she had been trying to get them to kick it all along. Even though it had been the first time she'd said a word to them.

Sheeda didn't want Sister Butler to go back and tell Auntie D that Sheeda hadn't talked to anybody except Kita and Mo the whole time, since the retreat was about fellowship and all that. Luckily, Auntie D (and apparently the other chaperones) were so scandalized by Yola and Jalen's growing relationship that by the time Sheeda got home, the only gossip going around was about how close they were.

Mo's merciless clowning of the alpha squad and how extra they were being had lifted Kita's spirits and stopped Sheeda from worrying the whole time. She was glad Mo had come.

She hadn't been sure how things would turn out. She'd forgiven Lennie, but couldn't help feeling like her and Mo's friendship wasn't the same. It wasn't until the second day of the retreat when they were doing a Blessing Circle—where everyone had to write down one blessing they were grateful for then show it at the same time. Sheeda had written "my aunt" partly because she meant it but, also, she knew Sister Butler went back and told the adults not on the trip everything. She wasn't above trying to get a few extra brownie points from Auntie D. Then she'd looked across the circle and saw that Mo had written, "my best friend," and felt bad for ever doubting their friendship.

She needed to cherish their friendship more than ever. Mo was looking at dance schools again. Black ones this time. And knowing Mo, once she set her mind to it, nothing could stop her. Thinking about Mo going away made Sheeda sad, but not as much as it had earlier that summer. Her worst nightmare had been losing Mo to dance. Instead, she'd almost lost her because she'd kept a secret. She never wanted to do that again.

Didn't have to. Now that they weren't in church all the time, she and her aunt talked more. While they ate dinner or played games, they talked about almost everything. Like how Sheeda was nervous about starting high school and how she liked church more now that she wasn't there as much. Her aunt's advice had been peppered with lots of "Luvvie's," stories about when she was fourteen, and encouraging her to create a drama piece for the church, maybe even start a theater ministry.

It was the first time she'd ever talked about using Sheeda's TAG skills in church.

Then, one day, Lennie showed up at their stoop in a polo shirt tucked into his pants. Except for liking a few things on his page, Sheeda hadn't talked to him in weeks. So, when he asked Auntie D if it was okay if he could come by and hang out sometimes, Sheeda had immediately texted Mo.

Rah-Rah:

Umm Lennie is up here like asking for my hand in marriage or something 😄

Mo'Betta:

😄 Not the hand in marriage tho. What ur aunt say?

Rah-Rah:

Right now they talking about how this isn't dating and I'm not allowed to date. I think she used the word date a hundred times already. .

Mo'Betta:

Do u wanna hang out with him?

                     Rah-Rah:

              If she lets me, yes. Is that okay?.

Mo'Betta:

👍

                     Rah-Rah:

                         🙂 .

Turned out, her Auntie D had a competitive streak a mile long. More shouting and noise came out of their row house on the nights that Lennie and Mo came over to play games or trivia on their phones than they'd made the whole time Sheeda lived there. No games with dice or playing cards were allowed because her aunt saw that as gambling. Sheeda had pretended not to see the side-eye that Lennie and Mo had given each other when she'd explained that.

One step at a time.

Auntie D was fun when she wasn't quoting the Bible. And if she was letting Lennie come over to play games, why couldn't buying a board game, with dice, be next?

Anything was possible.

That's why Sheeda was tempted to start calling her aunt "Mommy." Had even slipped and tried it. She wanted to show her aunt that she appreciated everything she did for her. Wanted her to know that she understood that the Auntie D she was now probably wasn't the Auntie D she'd always wanted to be. And also, that even though she had a mother six hundred miles away, Auntie D was the only mother she really knew. She was learning to be okay with that.

But Auntie D had wrinkled her nose and said, "Umm, no." She'd pulled Sheeda into a hug and pecked her forehead. "I don't need a title to love you. Besides, I'm honored to be your auntie."

It was what Sheeda needed. All she'd ever needed.